THE MAKER OF WORLDS

A Novel by

DAVID LITWACK

EVOLVED PUBLISHING™

www.EvolvedPub.com
Evolved Publishing LLC
Butler, Wisconsin, USA

Printed in Book Antiqua font.

BOOKS BY DAVID LITWACK

Along the Watchtower

The Daughter of the Sea and the Sky

THE SEEKERS (3-Book Series)
Book 1: *The Children of Darkness*
Book 2: *The Stuff of Stars*
Book 3: *The Light of Reason*

The Maker of Worlds

The Time That's Given

DEDICATION

For Terri and our new world,
and
For Amy, Lisa, and Sara, who may someday make their own.

PART 1 – THE MAELSTROM

When the cold of winter comes
Starless night will cover day,
In the veiling of the sun
We will walk in bitter rain,
But in dreams I can hear your name
And in dreams We will meet again
~ Fran Walsh

Chapter 1 – The Departure

All stories begin with a question, and this is mine: if you had the chance to remake the world, what kind of world would you choose?

Let me start from the beginning.

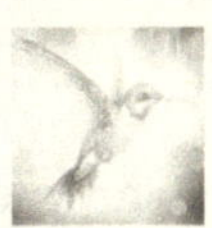

The day before my leap, spring had peeked above the horizon. A bolder sun had inspired buds to sprout on the branches, so tiny they stood out only when moistened by the morning dew. A smattering of flowers had bloomed as well, daffodils and the tips of tulips that showed more as promise. Forsythias bulged yellow, lilacs blossomed and spread their fragrance, and the air tasted fresher too, as if purified by the increased sunlight. A time for hope.

But not for me. The arrival of spring did nothing to remove the cloud that had shadowed my days and darkened my dreams these past six months.

Addy had always chided me for living only part time in the real world, the rest of my time filled with flights of fantasy.

I disagreed. My approach had always been a conscious choice, a matter of perspective. After all, what was so wonderful about reality?

Her answer: only in the real world would I find her.

I discovered too late how harsh my life would be without her.

I'd slept poorly that night, my sleep disturbed by dreams, but when I awoke well before dawn, my resolve remained. Though I'd sleepwalked through my coming of age five years earlier, my circumstance had now changed, replaced by a lingering sadness, a malaise that would not heal. I'd become inclined to imagine another life elsewhere, desperate to try out an alternate path. On this day, I intended to test the maelstrom.

The maelstrom appeared as a swirling circle of water for only three days each year, starting at the equinox—an unusual anomaly that behaved in a manner different from a proper whirlpool. This vortex hovered a foot above the lake's surface and, more bizarrely, stood vertical.

Townsfolk debated its purpose. The more rational claimed a perturbation of light, like a prism, caused by sprays of seasonal runoff and the angle of the sun. Others believed it to be magic, though none existed in our world.

Of course, what we called magic might be nothing more than a label for things beyond the boundaries of reason. Natural phenomenon might still be magic. The sun's rays lifted our spirits, and the advent of spring lightened our hearts.

Each year, as the equinox approached, young boys who'd reached their eighteenth year would boast about their intent to challenge the maelstrom. In practice, few did. By eighteen, most had narrowed their path through life, following the example of their elders, or rebelled and chosen a contrarian course. With age, the lust for adventure diminished to bluster, tall tales told to impress their younger peers.

Those who took the leap landed with a splash on the far side to the derision of their mates, but rumors alleged one had vanished years ago as villagers gaped, never to return. Philosophers speculated the swirling water might be a gateway to the gods, but only for those with sufficient faith.

At eighteen, I would never have abandoned Addy, but once she was gone, my desire for change stirred. While I lacked the required faith, this was caused by the cruelty of the world, and did not reflect my belief in magic. My desperation grew until, in the spring of my twenty-third year, I determined to go.

I'd leave before sunup, guaranteeing solitude on the shore. Should I stumble through the maelstrom to no effect, no one would witness my folly. Still in a daze, I stowed provisions in my backpack: a day's worth of salted mutton, a loaf of hard bread, two dried apples, a full waterskin, a knife, a flint, and a rain slicker to ward off the morning chill.

At the doorway of my Queen's Hill cottage, I hesitated. This morning's excursion would likely be a fool's errand, but what if it turned out to be something more, a journey to who-knows-where? As I gazed down to the lake, a sense of foreboding crept over me. No matter. Foolhardy or not, I was committed.

I slipped across the threshold and navigated the switchbacks in the dark.

The maelstrom hovered over the shallows a dozen paces offshore, in the dim light showing as nothing more than a disturbance in the air. I yanked off my boots, knotted the laces and slung them around my neck. As I rolled my trousers above the knee, I cast a lingering glance up the hill to catch a last glimpse of my cottage.

I waited until the eastern horizon reddened and waded into the lake.

An arm's length from the gateway, I reached out, keeping as far away as possible while my fingertips brushed its surface. It felt like... nothing, likely no more than an illusion. In half an hour, I'd be back in my bed, no closer to comprehending the universe. Yet I'd yearned for a portal to another world, one that might allow me to deviate from accepted norms. I longed to float off to a fresher fate.

Once, I too would have followed the safe path, with no risk of surprise, but then life did surprise me with a cosmic slap across the face that left me shattered—the taking of Addy. At twenty-two, misfortune had cleared the slate, leaving me alone and adrift.

I drew in a breath and plunged through.

In the light of pre-dawn, and in my half-awake state, no difference struck me at first, other than the chill waters deeper than expected, soaking the rolls of my trousers. Out of the mist on either side, giant evergreens loomed graceful as usual, rising until their tops blurred. The view so distracted me that several heartbeats passed before I realized the change.

Perhaps I was still sleeping in my bed, for where the channel to the west lake should have been, a broad flood plain spread. The water had washed over the banks and crept inland for a hundred paces, leaving the trees the only witness to what once had been dry land.

Beyond the trees, nothing.

Nowhere a dock or a mooring, not so much as a hint of early morning smoke rising from a chimney. Nowhere the cottages of Queen's Hill. Nowhere houses at all. As I gaped, the edges of branches shimmered as if undecided whether to remain intangible or become real. In a panic, I realized the folly of this quest. Better to return to a safer, albeit gloomier life, to go back through the portal at once.

Behind me, the maelstrom still swirled, a fleeting comfort as it had started to recede. While I stared at the last link to my old world, the orb diminished, shrunk to a size I could cover with my hand, and then to that of the tip of my thumb. Before I sloshed more than two steps closer, it winked out.

Now, to the north and the south, nothing showed but water. I stumbled to shore, my movements causing the slightest wake in the surface, which lay so still I could make out my astonished features in the reflection.

I'd spent much of my young life with Addy, like a mate sailing across a forever lake. She'd been with me through calm and storm. I'd yearned to find renewed hope on this side of the gateway and return home to a new life, yet now the gateway, like Addy, had vanished.

Chapter 2 – On Dry Land

I slogged through the muddy bank to the shore, settled on a flat rock, and rolled down my trouser legs to dry. After pulling on and tying my boots, I spread the contents of my pack on the ground and took stock of the situation.

This land appeared vast and lush, with dense forest on all sides. The lake may not be potable, but with so much greenery the rain must fall, and where it rained, bubbling brooks flowed.

Food was another matter. Staring at my scant provisions, I realized how poorly I'd planned. Despite my wild fantasies, I'd expected to return no later than sunset, though I'd ruminated on finding a thriving castle, one with an arched window high up in the tower through which I might behold a fair princess. I'd never considered the possibility of hunger or thirst. I eyed the modest chunk of mutton and decided to stow it away. Best to ration for now.

The sun cleared the treetops, spreading its beams across the land. I sat in less a clearing than a spit of sand where years of flooding had washed away the vegetation. The surrounding forest appeared impassable, until I spotted two intertwining trunks forming an archway. I crept toward it, peered through, and caught a path on the far side with pine needles pressed flat, as if others had passed that way.

I headed off through a tunnel of branches while the sun dappled the way, pausing only for an occasional sip of water. By midday, my pace slowed, and I plodded along on terrain so unchanging I worried the trail had circled back on itself. By dusk, I'd found no brook or stream, no trees bursting with fruit, and no bushes lush with berries.

Spending the night hungry, thirsty, and exposed held no appeal. With nightfall, the temperature would drop. Already the coming chill prickled my skin, and I longed for the meanest form of shelter.

How strange to find oneself in an alien world, cut adrift from every prior connection, blocked from returning home and uncertain of what lay ahead. The thrill of adventure sweetened the sensation at first, and the glow of youthful pride warmed it, but soon fear began to dominate. I spun about, peeking around and above to the trees. I was alone.

About to yield to despair, I stumbled upon what appeared to be a man-made shelter. Four poles had been stuck into the soft earth, two upright and two supporting them at an angle, an unlikely feat of nature. On closer inspection, the tops had been trimmed with a knife or axe and bound together with hemp twine, as I might have constructed myself.

I licked my dry lips. Now, if only I could find a stream. I spun around heel to toe, searching for some sign of moisture or the runoff of rain. I held my breath and waited, listening. Nothing. Tired and desperate, I squeezed my eyes shut and envisioned a bubbling brook.

No birds sang, but in the near perfect silence, a persistent murmur came wafting on the breeze, the splash of running water.

Its muffled presence came more as thought than sound, but inexplicably, I knew. A few paces behind the shelter, a path trailed away, so narrow I'd missed it before. I followed it, fighting off encroaching branches along the way. It dead-ended at the edge of a hill where, to my delight, a waist-high boulder stood as if holding back the hillside. Through a crack at its center trickled the purest stream.

I stuck my mouth beneath it and, without the need to ration, drank until my sides hurt. After I'd refilled my empty skin and surveyed the scene, a realization struck me. The rock and stream had appeared as I'd envisioned them, though I'd never viewed them before. My passage through the gateway had been improbable. How else might this world surprise me?

With a modest shelter and plentiful water, I deemed this a proper place to spend the night. The hill would protect my back, and the canopy of trees overhead would provide cover should the rain fall.

I'd gone camping in my youth, hiking inland from the lake to the mountains to stay overnight, but always in the warmth of summer. Now, as the chill set in, I gathered pine needles in a circle, cut small shavings from downed branches, and surrounded the bird's nest with a wooden tower.

Years had passed since I'd started a fire other than in my cottage stove. Now I clutched the flint a finger's width from the kindling and scraped with my knife. It sparked twice, three times, but my handiwork refused to ignite. I made a desperate wish, picturing a roaring fire, and struck the flint once more.

Sparks flew and, this time, the needles smoldered. I blew on them and the kindling caught enough to show tongues of orange. With added wood, the flames crackled and rose. I hovered over them, stamping on the ground and slapping my hands on my arms. I'd done it, my first accomplishment in this world, and with a sense of unwarranted bravado, I settled in for the night.

I'd slept poorly the prior night and awoken before sunrise. This day's hike had been long and confounding, and now a weariness overcame me. I gathered piles of hemlock needles, and spread them inside the shelter, clustering more at the head for a pillow, and slipped beneath the threadbare boughs. As I tipped up the waterskin for a drink, I marveled at the stately pines that rose to startling heights overhead. Their tops appeared to scrape the sky, seeming older than time, witnesses to creation.

Now if only that creation had added life to this place, even the smallest of creatures, I would not feel so alone. I closed my eyes and imagined a bird, the air filled with its song. When I opened them again, I caught sight of a tiny creature on the topmost branch, one I might have missed before, a sparrow perhaps, or a finch. As I gawked, it began a warbling song. This simple sign of life comforted me. If this world featured sun and trees and singing birds, how different could it be?

I gazed at the treetops, so familiar but so strange, begging them to reveal their secrets, but after the long day and with darkness encroaching, I gave up speculating.

The lulling birdsong acted as a lullaby, and when I placed my head upon my makeshift pillow, sleep crept over me, the blessed giver of oblivion.

Yet I was denied oblivion. Like the falling of night, the memories returned, and a harsh truth revealed itself. This world may be different, but I remained the same. The burden I'd hoped to leave behind had passed through the maelstrom with me.

Late one afternoon at the start of spring, I helped Addy outside. The sky had cleared after a week of rain, leaving a band of blue above the horizon. At its top edge, the setting sun leaked its dying rays. Our favorite bench lay nearby, situated by a notch in the trees. Though a short walk, the slope made the terrain a struggle for her. She'd take a few steps leaning on my arm and pause to rest before shuffling on. At last, we settled on the bench and beheld the western sky light up red and gold.

*"Nice... sunset," she said. The words came out one at a time —
she lacked breath for more.*

"Are you glad to be outside?"

"Yes... thank... you."

*That simple thought exhausted her, but through force of will,
she grasped my hand and squeezed.*

"The advent of spring always brings hope," I said.

*She stared at our fingers intertwined. Her lips formed the word
'perhaps' but the sound emerged as less than a whisper. She raised
her free hand, rested it on my cheek, and forced a smile.*

"My Lucas," she said as firmly as strength allowed.

*We'd grown up together, Addy and me. On summer days,
we'd race through chores, so we'd have daylight left to meet down
by the lake. Our favorite pastime was to construct a boat, small
enough to fit in the palm of my hand. We'd steal whatever we
could from our respective homes without alerting our parents to
the theft: a piece of parchment, a scrap of wood, or a roll of yarn.
As a final act, we'd gather a few twigs and bind them together,
crafting two stick figures, one for each of us. Then, we'd launch it
into the water.*

*On a windy day, we'd add a sail and stand transfixed as it
glided along the path paved by the setting sun. We'd follow it until
the tiny vessel drifted too far away to see, and make up stories about
where it had gone.*

"To a harbor with a castle soaring above it," I'd say.

"Not a castle," she countered. "A garden."

"A city with spires reaching to the sky."

"Or a dragon's lair."

"Or a wizard's tower."

*Always, we'd end the debate in agreement. It had sailed to the
land of dreams.*

*As we matured, the stories grew less fantastic, and our shared
reality shifted to firmer ground. We became more than friends, and
in my twenty-first year, we married.*

Now, as I stared into her moistened eyes, I searched for hope.

*"We'll have better days," I said. "You'll get stronger, and I'll
build us a sturdy boat, one we can sail away together on."*

"How... far"? she said.

"As far as you wish to go."

"I... can't... go far."

"You'll be able go to where I want us to."

Her eyes widened, flashing a spark brighter than I'd seen these past weeks. "Where's... that?"
"To the land of dreams."

I awoke to the chittering of birds. Most mornings, I'd strain to keep my eyes closed, resisting the urge to wake, challenging memories of reality to prove themselves more appealing than my dreams. Now I opened my eyes at once, eager to take in the view. This was, after all, neither dream nor real but a new world altogether.

I squinted up to a brightening sky and more birds overhead than I could count, circling and serenading the rising sun. I breathed in their presence.

But for the birdsong, the uncertainty of my situation still pervaded. With my bravado gone and my stomach grumbling, I scrambled to my feet, donned my rain slicker and pack, and set off to a destination unknown.

Now well rested, I added a spring to my step. The birdsong had cheered me and the sunrise had comforted me. Whatever this place, it obeyed familiar rules. With the discordance of the universe hidden, I believed for the moment I had stumbled into a more benign world, a land with a pleasing harmony. For now, I chose to pretend life made sense.

With no concept of direction, I needed to find food, but after two hours, the terrain stayed unchanged. By late afternoon, I trudged along, hungry, weary, and confused. I'd long ago accepted that the real world lacked purpose, especially after Addy had gone, but what was the purpose of this world? Why the gateway? Why did it exist? This trek through an ancient forest offered no answers.

As the sun settled once more below the treetops and the shadows darkened, I encountered the first challenge. Up to this moment, the path had changed little, sometimes straight, sometimes meandering, but always bordered by the same unending trees. Now, ahead, the way forked. Two identical paths presented themselves, offering no apparent way to choose one from the other.

What now? Would one choice reward me with the new life I sought, but the alternative cause me to wander for eternity? I closed my eyes as before and wished for a signpost to mark the way, but when I opened them, nothing had changed. What to do? I pulled out my knife and tossed it into the air, intent on picking the direction its blade pointed to. In a random universe, that approach seemed as sane as any.

It pointed to the right.

When I bent to pick it up, I was distracted by a faint buzz, almost beneath the threshold of hearing. I glanced up to find a hummingbird hovering at the entrance to the chosen path.

Tired and disillusioned, I determined to get on with it, but when I attempted to proceed, the creature barred my way. I tried to dodge it three times, on the third feinting one way and lunging to the other, but it blocked me each time. Its wings flapped in a blur, its existence challenging the boundaries of human understanding. What if on the other side of this boundary lay the end of reality? Why could this not be magic? For wasn't that its definition?

"You want me to go the other way?"

The whir of its wings slowed, becoming less frantic. It turned its back to me and started down the left path.

I followed.

After fighting through a tangle of brambles, I broke through to a clearing highlighted by a grassy lawn. Behind it loomed an immense redwood, so tall as to suggest the abode of a fairytale giant. Most distinct was its girth, the size of a rich man's cottage. The hummingbird hesitated a moment before flying to the far side, pausing every few paces to wait for me.

I drifted into the clearing like a penitent entering a cathedral. The tree had an aura to it and something more, the slightest trilling as the wind blew. As I came closer, the sound was joined by a tune played by some instrument, like a fiddle but more exotic.

I eyed the tree, wondering at the source of the music. The hummingbird edged near, so close I sensed the breeze from its wings on my face. Its humming became a murmur, and the murmur a whisper, almost forming words in a language too rapid to understand. It buzzed about my head, doing all but pushing me along, flitting back and forth, frustrated at my reluctance to proceed. At last, I followed.

With the fingertips of one hand brushing the bark, I circled the tree, its circumference beyond my ability to measure. I crept forward, shuffling one foot after the other, until I reached the far side. As I turned the final bend, I gasped.

A door.

Chapter 3 – The Custodian

It wasn't just any door. A block of cherry wood stood four paces high, capped by an ornate arch and bracketed by two golden lanterns, which glowed in the emerging dusk. Its surface bore sharp-cut geometric patterns winding around its edges, creating an illusion of depth. At eye level where a peephole might be, two bronze sculptures protruded, a vertical key, and beneath it a horizontal sword. On closer inspection, the key was hinged and along with the sword formed a knocker. For any who might doubt its intent, the blade blared the word 'welcome.'

What could I do? The waterway lay more than a day's hike away, and the gateway to my home had vanished. I had limited provisions, no permanent shelter, and no way back.

I blew out my cheeks, grasped the sword and knocked.

The music ceased and a moment later, the door creaked open.

At first, the chamber seemed empty, though a warm glow gave it a lived-in feel. The low-ceilinged lodging appeared comfortable in a leather-armchair sort of way, with lots of dark wood, by no means ostentatious, but more than expected in this rustic setting. On either side lay bookshelves filled with dusty tomes containing titles too faded to read. Framed portraits hung on the walls, of forest creatures great and small, all facing the viewer in an unnatural way, as if posing with a purpose.

A brazier rested on its tripod in the center of the space, its burning coals the source of the warmth. A pair of cushioned chairs bracketed it, each with a distinct back pillow embroidered with needlework pictures of fanciful beasts. The furniture appeared inviting enough, though undersized for someone of my height.

I crept closer and extended my hands toward the fire, hoping to warm my weary limbs, but in the process nearly tripped over my host, whom I'd somehow missed seeing.

A voice emanating from just above my waist let out a yelp, followed by a more polite clearing of the throat.

"So sorry. I—"

"Not to worry. Happens all the time. Hazard of my... ahem... stature."

I glanced down at a man with bead-like eyes and a nose so protruding from mutton chops it might have been the snout of a badger. A formal coat covered his body, starting at the top with a fur collar and ending with a broad bottom, obscuring all but his gloved hands and black leather boots. In his right hand, he grasped the instrument that made the music.

He eyed his guest, unsurprised at the sudden appearance of a visitor in such a remote location.

I gaped back. Before me stood what might have been a creature come in from the woods, who'd adapted to human ways. No. Not a creature. Beyond his ability to play a melody so sublime, his eyes bore a spark that gave doubt to the question of which of us was the wiser.

My host broke into a grin, revealing the mouth hidden within the facial hair. "Welcome to the borderlands," he said, in a voice like a prince delivering a speech from a castle wall. "I've been expecting you."

"Expecting me?"

He pointed to a set of crystal wind chimes above the door. "Yes, these trill whenever a visitor passes through the portal, an advance notice of sorts."

He collected a brass kettle from a back shelf, filled it with water, and hung it from a hook over the brazier.

As he waited for it to boil, I hovered over him trying to grasp my situation.

Once the water began to steam, the little man filled two floral cups containing a sack of tea and offered one to me, raising a finger in warning: "Best let it steep."

Soon, earthy scents flowed through the chamber, driving away all memories of the chilling breeze outside. I settled into a chair and wrapped my hands around the steaming cup, embracing its warmth.

The man raised his. "How about a toast to celebrate the occasion."

"What occasion is that?"

"The arrival of Lucas Mack to his new world."

I brought the drink to my lips but froze before taking a sip. "How... do you know my name, and what do you mean by my new world?"

The man set his cup down, and his bushy brows drew together in a dark knot. "Oh, bother, I've been doing this so long I sometimes forget and rush through the welcome. Let me slow down and explain. You've arrived at the borderlands, my home and a simple albeit boring place. I am its custodian, tasked with orienting newcomers and answering their initial questions before they move on. As you've already discovered, my realm consists of not much more than trees, a sort of blank slate where you can practice your newfound powers."

I had lived a hard couple of days with little to look forward to, slept poorly on the ground despite the pine needles, and after walking so many hours, my feet ached. I gazed half-dazed into the green liquid steeping in my cup, but his last words snapped me awake. "Newfound powers?"

"All who travel here are endowed with the potential to do magic. In the borderlands, you can dabble in the art, create structures, change the landscape, whatever simple pleasures you fancy. After a time, you may want to continue to the enchanted land. Now where would you like me to begin?"

I took two sips of hot tea, and let the burning sensation assure me this was no dream. The question sputtered out between gulps. "The... enchanted land?"

"Yes, of course. In the world you left, magic has faded over the centuries through disbelief, until it has all but vanished, but I suspect you've heard its stories from long ago. You likely considered them fairytales. Though embellished over time, it turns out most of them are true. So where did such wonders go?" He waved his hands to encompass the tree he lived in and all that surrounded it. "It's here!"

"You expect me to believe I can now do magic?"

"I expect nothing but know you've already performed some. Whenever an enchantment is used, the air vibrates a bit. Those of us more experienced can sense it on their skin. You must have felt it as well but are too new to recognize the sensation."

Images of odd events of the past days sprung to mind, all unexplained, yet I remained unconvinced. "Let's say I accept what you say. Why would I want to continue to this so-called enchanted land."

"Because nothing's here but trees and the changes you make, an appropriate place to practice the craft. If you take to the magic, you'll soon want to do more. The enchanted land is a world much like yours, with one exception. While its inhabitants have no supernatural powers, pilgrims like yourself dwell among them. The common folk call them wizards or sorcerers and either admire or fear them, depending on how these travelers have chosen to behave."

"Is that my fate, to become a conjurer in a strange land?"

"That depends on if it suits you. If not, you may choose to return home, but the power will be lost."

I pictured my cottage above the lake, once a cherished home but now barren and empty. My head spun. "What you ask me to believe is too much, and despite your claim, I feel powerless and worn out from the long day. My greatest dread right now is spending another night exposed in the cold on the ground."

A laugh emerged, starting from deep within the custodian's belly, more of a chortle, a sound discordant with my mood. "You misunderstand. *You* control the magic in this world. If it's a shelter you desire, you can conjure up tree branches, a rope, and a lean-to in the wink of an eye, as you did before."

Despite my tendency to be polite, I growled at him. "A lean-to? I don't want to live out my days in a lean-to in the woods."

"Nor shall you, unless you lack the imagination to dream of more."

When his words failed to lift my spirits, he rose to his feet and shuffled so close, his face lay a hand's breadth from mine.

With two fingers, he raised my chin until our eyes met. "Oh, bother, here I go again. Either I've lost my touch, or the new generation of pilgrims have grown more skeptical. I beg you to believe. This world is yours to make of what you wish, not a curse but a blessing."

My heart began to pound. I had believed in magic as a child, imagining alternative worlds, all more pleasing than my own, but these dreams became brittle with age and shattered. My prior life offered no magic, only vague hope that too often turned to despair.

Do I dare to dream again?

"If your world is such a blessing, can I banish death? Can I bring back the one I loved?"

The custodian's brows dipped at the corners. "I'm sorry. Like all things, magic has its limits. You may create most anything so long as you imagine with enough conviction, but you must stay within the rules: you may conjure memories as in your sleeping dreams, but these are ephemeral—you cannot change the past or violate the laws of nature. Your opportunity is to bring to life waking dreams fresh and new."

I sat up straighter, pressing my back to the chair. Could it be, a world to make as I saw fit? The maelstrom had proved to be a form of magic I could not otherwise explain. The brook and the birds in the trees *did* come to pass as I'd imagined them, but even if true, would such power be enough? The borderland was verdant, wild, and unknown, a blank slate—possibly a paradise, maybe an illusion. I recalled the world I came from, plagued by discord, illness and death, less paradise, more hell. Was that the nature of things?

I took in a breath and released it in a long stream. "I seem to have no choice."

The custodian took a step back and drew himself up, seeming taller than his limited height. "No choice? My boy, you've been given a wonderful opportunity. You should be rejoicing like—" He stopped in mid-sentence and took a moment to reflect. "Forgive me. I'm so much more accustomed to this world than you who just arrived. It's late now. You're weary from your journey and confounded by the sudden change. I have a modest guest room. Stay the night with me. Get some rest and ponder what I've told you. Perhaps in the morning, things will be clearer, and you'll be more enthusiastic to start on your way."

He led me to a small room with minimal furnishings: a bed not quite long enough to hold my frame, a wooden table with two drawers, and a desk with a brass candle holder. Not a place for guests to linger, but preferable to the shelter from the night before.

I kept the candle lit and lay down, staring at the flickering shadows it made on the rafters of the ceiling.

I might cause memories to appear, but these would be ephemeral. The past cannot not be changed, but whatever else I can imagine with conviction will come to life. No choice. I'll go out tomorrow and explore this new world, magic or not, and see if I can do a better job than the gods did with the old.

I rose and blew out the candle. As I lay back in the dark, I whispered to Addy: *"Illusion or not, I may have found the land of dreams."*

I arose the next morning well rested but only a bit less confused. The custodian served me a biscuit with jam and honey and a fresh cup of tea, and waited until I finished before offering to answer my questions.

I glanced around the chamber, an unlikely hollowed-out tree that a hummingbird had guided me to. The whole experience from the time I'd made the leap had been strange. Once I exited this front door, I had no idea what to expect, but likely would be on my own. Or would I?

"Will I meet others like me in the borderland, travelers from the real world?"

The custodian stood and circled the room twice, as if making certain to phrase his answer better than the night before. At last, his lips curled into a curious smile. "Fewer pilgrims pass through the portal these days—too many skeptics and non-believers. Those who come stay here a brief time, and either move on to the enchanted land or return to their homes, so meeting someone here is possible but rare. In the enchanted land, you will meet lots of ordinary folks, but they will not be like you. Other conjurers, however, settle there, all much more experienced. For better or worse, you will encounter them."

"Why for better or worse?"

He paused and gazed up at the rafters. When he looked back, his pleasant smile had turned into a frown. "If you stay long enough, you'll discover how the power can change you. It brings out more of your character, both its strengths and... its flaws." His frown deepened, and his brows drooped. "For what is magic if not the bending of reality to one's will. If one's will becomes corrupted, so too will the magic, and thus evil defiles an otherwise peaceful world."

I raised a hand to query him further, but before I could state my concern, the smile returned.

"And you may meet Lyra."

"Lyra?"

"The transition can be challenging for pilgrims—a multitude of choices. You might achieve your dreams in the end, but many are unsure of what to wish for, so the forces that created this realm provided Lyra, part guide and part helper. Of course, you may never meet her. You may be one of those so sure or your intent as to have no need. She was put here as a facilitator but has developed a mind of her own, and appears only to those she deems needy."

A multitude of choices.

I knitted my brow. "After I pass through that door, which way do I go. North? South? Can you give me some direction to start."

"The choices are yours, not mine."

"Then at least lend me a map?"

"A map?" His voice rose an octave. "To the world you've yet to create?"

I sighed and gave a deep shrug. "How about provisions to last a day or two while I figure this out?"

"No need."

He urged me to stand in front of the small table fronting the brazier.

"Place you pack here, close your eyes, and imagine what you'd like to have in it."

I set the pack down, grimacing as it settled, half empty with little left inside, closed my eyes, and waited a few seconds before opening them. The contents remained unchanged.

"Remember," the custodian said, "always with conviction."

I squeezed my eyes shut again and held them this time, thinking of Addy at the lakefront on a blanket with a basket of food she'd prepared for a summer outing. I pictured the feast in such detail my mouth watered.

When I opened my eyes this time, I gasped.

The pack on the table bulged with provisions.

Chapter 4 – Visions

I hoisted the pack and went outside, but before starting out, I glanced over my shoulder at the open doorway. The custodian avoided my gaze, staring at the ceiling, and shut the door behind me. I suspected if I knocked again, he'd deny me entrance, like a mama bird tossing her chick out of the nest to fall or fly.

Time to fly.

I placed one tentative bootstep on the spongy moss and let it settle, checking for ground solid enough to support my weight. Perhaps he was spying on me through a peephole in the door, fascinated by the launch of another of his proteges. Determined to avoid embarrassing myself, I set out with a brisk pace on a path I swore did not exist the evening before.

The rising sun foretold a more comfortable day, and as my sore muscles eased, my stride lengthened. I tramped on the unchanging trail until out of sight of the tree, where I paused to take stock.

This is my world, to change as I see fit, but only if I have conviction. Time to consider what I want.

For a start, I removed the pack and set it on the ground, curious what my newfound power had provided. Much as I guessed, it contained what Addy might have stuffed into her basket: succulent slices of ham; a loaf of pumpkin bread still warm, though I'd spotted no oven; a stick of butter and a jar of raspberry jam; and two pears, each with a pink blush signifying their ripeness.

The magic had worked, albeit with a modest request. What next to wish for?

Hope is a persistent thing. Even where there should be none, it flashes its wings and attempts to fly. After a fashion, Addy had stayed with me since the day she died, first in my minute-to-minute thoughts, and then day to day. As I busied myself trying to rebuild my life, I thought of her less, at least in my waking hours, but I couldn't move past the night dreams.

Their settings varied and the circumstances changed, but one common thread remained: she would appear as clear as when she was alive. We'd meet for a moment but never touch. Always in odd ways, she'd fade away.

Many a night as I dozed off in my cottage bed, she'd visit me in the twilight between wake and sleep, her presence vivid but always beyond my reach.

I'm sitting at a table with neighbors at the harvest festival, surrounded by signs of fall — hay bales and corn stalks, pumpkins, and multicolored gourds. On a platform in the front, musicians play a lively reel with fiddle and penny whistle on a wooden platform. Children twirl and dance to the music, their laughter filling the air.

I tap my foot to the rhythm and say, "Such a lovely tune."

Addy's voice behind me says, "Lovely." After a pause, she adds, "I have to go away for a while."

"How long?" I say. "A week or two?"

"Longer."

"I understand. You need to rest, but I'd hope no more than two."

When she fails to answer, I wait three more beats and turn around to look. Nothing but an empty chair.

I'm outside our cottage, stacking firewood I'd split on the chopping block, piling it in alternating rows to dry for winter. From inside, Addy hums a tune, likely as she worked on a new quilt to keep us warm. I go to check on her progress, but when I reach for the door, the knob is gone with no way to release the latch.

I knock. No answer.

I pound on the door. "The latch is broken. Please let me in."

The humming stops.

We're hiking in the mountains to the north of the lake, as we'd done on a many a summer day. In this dream, we attain the summit, admire the view in an open field of daisies, and pass around a wineskin. After we head back down, we come to a crossroads, one marked on our map. The left path is shorter, steeper, but exposed with better views. The right path is gentler, meandering through the woods before rejoining the trail.

Addy had always been skittish about heights, avoiding those with broad vistas and steep drop-offs, so she chooses the easier way. We agree to meet below.

I wander down my hike of choice, wishing we'd stayed together. At the convergence of trails, I rest on a rock to wait.

In dreams, time has no meaning, so I have no sense of how long I wait, but I grow impatient and consider setting off on my own. After a time, she emerges from the trees. I rise to greet her, but she passes by without acknowledging me.

I follow, but she speeds up, faster than I can move. As the space between us lengthens, she thins and becomes translucent.

The trail grows thick with mist. The lines of the mountain blur, and the sky turns threatening. Ominous clouds billow overhead, and thunder rumbles. Somewhere in the distance, a dog barks, and a passing rain sweetens the ghost fog. Then she's gone.

The custodian had insisted this was my world to create if I had enough conviction, but I could never change the past. The custodian be damned.

I raised my eyes to the heavens and imagined a loftier goal than provisions, more miracle than magic.

When I glanced back down, I caught a shimmering in the trees lining the path, less tangible than the surrounding terrain, more like those bordering the lake when I'd first arrived. As I gaped, they turned into bushes and the bushes bloomed, brightening the setting with roses, yellows and reds.

I approached and picked one of the brightest, bringing it close until its petals tickled my nose. Its perfume made me light-headed. As I staggered, grasping at the flimsy branches to steady myself, I caught movement ahead. I stared harder, unblinking. Yes, a shape, for sure, moving toward me on the path.

All sound ceased. No birds. No crickets. The wind itself held its breath as the shape took form.

Addy.

She drifted by, stopping to smell the roses on either side—she so loved roses. I stepped closer, but as I reached for her, she passed right through me. When I spun around, she was gone, along with the flowers.

Chapter 5 – Lyra

For the next two days, I refrained from magic, confounded by my last attempt, but by the morning of the third day, I'd eaten through my provisions. Rather than refill the pack in the same manner, I chose an alternate approach. The borderland may be devoid of people, but it had rich soil and plenty of sun and rain. I rejected food on demand, and instead determined to enhance this verdant land with growing things.

Whether through conviction or hunger, I let the magic fill me and envisioned bushes ripe with berries. A popping noise sounded, followed by a rumble like the earth moving. Before me, in an area ten paces by ten, the trees vanished, trunk and roots, branches and leaves, as if swept away by a raging flood. In their place, the ground churned and eight bushes burst forth, grew to knee height, and then to my waist. Tips of green buds sprouted, blossoms bloomed, and in less than a minute, strawberry beds hung heavy with fruit grown ripe and red.

I picked one and sniffed. Its fragrance delighted my senses. I bit down, and my mouth reveled in its flavor. Unlike my prior vision, I'd created something real.

The newfound power pulsed though me with an energy I made no effort to contain. I twirled around, heel to toe, waving my arms as I imagined a seasoned wizard would. Additional bushes appeared, lush with blueberries, blackberries, and raspberries.

Now how to gather the food? On a fine summer's day, Addy and I would head into the woods, basket in hand, and harvest bright red strawberries, so plump we thought they'd melt in our hands. More confident now, I waved a hand and conjured a cedar bark basket identical to the one she'd brought on our outings.

I set about filling it, shuffling along the pathway as if better to appreciate the loamy ground, relishing the sheer joy of it. I hadn't been this happy in a long time.

Lost in this reverie, I wandered far from my creations, until I stumbled upon a narrow path, the kind worn down by animals frequenting a watering hole. To my surprise, it bore a clear sign of tracks, not animal tracks but those made by bare human feet. At least, they appeared human, although so small as to have belonged to a child and so shallow they barely left a mark.

I glanced about to get my bearings. Thick ferns loomed overhead, their fronds fingering the air. These clustered on either side so they shadowed the way, letting through only an occasional shaft of sunlight. As I narrowed my eyes, trying to scout ahead, I caught a fluctuation in the light, or more likely some deviant vegetation defying the unending green.

Perhaps like the hummingbird, the footsteps were leading me to something important. I quickened my pace. Around the third turn, the vegetation opened enough to make out the far edge of a clearing. The splash of color that had drawn my eye had come from a cluster of rhododendron bushes, each twice my height, with bright blue blossoms the size of grapefruits. A bench nestled among them, and on it sat a person.

I drew in a sudden breath and stopped in my tracks. While the scene remained obscured by fern leaves, I recognized the apparition.

Addy again, though I'd not summoned her this time.

She rested there as she might have in life, ankles crossed and hands folded on her lap, her face framed by the flowers. A strand of golden hair had slipped down and caressed her cheek. A dreamy expression masked her features, a look of being on the bench, but also being elsewhere—of being real but not real.

I crept closer, not wanting to startle away this latest vision.

If this is a mirage, let the illusion last forever.

At arm's length, I stopped and whispered, "Addy?"

No response.

I closed my eyes and inhaled, hoping to sense her perfume.

Nothing.

I reached out to touch her, but once more, the vision rippled and disappeared.

My knees buckled and I slumped to the mossy ground, struggling to catch my breath, focusing on the song of birds that had reappeared as if to soothe a distressed mind.

As my breathing eased and my heartbeat slowed, I recalled something I'd read: everyone dies three times—the first when their body fails; the second when the last person who loved them recalls them no more; and the final time when no one is left to say their name.

By that standard, Addy still lived, because here on this mossy ground dwelled one who had loved her and moments before believed she sat nearby.

I staggered to my feet and collapsed next to the spot where she'd appeared, brushing the wooden slats with my fingertips, hoping to find its surface still warm. I was new to this magic. Was my conviction insufficient, my imagination too vague to bring her back to life?

I pictured the time we hiked in the mountains when the heather bloomed, resting at a viewpoint on a rock ledge, her with her speckled kerchief tied around her hair. Her cheeks glowed with the rush of blood, and her eyes sparkled.

I cried aloud with as much conviction as I could muster. "If I can recall you so alive, why can't I bring you back to life?"

I waited for an answer, but only the birdsong replied.

Then I heard it, not the sound of a bird's wings flapping through the air nor the swish of silken fabric rubbing together, but of someone slipping through the tall grass circling the clearing.

The motion stopped, and a voice sounded behind me, as melodious as the birdsong. "You can't because she can never be part of this world."

I turned to find a young girl approaching, half hidden in the shadow of the ferns. After a moment, she emerged into the sunlight, taking her time, as if afraid to scare me away. Her skin shone as if lit less by the sun than from within. Her flaxen hair drifted straight down to the small of her back and was broken only by two tiny ears, which I expected to be pointed like an elf's.

She flicked her gaze up to meet mine, and I regarded her long enough to be uncomfortable. I fixed on her eyes, irises almost gold in color, with what appeared to be an amber ring around their centers. Dark lashes highlighted the eyes.

Though more real than my vision, she moved without sound, stepping so lightly the grass hardly bent beneath her bare feet—clearly the source of the footprints.

"Why did you lead me here to tempt me into what's forbidden?"

"To teach you a lesson." When I gaped open-mouthed, she gave a hint of a bow, no more than a gentle nod of the head. "My name is Lyra."

"Lyra. The one the custodian spoke of. I hoped you'd find me, since I'm as confused as any of your pilgrims. I can use your help. What took you so long?"

"I can't teach a pilgrim who isn't ready to learn. You weren't ready."

I pondered her words, wondering what lesson I was meant to learn. "You haven't answered my question. The custodian insisted I had the power to create anything, limited only by my conviction. While I can't change the past, why can't I add to this new world someone from before?"

She stepped closer so a bar of light fell across her face, revealing a compassion hard to explain, one part wonder and one part sadness. "This world must be built from aspirations, not memories."

When I scrunched my brow—the rules too obscure for me—she rested a hand on my arm to reassure me. "Memories of past people lack substance like bricks or stone. You can't build with them. You can only cast a smile or shed a tear before they dissipate like fog in the morning sun. You need to create your world anew."

"I don't understand."

"Let me show you an example."

With a wave of her hand, she conjured a blank canvas on an easel and a paintbrush with an engraved silver handle.

As she waved the brush across the canvas, a picture appeared, a scene of her sitting by a river's edge at noon. A full-grown maple provided shade overhead, and behind it spread a meadow lush with green grass and sprinkled with buttercups. A little way downstream, a row of willows grew, their branches swaying in the breeze.

I gaped at the fine detail, the rich colors, and the sunlight sparkling on the water, but I gasped when the clearing I stood in changed to match the image. A river now flowed alongside us. The sun shone over the water as it had on the canvas, and flowers bloomed in a grassy meadow.

After she finished, the painting beamed worthy of a master, but as she handed the brush to me, the picture vanished, along with the riverside scene.

"What happened to your picture?"

"It's temporary... like me. This is your world. You can paint anything you like. That's why you're here, to create your new reality. Show me what you desire the most."

What I desire the most? To turn back the clock to a time when I still had dreams, to the point before my heart froze over.

As I accepted the brush and approached the canvas, a gust kicked up, making the grass sway, but the wind had no effect on the girl. Her loose-fitting smock hung limp on her slender form and her hair never budged, laying still about her shoulders.

I held the brush over the canvas, its tip hovering a thumb's width above the surface but never touching. After a moment, I returned it to her.

"I can't."

She shook her head, sighed, and settled on the bench beside me, where the vision had sat moments before. "Now I understand. You're one of the lost, one who came here not to find a new world but to escape the old." She twirled a lock of hair around her finger and glanced away, fiddling with a pendant hanging from her neck on a golden chain. "Here. Perhaps this will help." She removed the pendant and offered it to me.

"What is it?"

"A pilgrim's locket, made to help define your goal."

"May I open it?"

"Of course. Release the clasp here."

I pried it apart, careful not to break it. The locket opened into four oval compartments holding pictures: the first with a picture of a toddler, the second an awkward schoolboy, and the third a foolish adult. The fourth was blurred with mist."

"Do you recognize them?"

I checked again, and gasped. "They're me, but how?"

"A locket comes into being for each traveler, a reminder of where you've come from, for though you can't change the past, you can't create a future without it. The fourth picture is yours and will come into focus as you decide who you want to be."

I clutched the locket and stared at the blank frame. "I thought you were supposed to help me with that?"

Her eyes rounded, a look of feigned innocence. "Me? It's *your* magic."

I winced and slipped the locket into my pack. "At least help me search for the answer. Let's leave this place of false hope and find out what lies at the end of this trail. You're supposed to be my guide. You lead."

She gave me an unnerving glare, this time letting her gaze pass from my head to my toes before relenting. "Very well. I'm here to serve." She rose in a huff, turned, and loped off down the path, calling back over her shoulder. "Follow me."

For the rest of the day, she set a frantic pace, with me struggling to keep up. At times, she pulled so far ahead, I glimpsed nothing more than a swatch of flaxen hair in the distance.

"Wait," I cried at my limit, and she stopped. "How much farther?"

"Forever," she replied, "for this trail doesn't end until *you* decide where it leads."

Chapter 6 – Shooting Stars

For the rest of the day, I followed with little respite, until I arrived at a clearing with an inviting flat rock. I collapsed on it and refused to go on, hoping this so-called helper would forget about me, but after a few moments, she circled back.

Small as she was, she loomed over me, hands on hips. "Well...?"

"I won't go any farther with no end in sight."

"The end is yours to create."

"You're supposed to help."

"Prod might be a better word, because only you can define your future."

Absurd as it seemed, she was intent on convincing me this world was a blank slate. I remained skeptical, but in my desperation was prepared to play along.

I sighed. "I... may have an idea. Lend me your canvas again."

With little more than a wink, she made the easel, canvas, and brush reappear.

I accepted the brush from her and let my hand wander across the canvas. A picture emerged of a boat on a lake, but the image lacked definition, with ragged lines and sloppy form, as a child might draw. As a further insult, no replica appeared on the horizon.

"I painted my goal. Why doesn't the magic make it real?"

"Because it's made up to please me, not created from your hopes and dreams. It's no more real than your memories because it's not real to you."

She was right. What I'd drawn came not from my current life but from old fantasies shared with another. After she died, those passed with her. This insincere attempt at sketching my future had failed because I'd painted a false vision without conviction.

I tossed the brush back to her and buried my face in my hands. "I have no hope. My dreams ended in the past."

She stepped closer and settled next to me on the rock. Whatever condescension had possessed her was gone, replaced by compassion.

"Sometimes, a pilgrim needs more time to find his purpose. You should rest. We'll go no farther today."

It turned out that Lyra required no food, drink, or sleep, but accustomed to travelers from the real world, she helped me set up camp for the night.

Beneath a canopy of oak branches thick enough to protect me from all but the heaviest downpour, I prepared the clearing by hand, as I had that first night. I swept the leaves into a pile to create a soft bed, but quit with the task half done, my shoulders slumping and my eyes downcast.

Lyra approached me concerned. When I refused to acknowledge her, she gave a cough. "Why do you stare at the ground, Lucas, when you can behold the heavens instead?"

Though her intent remained a mystery, I determined she had my best interest at heart, so I did as she asked. The universe above sparkled, a clear night with a blanket of stars so dense they formed a gem-like mist. Then I caught the reason she'd made me look up. Across the sky, streaks of white appeared, flaring and vanishing by the dozens, shining like silver rain.

"Do you realize what they are?" she said.

"Our philosophers claim they're rocks flying through the air and catching fire when they come too close, the gods' way of protecting us."

"I know nothing about your gods, but I know shooting stars. They're a wonder of the night, and at least in this world, if you wish upon them, you're wish may come true."

I beheld the streaks anew. The night was laced with them, so many I could almost hear them calling to me. My breath came in short bursts.

What happened to your sense of wonder, Lucas? Where has it gone?

Did I dare? The custodian had said anything I imagined might come to pass, but if I were to dare, what would I wish for?

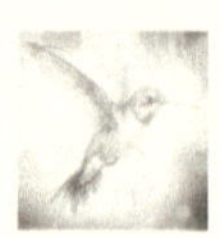

That night, I dreamed I awoke on the banks of a pond, with a bed of white lilies floating near the shore. Its surface mirrored the light of a crescent moon and the surrounding trees showed in reflection. A trilling wafted on the breeze like the music of the custodian's wind chimes. I rose and followed the sound to a familiar cottage, whose yard lay barren, as if abandoned. As I gaped, I

detected a padding from within like someone bustling about wearing slippers. Through the open doorway, I caught a shadow cast from the rays of a lantern. When I poked my head inside to discover its owner, I found nothing but a disconnected shadow.

A sigh sounded behind me. I turned to find the likeness of Addy at the edge of the clearing, her hands hugging her arms as if cold. No more than a likeness because she lacked color or definition, with skin grayer than flesh and the edges of her body shimmering, an image as malformed as my attempt at painting the lake on canvas.

"Come in with me," I begged, a tremor in my voice, perhaps from the chill night air. "Come in and be warm."

She demurred, never speaking, but gave the slightest shake of her head, enough to make her golden hair swish about, and pointed to the cottage behind me.

Inside, the orphan shadow had extended an arm and, with one finger, beckoned me to come in. I wanted to refuse, to insist I wouldn't go in unless she came with me, but at last I understood. I entered alone, for in this world, as in my home, she would never join me again.

From the doorway, at the far side of the threshold, I gaped as she faded into the night.

I awoke to the gentle lapping of water, and farther off, to a trilling like in my dream. I kept my eyes closed, fearing I'd find everything had changed. I tried to deny the change, to make it fade away, but the sounds persisted.

At last, I opened my eyes and found myself lying on the sandy shore of a pond, though I'd fallen asleep surrounded by forest. I startled to windchimes in the distance, too distinct to be imagined.

I staggered to my feet and followed the sound. After making my way through a gap in the trees, I discovered a clear path, hushed and peaceful but dense with fog. Thin white wisps wove about my ankles and muffled my footsteps. Not far ahead, a light twinkled through the branches in the musky dawn.

Shortly, I came to a barebones cottage set in the center of a clearing, much like my former home but lacking any embellishments. It had a single door in the middle at ground level, bracketed by a window on either side, each bearing a flowerbox. These appeared untended, containing nothing but a smattering of decayed geraniums, adding to the abandoned nature of the washed-out façade. No curtains hung across the windows to shroud what lay inside, their open frames revealing nothing but a brass lantern, the source of the light.

I reached out and tested the latch. The door yielded to my touch with the slightest pressure, but I hesitated to go in.

I 'd conjured streams and flowers, followed a persistent hummingbird that led me to the custodian, and witnessed buds bloom into fruit in seconds. The pond had appeared overnight while I slept, after making unconscious wishes upon shooting stars. In such a world, was anything impossible?

A familiar voice tipped the balance for me — Lyra, appearing as usual from nowhere, as if possessing a mystical ability to find me in need.

"Aren't you going in?" she said.

"I wouldn't want to intrude on someone else's home. I couldn't—"

She cut me off, waving her hands as if to clear a noxious mist. "It's waiting for you. No one is inside."

I eyed the flickering flame and turned to face her. "Then who lit the lantern."

She answered with the same infuriating tone. "You did, Lucas, the maker of worlds."

Chapter 7 – Apples

Inside, the cottage lay bare, its bones all but exposed to the weather, with nary a splash of color to brighten it. Encouraged by the triumph of my dream, I set about making it more like a home.

To warm the place, I conjured a fireplace, first of modest brick, but on second thought replaced with a more impressive one of stone. Before the hearth, I placed an oaken table and two rocking chairs with a couch in between. Outside, I populated a rack with two cords of wood but stopped short of finishing the job. Instead, I added a wedge and chopping block, and split the logs by hand. As I swung the wedge, the muscles of my shoulders sang.

After filling the fireplace, I lit the fire with a wave of my arm. The room warmed, so much cozier than my lean-tos in the forest. I sprawled on the couch, gazed into the crackling flames, and let the world go still. The piney scent brought back visions of things I wished I'd done and raised my hope for the future. Tomorrow, I'd make this cottage more of a home, adding a garden in front. For the first time in months, I looked forward to the next day, but now, exhausted, I readied for bed.

I lay down and stared at the ceiling beams conjured from nothing. Now, as I waited for sleep to come, I wondered how solid this creation might be. Years before, I had taken half a year to construct our cottage, often with neighbors' help. Would this structure, constructed from nothing but magic, withstand a storm, or would it be as insubstantial as a dream? Would it keep out the rain?

Addy loved the rain, how it drummed on the timbers above us. At night, we'd snuggle in bed and listen to how the storm argued with the wind demanding entry, and how the fire in the hearth snapped back, telling it this home had no place for its fury.

My breathing slowed, and with it, the forest outside gave itself over to the gentle rustle of night.

While I pondered the accomplishments of the day, I caught drumming on the beams, which brought a smile to my face. Conscious or not, I had made it rain.

My bed had no lumps to cause discomfort. This room I created held no fears. Weary and content, I fell into a deep sleep.

I awoke to morning sunlight streaming through the window.

I enjoyed the cottage the next couple of days, sleeping well and relishing fresh food from my conjured garden. I cleaned out the debris in the flowerbox by hand, but unwilling to wait for nature, willed a smattering of mature geraniums to fill the pots. I covered the windows with curtains, each with a unique floral pattern.

I continued to try out my powers, adding a waterfall to the side of the pond, fed by an underground stream. The newfound current rippled across the surface before disappearing into the woods, perhaps flowing all the way to the flood plain where I'd first arrived. Along the path, I created bushes lush with berries. For fun, I conjured a pair of golden swords and swished them about in the yard, but feeling foolish dueling alone, I hung them crosswise above the mantle instead.

With a twirl of my fingers, I produced a journal, a quill pen, and a bottle of ink, intending to catalog how this world would differ from the old. I took up the pen but hesitated, its tip hovering over the page. I wanted to write, "No sorrow allowed," but sorrow had accompanied me here. In its place, I scribbled, "Sunshine daily, rain at night." I tried to compose more, but no words came, only a lonely phrase blotted out before the ink dried.

By late afternoon, daydreams replaced rational thought. Memories flooded in of apple picking in the fall. I recalled rows of trees with branches bending under the weight of fruit, red and ripe, and a shack below from where smoke would rise, sending forth the aroma of cider steeping and pies baking in an oven.

This vision filled my mind with such need, I suspected my ruminations might have brought it into being, though I hadn't conjured it like my other feats of sorcery. I went outside to check and found a new path had appeared behind the cottage.

My previous tricks had surfaced as envisioned, yet now I noted how this latest differed from what I'd imagined. The custodian had insisted this world was mine to define, but it seemed to possess a plan of its own. Sometimes, like Lyra, it nudged my wishes in a preferred direction.

I followed the path as it veered into a glade, and a hilly grove loomed above me. Trees lay in neat rows laden with apples, but something was missing. No shack appeared at the bottom of the hill and no people to make the cider and bake the pies. Here in the borderland, I stood alone, surrounded by the scent of the fruit.

I reached up and picked three of the ripest apples, stored two in my pack and bit into the third. It tasted juicy but tart. I recalled how Addy used to bring along a pot of honey. I waved my arms and wished for honey, but for some reason, no matter how hard I tried, none appeared.

Why does the magic fail me now? Had I violated some rule?

Lyra snuck up from behind, wandered past the unspoken question, and stopped before me, hands on hips. "You know why."

I glanced back at the familiar cottage with its flowerboxes and curtains, its hearth, and bushes ripe with berries, and realized the answer. Instead of focusing on aspirations, I'd been trying to recreate my life back home, and yet I remained alone.

"Come walk with me, Lyra. There's something I need to do."

We headed down the path toward the pond. At the shore, I stood for a moment in silence as the trees above me stilled. At last, I removed my boots and rolled up my pants, as I had when I first passed through the maelstrom. With a sigh, I waded in and picked the most beautiful lily. My eyes misted, but I pressed on, deeper until I reached the current. The water swirled around my knees as I set down the flower and let it float away like the toy boat of my youth.

You will always dwell in my memory, but you can never be part of this world.

Chapter 8 – Honey

The young woman drifted through the trees, breathing to a measured rhythm. Her breast rose and fell like a tree filling with wind and settling with the calm. After a time, exhausted and without direction, she rested on a rock and considered her situation. The man who called himself the custodian had insisted she controlled this world, and in some respects, she had. Bubbling brooks appeared to quench her thirst, berry bushes to sate her hunger. When she wearied for the night, a shaded clearing opened, with soft ground and plentiful pine needles to make a bed.

Yet something was lacking.

She removed the sack from her back, other than her clothing the only remnant of her old life—she had not planned to come here and had arrived unprepared. From inside, she withdrew the last of the berries and determined to resist conjuring any more. The little man had said she must use magic with conviction, but how could she have conviction without purpose. She pondered this as she munched on the berries, wincing at their tartness. If only she had something sweet to add.

She was startled as a bee appeared, yellow- and black-striped and about the size of a walnut. It buzzed around her head, but not in a threatening way. In this strange world, she'd found little life beyond the custodian and Lyra. If she felt lonely, a squirrel might appear, or a robin might hop about in the high grass and sing a tune, but she'd never encountered a bee.

The bee stopped an arm's length away, hovering before her and making a buzzing noise. If she closed her eyes, it sounded almost like words as it flitted to the edge of the clearing and waited. When she failed to understand, it repeated the routine.

"You want me to follow?" Despite the oddities of this place, she felt foolish speaking to an insect.

The bee bounced up and down like a nod and flew off.

She followed.

A little way down the path, it led her to the trunk of a gnarly tree. Inside a hole in the knob, she found a honeycomb. She hesitated to reach in, afraid to disturb the hive, but a beam of sunlight broke through the branches of the overhanging trees and revealed the nest abandoned. Cautiously, she reached in and snapped off a piece of the comb. It dripped with nectar.

As she puzzled what to do, a clay pot appeared in her spare hand. It bore a painting of a scene from her home—ocean waves, amber-colored sand, and high dunes. She let the honey drip in and gather more, until the pot was full.

She returned to her perch on the rock where she'd left her pack and dipped a berry into the honey—less tart, but not quite right. She realized the problem—honey went better with apples. Besides her reluctance to engage in more magic, she'd never conjured more than a few bushes and now worried a fruit tree might be beyond her power. She tried. Nothing happened—too complex a task, or as the custodian would say, too little conviction.

She brushed away a lock that had fallen across one eye and stared into the distance, where she spotted a familiar figure emerging from the trees, a girl with flaxen hair.

Her features tightened. "Hello, Lyra, are you ready to guide me to my new goal?"

The girl stamped her bare foot and circled the clearing twice before stopping to face her. Her eyes shifted from side to side—not an encouraging sign. Lyra had been less than forthcoming with her.

Lyra took a breath, and the words rushed out. "Yes, why not. Follow me. I'll lead you to where you need to go." She spun about and reentered the trees but at a more leisurely pace than their last encounter.

Why not, indeed? Lost and without direction, what other choice do I have?

The young woman followed.

Chapter 9 – Apples and Honey

As I sat on the soft sand by the banks of the pond, the afternoon sun kissed the top of the trees and cast a golden path on the water. With the music of the waterfall filling the air, my cottage brightened by geraniums, and my conjured orchard bursting with fruit, I should have been content. I bit into a slice of apple and winced—juicy but too tart. With my pack open between my knees, the two remaining apples I'd picked gaped back at me like accusing red eyes.

Why am I so restless? Why this emptiness in my chest?

Lyra had called me one of the lost who came here not to find a new world but to escape the old. Now I'd determined to move on but was unsure where to go, and time was passing me by. One day, I would wink out like a firefly, despite my cottage, my pond, my orchard and garden, never leaving a mark.

The space in my chest filled with longing, an emotion I'd been too numb to feel these past months. The longing swirled, now a maelstrom, now a whirlwind, and like a whirlwind or maelstrom, it spun in circles, longing without direction.

I dug into my pack and pulled out the locket. Where the fourth picture had been blank before, now a vague fog showed—small progress there.

Now that I'm alone, who am I, and who do I aspire to be?

The sound of footsteps tramping along the path interrupted my reverie. Likely Lyra come to nag me to find a goal, to prod me, but to what end? Better to leave me to brood.

Wait. No.

Steps too firm for Lyra.

I twisted around and caught movement through the trees, different from my visions of the past. Those others had floated through the world. This figure made the grass bow beneath her feet and the branches rattle, bearing not an air of ethereal contentment, but a troubled frown. Rather than float, she trudged toward the pond, head down, too preoccupied to notice me.

She stopped when almost upon me, and her brows rose. The index finger of her right hand reached out an inch at a time, until it brushed my shoulder and jerked away, a gesture a child might make on touching a hot stove for the first time.

While she stumbled about in small circles as if searching for an explanation for what she'd discovered, I took her in—taller than Addy by a hand, with flashing brown eyes rather than blue, and raven hair marred by bits of twigs and leaves. She wore a light jacket pulled tight about her, causing the content of one pocket to bulge. Neither vision nor memory—a person I'd never met before.

At last, she steadied and spoke, though in a halting voice. "Are you... real?"

I groped for an answer, unsure myself, so I nodded instead, my heart pounding so hard I feared it would burst from my rib cage.

She crept closer, reached out a hand, and rested it on my shoulder. "You *are* real."

I fumbled for how to respond, certain I hadn't conjured her, yet here she stood. Only one explanation.

"Did you come through the maelstrom as well?"

"I... don't know what you mean."

"How did you come to be here?"

The light was failing. She gazed up at the twilit sky, still with streaks of orange, and fixed on the red glow burnishing the surface of the water. She spoke with her face turned away from me, her words tumbling out like the waterfall.

"I... have a small cottage at the edge of the dunes. These past months, I made a habit of walking on the beach around sunset to search the ocean. The dunes are high where I live, with only a few trails through. That evening was low tide, and the waves were little more than a ripple, so I decided to stroll along the waterline. I'd had a bad time of it lately and was distraught, lost in thought when a strange fog blew in, the kind I'd only seen once before. It lay thick, as if the bowl of the sky had spilled all its milky clouds onto the sand.

"Despite the years I'd lived there, I became disoriented, and as night fell, I panicked, racing up and down the beach, unable to find any path back through the dunes. When I finally stumbled upon one, I lunged toward it, anything to escape the ghostly fog, but when I tried to enter, my way was blocked by a swirling orb. Exhausted and longing for rest, I burst through. On the far side, my home and all I'd known had vanished. In their stead, I found a place I'd never been, a broad body of water, not like the ocean—smaller waves—but the largest lake I'd ever seen, surrounded by pines and spruce. I started to turn back, but when I glanced behind me, the world I'd left was gone."

"The maelstrom," I said.

"What?"

"The same orb I passed through. From that spot, was the only choice a path through arched trees leading you on?"

Her eyes widened. Their intent was difficult to fathom, as if she used them to search other people's thoughts rather than reveal her own:

"Yes," she said. "With nothing else to do, I followed it."

"As did I."

"I staggered around half the night until I fell asleep with exhaustion, and awoke expecting to be home in my bed after a disturbing dream. Instead, I found an unending trail. I almost gave up hope when—I feel foolish saying it—a hummingbird appeared and led me to... No, you'll think me crazy."

I grasped her by the shoulders and turned her to face me. "The hummingbird led you to a tree with a door, where you met a little man, the custodian."

With a hand to her forehead, she wavered as if about to fall.

I caught her, lowered her to the ground, and sat back down next to her. Noting her parched lips, I offered her my water bottle.

She clutched it in both hands and took a few eager gulps.

I eased the bottle away. "How long has it been since you last drank?"

She screwed up her face trying to remember. "I've lost track of time. Could it be yesterday when I met the custodian, or two days ago?"

"And food?"

"The same except for a few berries."

"Why didn't you use the magic he taught you to conjure up provisions."

She grabbed the bottle back from me and emptied it, then took three breaths to settle herself. "I was afraid. The little man insisted I needed conviction to do magic, something I did only under his tutelage, but my life has had little conviction these past months."

She eyed me as if expecting me to judge her, but my own conviction had been in short supply.

I said, "When I first arrived, I doubted like you, but now I've managed to conjure this pond and waterfall, and nearby a garden and an orchard."

She noted the apples in my pack. "An orchard? Is that where those came from?"

I nodded.

She fumbled in her pocket and pulled out a small clay pot, decorated with the ocean and dunes. "I created a few berry bushes, though I suspect they already existed. Then, as I longed for something to sweeten the berries, a bee flew by and guided me to a nest bursting with honey. Does such a trick count as magic? But when I wished for apples to dip in it, nothing happened. Sensing my frustration, the helper girl, Lyra, appeared and brought me here."

She gaped at my pack, while I eyed the jar in her hands. I pulled out one of the apples, polished it on my sleeve until it sparkled in what was left of the setting sun, and held it up for her.

"I've had an extra three days to adapt," I said, "but I remain a novice. You, who've had less time, have managed to find what has escaped me—honey. Shall we partake in the fruits of our sorcery?"

A sparkle came into her eyes, and for the first time, she smiled.

I took out my knife and cut a quarter moon slice for each of us while she uncovered her jar. As we sat by the pond in the twilight, we partook of apples dipped in honey, like two children tasting their combined goodness for the first time.

After we finished, I turned to her. "We haven't been introduced. I'm Lucas."

"I'm Mia, or at least I was in my old world." A breeze gusted off the water, making her scramble to her feet and wrap her arms about her for warmth. "And Mia, or whoever I am, dreads spending another night outside in the cold."

I stood as well and gestured to the path, now almost invisible in the failing light. "See that? I created it, and at its end, I conjured a place where you can rest for the night. I'm not much of a wizard yet, so it's no palace, but I did manage to add a fireplace to keep us warm."

The sun dipped below the horizon and a silky darkness slipped among the trees, enveloping the two of us. Dusk was a magical time, a thin time between worlds.

I rose and headed to the cottage.

After a brief hesitation, she followed.

In the cottage, she collapsed on the couch, while I lit the fire and stood over it until it burned hot and strong. Then I settled beside her, but not so close as to be touching, being not yet so familiar with her, nor quite convinced she existed.

Moments later, she leaned her head back and dozed off, her breath making purring sounds.

I fetched my journal, pen, and ink, and squatted on the rug in the firelight. Beneath the prior words, "Sunshine daily, rain at night," I scribbled, "Someone to share this world with." I stared at the phrase for a few minutes, unsure whether to blot it out or not.

The ink dried. I let it stay.

My past held storm clouds, and my future lay hidden in haze—the same, I suspected, with Mia. Perhaps the answer lay in discovering the future together.

Chapter 10 – Hopes and Dreams

The following day, I gave Mia a tour, and she made suggestions on how to improve my handiwork. In her eyes, every aspect of the landscape had the potential to be enhanced. She had me add quartz boulders to mark the cottage entrance, angled to glisten in the morning sun, and a double curve in the path to the front door, lined with white stones.

Next, she proposed the cottage's exterior needed more color beyond the garden and flowerboxes.

I balked, saying, "Enough. You have the same power as me. Your turn to try."

Her eyes shifted up to the top of the chimney and, after a deep sigh, down to the ground at her feet. "I can't."

"Why not?"

"Before I came here, I'd lost hope. Without hope, you can't have faith, and without faith, no magic."

How can she have less hope than me? Yet my magic works.

I grasped her hands in mine and forced her to face me. "I suspect If you had no potential, the maelstrom would not have let you through. "Let's try together."

We focused our combined wills, with her likely wishing for flowers and me for hope to return to the both of us. After a moment, a sweet scent filled the air, and the grounds of the modest cottage took on the appearance of a lushly maintained manor awash with lilacs and rhododendrons, a mix of pinks, purples, and reds.

Encouraged by our success, we expanded the garden with cucumbers, summer squash and tomatoes, all staggered so they would ripen a little at a time. At my prompting, she added sunflowers, which towered over all as if standing guard.

As we admired our work, birds in the forest chirped, seeming to join in our celebration.

Mia glanced up to the treetops, searching for the source of the sound hidden in the canopy. "We need more wildlife to populate these woods — nothing dangerous, squirrels and chipmunks and a few rabbits."

"Rabbits are cute, but they scavenge gardens."

Mia's mood, which had been restrained until now, brightened. "I love rabbits."

"But our vegetables—"

"All good things have adversity, else we learn to take them for granted. We can make a fence to protect our crop."

I agreed, but much like I'd relished chopping the firewood or cleaning out the flowerboxes by hand, I needed to be useful on my own.

"All right. We'll make one but without supernatural aids. We'll build it by hand, so when complete, we can take pride in our efforts."

I confess I gave in to some shortcuts, conjuring up the posts and wire, and two sturdy shovels. We took turns digging holes in the soft ground and placing the poles. Once the garden was surrounded, we strung the wire.

Despite a bit of cheating, the effort took up the whole afternoon. When finished, we hovered over our handiwork, hot and tired but satisfied with overcoming the challenge. As we stood in silence, near each other but shoulders not quite touching, a breeze stirred Mia's hair.

She turned to me. "We haven't been to the pond since we first met, and the setting was so pleasant at twilight. Can we go back now?"

The thought had entered my mind as well. I nodded.

Back at our favorite spot, I squatted on the ground, absent-mindedly plucking at the grass.

She remained standing, pacing the shore and picking up small pebbles. After she'd gathered a fistful, she began tossing them into the water one at a time, waiting after each until the ripple settled before tossing another.

After a while, she spoke without facing me. "I understand why I've been brought here. I'd lost interest in my prior life, but now that I'm here, I'm not sure what I'm supposed to do. It can't be enough to grow plants and make your cottage more beautiful."

I waited for her to continue.

She quieted and threw a few more pebbles, this time one after the other so the ripples overlapped.

I could contain the question no longer. "What made you lose hope?"

She hesitated, staring into the water.

I wondered why the birds kept on singing—not pausing their songs to catch the expected revelation, but they would have had to wait too long, so drawn out was her silence.

At last, she spoke as much to the ripples in the pond as to me. "My father was a fisherman. Five days a week, regardless of season, he'd head out on his boat before first light. He sailed in rain and snow, when the leaves had fallen and when the trees had leafed out again and the bushes were flush with berries. He sailed when the seas were calm and when the whitecaps raged. He'd leave with a vessel empty but for the tackle and netting, and return at dusk with caskets full of mackerel, so much this little girl thought it to be magic. That magic provided a modest home for our family, plenty of food and extra to sell at the market.

"As I grew older, he'd take me out with him, but only in perfect weather. He insisted the sea was no place for a child when it became angry. On stormy days, my mother would wait on the shore for him to come back, arms wrapped around her for warmth and squinting into the setting sun. After I was old enough to stay on my own, she begged to go with him in bad weather, so she could help with the catch, but I understood the real reason--she couldn't bear the waiting. On those days, I replaced her standing watch by the dunes.

"Two months ago, they failed to return. A fog had rolled in, so I could see no more than a hundred paces into the sea. I stared out until my eyes watered and began to play tricks with me, teasing me with a flash of reflected sunlight or the hint of a white sail on the horizon. I stayed through the night, trying to conjure a boat through force of will, breathing in small bursts of cold air that stung like needles in my lungs.

"The night before last, a similar fog rolled in. When I first landed in this world, I prayed I'd find them here, believing they couldn't have just vanished. At first, I'd catch glimpses of them floating through the woods, more phantoms than visions. Lyra told me they were nothing but memories, but when memories are all you have, they're a great deal more than nothing."

She flung the remaining pebbles into the pond, making the water churn and froth.

I longed to put my arm around her, to tell her I too understood the power of memories, but a darkness accompanied her, standing beside her like an unwanted acquaintance who refused to leave. How could I tell her I had a darkness of my own?

We're all a collection of our stories, our joys and sorrows, the sum of our loves and losses. The losses too often leave a mark, like scars on the soul. That's why we were kindred spirits, Mia and I—our scars.

When the water calmed, she turned and hovered over me. "Look at you. My story has made you sad, head bowed and squatting on the ground. This spot deserves a bench, so we can sit and watch the sun go down."

"You have magic. Wish for one."

"I don't want any bench. I want one that will please you. What kind do you favor?"

I massaged my forehead with three fingers, too tired to play along, but she'd become so earnest. "A stone bench," I said, "with arms in the shape of eagle heads."

"Stone? Too harsh. I prefer a wooden one, with the sides curled into coils like flowers, and a high back in the center with a carving of a rose."

I sat up straighter. "Wood it is, but enough of flowers. I still want my eagle."

"Not on the arms. The back should taper up with wings on either side and at its peak, an eagle head as if ready to take flight."

"A symbol of hope?" I offered.

"A symbol of hope."

With the plan agreed, the bench came into being.

We settled on it and gazed at the water now mirror smooth. As the sun's last rays sputtered and flared, we lingered by the pond, and I told her about growing up with Addy, about her illness and death, and how I'd struggled ever since.

Now she knew. We both had scars. Scars were part of nature, accumulated throughout life, as a child on the elbows and knees, and as an adult on the heart.

Isn't that the way of life? You accumulate scars and move on.

She shifted closer so our shoulders touched, and began to sing. Her voice filled the damp night air and lost itself in the droplets of darkness.

> *Sail in the sunrise through golden rays,*
> *Return on the tide at the end of days,*
> *Sleep in the moonlight when the stars do shine,*
> *Linger with me till the end of time,*
> *And if the ocean should steal you away,*
> *We'll meet in our dreams I hope and pray.*

"What was that?"

"A song my mother used to sing by the shore while waiting for my father."

A song of loss, a song of longing.

For most of my youth, I'd sought to make sense of life, to discover its meaning. So much of what mattered to me had been invested in Addy. After her passing, life offered more mystery than meaning, but since entering this world, the longing had returned.

"So, Lucas, what do we wish for next?"

I turned to her, my eyes glistening. "Maybe what we've been wishing for is too easy. We wave our hands and make flowers grow or waterfalls flow, but what was more satisfying? Building the fence together. What if what we're searching for must be hard to find?"

She stirred. "Like in the stories my father told me at bedtime when I was little, tales of knights and dragons, of witches and fairies with wings. The ones I loved best were always scary. They'd keep me awake at night wondering how they might turn out. Sometimes the story would last three or four nights, and I had to wait, afraid to learn the ending, because how could such a sad tale end well? Isn't that like in our old lives? After all that's happened to us, how can we expect to be happy again? Yet each time in the stories, the dark part was a passing thing, and the heroes found a way to thrive."

"I remember. That's how all fairytales end."

"Yes, but not in the real world."

"Well, Mia, we're no longer in the real world."

A voice sounded behind us. "Now you're getting the idea. Not the real world indeed. So, are you two lost souls ready to move on to a place of possibilities?"

No need to turn. While Lyra's movements made no sound, I'd learned her presence caused a tingling on my skin. "Hello, Lyra. To where? A vast lake?"

Mia added, "Or a golden tower?"

"No. To the enchanted land."

We gaped at each other, open-mouthed. Were we ready to become sorcerers in a land otherwise not so different from our own?

Our mystical helper, impatient as always, spun about and called back over her shoulder. "I can't decide for you, but when the time is right, summon me, and I'll guide you there."

Back at the cottage, I lit the fire as the twilight shadows dimmed. Once the logs caught and the sparks flew, I turned to Mia. "Perhaps that's the answer. Not a boat sailing off to the land of dreams or a golden tower, but a new life in a place like a fairytale with a quest of sorts."

She shook her head, making her raven hair swish across her eyes. "Not a quest."

"Why not? Knights and dragons aren't memories, but flights of imagination, something we can conjure with conviction."

"Quests require hope."

"No. Most start with little, but hope grows over time. That could happen to us."

The firelight flickered off her features and cast a glow, but quickly followed by shadow. "You don't realize how little hope I've had, how my days crawled by until I would go stand a futile watch each sunset for a boat that never came. You didn't hear the words I've spoken in the middle of the night, when the walls of darkness closed in."

"Yes, but then, you were alone."

As I spoke, the top log of the fire crackled and collapsed, sending up a surge of flame that brightened the room. The color came back to her face like the blush of red along the underside of a cloud at sunrise. She turned to me, the shadow gone, and the spark in her eyes reflected the firelight.

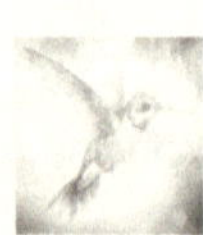

The next day, I summoned Lyra. "We've decided. We're ready to go."

She raised one brow and smiled her sideways smile. "To be sure, what do you expect to find?"

Addy's funeral had passed with all its pageant of black crepe and prayers and solemn faces; afterwards, the dull clouds of everyday life had rolled in. My night dreams became preferable to the harsh realities of the day. I slept and woke, washed and dressed, and went through the motions, avoiding the looming question: What do I do next? Now, at last, the time to choose.

I glanced at Mia, and we answered together. "Hope and meaning."

Lyra leaned against the wall and crossed her arms, but her gaze, rather than softening, hardened, like someone about to impart bad news.

"Very well," she said, "but a word of caution. So far, this world has been a blank slate for you, an unending forest with pathways waiting to be embellished, more like a game. In the enchanted land, your power may affect the lives of those who dwell there. To meet your demands, the magic will tap into your innermost heart. Deep within lay many notions, some brimming with hope but others in shadow, demons you may wish to never unleash. Hope and meaning are not the stuff of magic. You cannot conjure hope. You cannot summon meaning. Magic can only drive events. Hope and meaning, if they come, emerge from those events. But beware: where you find hope, you may also find despair. Where you find meaning, you may also encounter the void, because the one cannot exist without the other."

She turned to leave, but before passing through the door, she paused and spoke more to the fireplace than to us. "It's a long trek and an important decision. Sleep on it tonight. If you still choose to go, I'll take you in the morning."

PART 2 – SEARCHERS

*"The truly unique trait of Sapiens is our ability to create and believe fiction.
All other animals use their communication system to describe reality.
We use our communication system to create new realities."*
~ Yuval Noah Harari

Chapter 11 – Beginnings

That night, I tossed and turned, not dozing off until the crickets quieted and the breeze calmed. Too soon, night bled into morning, and I awoke to the comforting aroma of tea brewing.

Mia had risen before me and conjured a floral teapot and two cups on my oaken table. Steam emanated from the pot's spout and with it the scent of apple cinnamon spice.

After a modest breakfast, the time had come to decide. Lyra's opaque caution had unsettled us, but our choices were few — to live out our lives in the borderland in an attempt to recreate our past, or to follow Lyra for a chance at adventure.

We gathered by the bench at the pond and discussed what to bring. I suggested taking the two golden swords from above the mantle for protection, but Mia balked.

"We may be entering the unknown, but let's not assume the worst. How about packs and two days' provisions"

"No need to carry so much. We can conjure whatever we need."

Recalling how our powers oftentimes produced something different than expected, we determined to let the magic choose. We concentrated, counted to ten, and were surprised once again. On the ground before us lay two pieces, neither of which we'd requested: a gold necklace for Mia with a heart-shaped amethyst hanging down, and for me, a broad belt with a burnished brass buckle and an eagle at its center. The magic seemed more concerned with the sorcerers' appearance than their earthly needs.

Time to summon Lyra.

She appeared at once, wearing what she called her traveling attire: maroon leggings tucked into calfskin boots, a brief jacket so light as to provide little warmth — although I suspected she was unaffected by the elements — and a peaked cap with a yellow feather.

"Are you ready?" she said. "The way to the enchanted land starts here."

She spun around, taking for granted we'd follow, and led us to a hidden path behind the waterfall, one we'd never have found without a guide. Indeed, it scarcely qualified as a path, winding up a steep, overgrown hill with young saplings growing in the middle of it. Their branches acted like rods to lash us as we battled our way through.

To my relief, the terrain flattened at the top, returning to the familiar pine needle-covered trail. That lasted until noon, when the landscape changed in a way that made me miss the lush forests of the borderland.

First a fog rolled in, erasing all color. Earth and sky blended into a ghostly grey, a malevolent fog, I imagined, like the one that had taken Mia's parents. Next, the trees themselves vanished, and on either side of what had become a crusty dirt road, bleak moors stretched to the horizon. On occasion, a ray of sunlight pierced the gloom, revealing a smattering of misshapen boulders strewn about like ancient sculptures worn away by time. Here and there, we encountered a pit filled with boiling sludge that sent foul-smelling steam into the air.

Mia caught up to Lyra and blocked her way, forcing her to stop. "Can this be the enchanted land?"

She laughed a know-it-all laugh. "Of course not. We're still in the borderland."

"Then why the change?"

She sighed as if she'd explained this many times. "The borderland is not as you've seen it. It's an illusion maintained by magic, a combination of the custodian's skill and the whims of the travelers who enter. The result is a non-threatening transition where you can practice your newfound powers but not wish to stay too long. Where we're going, you'll have no need for such reassurance."

"So we can't do magic here?" I asked.

"You can, but no one wants to so close to moving on." She waved her arms to encompass the place. "Would you want to create your new lives here?"

Both of us shook our heads.

"Then follow me. We're almost there."

After a time, the fog cleared a bit and we could see farther ahead. I squinted, hoping to catch a glimpse of the turrets of castles or the spires of palaces, but only unending moors spread before us. At last, one exception broke the horizon, a modest structure blocking the road. As we came closer, I realized it formed an archway.

According to our guide, here lay the entrance to the enchanted land. On the far side, we would find a more familiar world, with people and livestock, farms and villages, though we'd also run into the effects of magic performed by travelers like us who'd chosen to stay.

This uninspiring gateway defied my expectation, too plain to herald a promised future. Made of bricks and dried mud, it bore no markings or artwork, and if incantations had been etched upon it, they'd long ago been eroded by wind and rain.

I gaped through the opening, which revealed nothing but the same stark landscape. "This is the entrance?"

"Time for the two of you to abandon your preconceptions and believe." Without waiting for our response, she slipped through, vanishing on the far side.

Left alone, I glanced at Mia. Her brows rose and her lips parted, but no sound emerged. I extended my hand and mouthed the words, 'a new life.' She accepted my hand, and after a deep breath, we stepped through.

Everything changed. The vista expanded and the dome of the sky grew large. Where my arrival into the borderland had blurred the vegetation, here the points of leaves and the blades of grass screamed with a green reality. Sounds of life filled the air, not only birds, but the chittering of insects. An aroma of planted things pervaded along with the loamy scent of moss beneath our feet, and my heart swelled with an overwhelming sense of being alive.

We rejoined Lyra, who now let us set the pace. We sauntered along, gawking to our left and right as the surrounding woods rang with sound: the bubbling of a brook as it flowed between rocks, the wind among the pine needles, and from time to time a gust that made the fir branches rub together.

Our anticipation heightened. We imagined every stream might be home to a troll, every tree a gnome, every flower a pixie in disguise. Anything had the potential to be enchanted, but in this, we were disappointed.

I quickened my pace, eager to reach some destination, but Mia grabbed me to slow me down and pointed at the sky. Overhead, an eagle soared past with a twig in its beak. I followed it long enough for the bird to complete a full circle before heading off to finish its nest.

"Did you conjure that eagle?"

She shook her head. "No. There's magic here neither of us controls."

We traveled until the sun sank behind the treetops, threatening to give up on the day. The excitement of a new place had drained us, and we needed time to rest. As the shadows lengthened, dozens of crows circled overhead, squawking as if to warn of an impending night. Dark clouds more ominous than twilight blew in on a gust, portending a storm. With a little effort, Mia and I conjured a wooden hut sufficient to shelter the two of us.

That night, I lay on my makeshift bed, listening to the rain drumming on our roof and focusing on the hoot of an owl, perhaps searching for his mate. I followed his call, letting my memories stray through the night, yet no sleep came.

I tried a different approach.

What were my expectations for this place? What was I searching for?

One summer, when I was a boy of seven, an infestation of crows flew in. People had never witnessed their likes. They arrived in black batches from the lake and invaded the town, scavenging for what was dead, or diving into trashcans for anything edible before roosting for the night in the trees.

They frightened me with their shadowy presence outside my window, and afraid to sleep, I lay awake and wondered what their arrival portended.

My father came in and rested on my bed to calm me. He was an unassuming shepherd who went to work in the morning and slept well at night, knowing he'd completed the day's tasks. Lacking the restlessness of his son, he never bothered with fantasies. That night, he urged me to grasp the simplicity of life, with only four possible quests: for love, for power, for treasure or meaning. For love, he had his children and an unquestioning devotion to my mother; power was to be avoided, too often coming at the expense of others; treasure he had in abundance, enough to provide for his family; and as for meaning, on those fine days he'd bring me to the mountain pastureland, he'd wave an arm at the view and ask what more can one desire. And though evil may arrive unannounced like the crows, a man had no need for more.

My eyes popped open, staring at the shelter roof as if trying to peer through it to the stars. I listened to Mia's soft breathing at my side.

What quest am I on? What goal do I seek?
With no answers, I slipped into a dreamless sleep.
I emerged the next morning to find the grass covered with dew.
Mia's clothes and skin had a velvety bloom, and her hair had added the sparkle of a million tiny spheres of water to its customary sheen. She appeared to be wearing a jeweled halo.

Moreover, the whole world had changed. While we sheltered inside, a magic greater than what we'd wished for had occurred. Above us spread a stunning sky, blanketed not with the usual white clouds but a rippling mixture of slate-blue and sea-green. This curious coloration differed from the norm, more as one might imagine in a fairytale.

"Where's Lyra?" I asked.

"Gone. I tried calling out to her but no answer. We're on our own."

After a small breakfast, we started off. Soon, the narrow path turned into a well-traveled dirt road that ran along a river. The distinct markings of wagon tracks foretold the eventual presence of others. This world now teemed with life. The branches of surrounding trees stirred with birds hidden behind the leaves.

The travel came easier than the day before because we'd both slept well and awoke refreshed. With the wind at our backs and the sun on our faces, we quickened our pace.

Around a bend, I encountered a blue heron standing on one leg knee-deep at the edge of the riverbank. He eyed me for a second or two, long enough so I wondered if the creature would speak and help make sense of our circumstance. Instead, showing no curiosity about our fate, he spread his wings and lifted off, flying to the horizon and beyond.

By mid-morning, we came to the crest of a hill. On the far side, a thin wisp of smoke arose as if from a fireplace. I dashed to the top, eager to discover what awaited.

Below lay a lone farmhouse, but soon after, other farms followed, with split rail fences surrounding fields of crops guarded by scarecrows. A short distance later, we reached a village.

We strolled along the well-used dirt road, between rows of thatch-roofed cottages and the occasional stone-built windmill with brown canvas sails. Any suspicion the place lacked people was dispelled by smoke wafting up from every chimney. Chickens clucked at us from their coops, and goats craned their necks from their pens as they took in the newcomers. But though smoke rose from each cottage, we detected not a soul. Doors remained shut, and windows shuttered, as if the villagers were hiding from our passage.

Halfway through, we caught the first sign of life. A boy peeked out from behind a shutter, showing one eye and the tip of his nose before his parents pulled him from the window.

"Better to be unseen," his father whispered. "Better to let the sorcerers pass."

Then he closed the shutter and secured the latch.

Chapter 12 – The Village

When no one emerged, I surveyed the village from one end to the other. In the center, a larger structure arose capped by a bell tower, what in my home would have been the central meeting place. A fountain bubbled in front of it, skirted by a knee-high stone fence and surrounded by freshly cut grass, more proof the settlement was inhabited. This tranquil setting appeared well-kept but for the structure's ravaged front door, which had been wrenched off its hinges and split in half. An angry black scar sliced across it as if struck by lightning.

I frowned at the dozens of cottages all shuttered tight.

How have we become so fearsome?

Mia tapped me on the shoulder and pointed at a possible answer. The road, which had been flat until now, turned uphill past the village and twisted around a bend into a grove of immense pines. Above their tops loomed the turrets of what had to be a castle.

I'd eagerly anticipated my first castle, but this one had an unexpected effect. I shivered at its presence, and the small hairs at the back of my neck stood up.

We settled on the fountain wall and let the flowing water calm us. Perhaps by appearing unthreatening, the locals might engage.

When not so much as a shutter unlatched, I determined to show we were friends. I rose and in a dramatic wave of my hands, applied my magic to fix the broken door. The shattered timber groaned, and the old hinges complained, resisting my enchantment for three heartbeats before the blackened wound healed, and the repaired door swung back into place.

Not a soul came out to thank me.

"I guess we're not welcome here," Mia said. "Perhaps we should move on."

"What if the next village is the same, and the one after? What do we do then? I'd hate to give up on our first encounter without learning something and leaving a mark."

I stood and approached the cottage where the boy had peaked out, making no attempt to soften the crunch of my footsteps on the gravel walkway. Late-blooming tulips danced in pots by the entrance, and sweet peas clung to their canes, decorating the walls with shades of powder-blue and lavender. I paused to inhale their fragrance. But for the telltale tingling on my skin signaling the presence of magic, the familiar scent of the flowers would have made me believe I'd returned home.

A sliver of light from a candle flickered at the bottom of the door frame.

I drew in a breath and knocked, keeping my demeaner as pleasant as possible. "Please open. We're simple travelers who mean you no harm."

A raspy voice answered. "You're no travelers. You're sorcerers. We can tell by your buckle and the witch's pendant. Go away and leave us alone."

Mia joined me. "I don't know what sorcerers have done to you in the past, but we're new to this world, just finding our way. You've seen how my friend has repaired your door. Do you think this door would keep us out if we wished to enter by force? Please let us in. Our intentions are pure."

Muffled bootsteps creaked along the floor, followed by hushed voices and a scraping sound like furniture being dragged across the room. At last, the latch clicked and the door opened.

A modest living space lay inside, with an eating area at one end and a fireplace at the other radiating welcoming waves of warmth. By one of the shuttered windows, a wooden table rested with benches on either side, with space for a family of six. The table, however, had been set for four, with a bowl and spoon at each place. An iron pot hung above the fire, bubbling with a stew whose scent made my mouth water.

At the rear wall, a doorway opened to the sleeping quarters, the only other room in the cottage.

Across the threshold waited a man of middle years with thinning hair starting to turn gray at the temples. His wife hovered behind him, one hand pressing on his arm as if urging him to fall back a step. They appeared no different from farmers I might have encountered near my home.

"Thank you," I said. "As my friend mentioned, we're new here and trying to find our way. May we come in?"

The two shuffled aside, a weak invitation without saying a word.

"Whatever problems you've had, we're your friends and would like to help in any way we can."

"Tell him about the castle," the woman said, loud enough for me to hear.

The man waved her off. "Hush, Natty, don't talk of such things."

Her next words were quieter still, but I caught a single phrase: "...may be our only hope."

While the two debated how to handle these frightful sorcerers who had appeared unwanted in their midst, Mia circled the room, peered into the sleeping area, and returned to my side.

She leaned close and whispered in my ear, "Where is the boy?"

I inched closer to the two and kept my voice steady despite a burning curiosity. "Where is your son, the one who spied us from the window?"

The man shook his head and retreated to a corner of the room, lingering over a woven rug, doing his best to avert his eyes.

The woman, more desperate, approached Mia. "In the past, several enchanters have passed this way, most haughty and caring nothing for simple folk, but now and then, a kind one would come by. Once, when we suffered from a drought, a sorcerer conjured a feast for the entire village, and the next day, before departing, he made it rain. You have sympathetic eyes. Might you be a kind one?"

Mia grasped the woman's hands and clutched them to her breast. "I'm new to magic and doubt I could feed so many or make it rain, but I've always been kind to others. I'd be happy to use my limited powers to help."

The woman twisted around to her husband, her eyes pleading. "Do we trust them, John?"

John peered past me through the open door, eyeing my handiwork at their meeting place. He closed the door and nodded, slowly at first, and then with more conviction. With a sudden decisiveness, he stepped aside and removed the rug, revealing a trap door to a root cellar. When he flipped it up, the boy from the window crawled out, stiff from being constrained in the small space.

The man turned to me. "This is Caleb, our youngest son. We hide him from strangers to protect him."

Youngest?

I eyed the four settings on the table.

The man caught my gaze. "We hold a place for Isaac, our oldest, in the hope he'll soon return."

Mia stepped forward and embraced the boy. "Welcome, Caleb. You're safe with us."

Caleb glanced from his parents to Mia, his brows raised and eyes wide. "Does that mean you can help my brother?"

I turned to his father. "Where is Isaac now, and why does he need our help?"

John studied his boot tops for a moment, then faced me. Blood rushed to his cheeks as he spit out the words. "You've seen the castle on the hill. That's where he is, if such a place exists, rather than being a portal to hell."

"But why...?"

The woman, Natty, led him away from me to the table. "You two *are* new to this world but still our guests. I caught you eyeing my stew. Come, hungry travelers, and share our meal. It's hot and ready, and we have plenty for all. We can discuss as we eat."

She fetched two more bowls and set them before us. I noted how she left the missing son's empty plate on the table. One by one, she brought a bowl to the fireplace and ladled in an ample helping, serving the visitors first. When all had been served, and we'd partaken enough to sate our hunger, a silence settled over the room.

John broke the silence. "Three years ago, he came to our village, strolling in from nowhere, same as you two. He seemed friendly at first, chatting with us, conjuring gifts, and playing with the children. When he stayed too long, we became anxious and hoped he would move on, but he decided to settle here. After staying in our homes and sharing our meals, he vanished one day. We thought he'd gone, but when we rose the next morning, we discovered he'd conjured that castle overnight.

"Now, when you're simple farmers, an immense castle popping up out of nothing can be unnerving, but we hadn't seen the worst. Once a month, at the start of the waning crescent of the moon, when it shows a mere sliver before the darkest night, he casts a spell on one of the children. The lad or lass would grow somber regardless of prior disposition, speaking to no one. In the middle of that night, no matter what precautions the parents took, the child would sneak out and be missing by morning. We later discovered they'd wandered off to the castle as if in a dream."

He licked his lips as if his mouth had gone dry, silenced by his oppressor.

His wife chimed in. "We learned to hide our children at that time of the month, to protect them from being taken, but to no avail. His magic found a way to steal them."

She dipped her spoon into the stew and raised it halfway, but paused and returned it to the bowl. "You question how we allowed such a thing to happen. At first, we assembled at the commons, every man and woman, with rakes and scythes and pitchforks. We had no other weapons. After some speeches and a whole lot of grumbling, we gathered our courage and marched off to confront him, prepared to fight and die to protect our children, but the simplest of enchantments barred our way. The one oaken gate allowing entrance contained neither latch nor knob, with no way to open it. We cut down a stout tree, hoping to batter it down, but it refused to budge. We tried to burn it, but protected by some black magic, it failed to catch fire. When we returned to the village, the grand door to our temple hung loose, a burnt crack in its center, a smoldering warning. Our efforts had accomplished nothing, and more children were taken." Her eyes misted. "Three weeks past, our Isaac fell under his spell."

I held my breath, waiting for more.

When no more was forthcoming, Mia spoke. "Yet you keep a place for him and hope for his return. What happened to the other boys?"

"Those lured away eventually come back, some within weeks, some after more than a month. They appear well-fed and unharmed, but none recall what transpired, what dark rites he'd performed."

My blood rose. I doubted our newfound powers would match those of an experienced sorcerer, but I vowed to help in whatever way possible. Why else had we come to this world?

A glance at Mia showed her thoughts matched mine.

"In the morning," I said, "we'll go to the castle and see what we can do."

John approached and embraced us. Natty followed, kissing each of us on both cheeks, before insisting we stay the night. She asked for no payment, only that we refrain from magic while on the premises.

After the others retired for the night, we spent the rest of the evening in silence, Mia warming herself by the fire, and I making entries in my journal. The only sounds were the wood being consumed in the grate and the scratch of pen against paper.

She settled in for the night, but I remained restless. I slid open the door and stepped outside, needing to inspect the castle one last time before sleep. An inky gloom had spilled over the village, with dark clouds blocking any light from the moon or stars.

Can our adversary be so powerful as to detect our presence and block his abode from my view?

By the time I lay down, I was too tired to dream. I woke only once, when the wind raved in furious gusts and torrents of rain fell.

- 68 -

Chapter 13 – The Castle

The next morning, our hosts sent us off with hugs and tears. To our surprise, they'd spread word of our mission, and we departed on a road lined with villagers. From each doorway came the young and old, men and women and barefoot children with mud on their faces, all cheering us on and adding to the unbearable expectation of hope.

The parade of our admirers led us out of the village and several hundred paces beyond, to where an unremarkable side path headed uphill into the woods. At its entrance, the celebratory mood withered and the cheering ceased. Bright expressions paled as our escort shrank from us. We were on our own.

I'd witnessed how much our powers had grown in the borderland. How much stronger might the lord of the castle be after three years?

The narrow path appeared unthreatening—no signs warning trespassers away, and no skeletons of past victims hanging from trees, only a mossy trail a sleepy child might navigate in the dark.

Sunlight filtering through the leaves warmed the dew-soaked ground, raising streamers of fog that swirled about our ankles. Along the way, we encountered a cave tucked among the roots of a massive tree. Spider webs weaved across its entrance, showing it abandoned. On either side lay an assortment of totems—dried flowers, polished rocks, and torn pieces of cloth, suggesting a holy man had once dwelled within. I wished he still lived there. I could use a wise man now.

I lingered, pretending to contemplate exploring inside, but Mia suspected my real reason.

"We can still go back," she said. "We can wait until everyone's gone and sneak back to the road. No one would ever find out."

I shook my head. We'd learned everything possible from the villagers and now faced a dilemma: to move along as if we'd never heard of their plight, or to confront their oppressor. No. The magic had brought us to this village for a purpose, and unless we were prepared to give up our quest so soon, we needed to go on.

As we climbed the path, the weather turned. Clouds rolled in and a sudden headwind lashed our faces, the kind of gust that moans in the chimney as you hunker indoors from a storm. Again, we thought of turning back, but the way forward offered the nearest shelter, and we believed we were close.

The next turn brought us out of the trees and within sight of the castle. We quickened our step until we reached the gateway and ducked under its overhang. While we caught our breath, we studied the black door that had confounded the villagers. This stood three times the height of their temple door but, as they'd claimed, presented no latch or knob. I rapped with my knuckles but it made no sound. This barrier would not be breached by normal means. One hope remained to get inside.

Magic!

I confronted the gate, consumed by doubt. Would the two of us have sufficient conviction?

I pictured the boy, Isaac, alone with a wizard of unknown intent, and my blood rose. "This place seems too harsh for a child."

Mia grasped my hand, and we squeezed our eyes shut.

Before we could exert our will, the tingling on my arms quickened, and my eyes sprung open at the sound of hinges creaking. The door swung wide. Of course. He'd sense our powers as we'd sensed his. Like us, he'd come from some sorry prior life, and was now inviting his kindred souls in.

But for what purpose?

The entrance opened into a courtyard where stood a fountain more ornate than the one in the village, with cherubs gracing the rim of a stone border. An angel rose in the middle with wings spread. It appeared water was supposed to spout from piping protruding from its mouth, but the basin beneath it lay dry, a testament to a master who'd grown bored of his handiwork and abandoned it.

An archway at the rear opened into a high-ceilinged anteroom. With no guard or gate blocking our way, we stepped through.

The two of us spun around, gazing in all directions, worried about somebody spying on us, but more so because of the spectacle presenting itself.

Carved figures embellished the ledge above us, fanciful creations of their master's whimsy — part dog, part lizard, a ferret with a row of spines along its back, a dolphin with wings, and a reptilian creature I took to be a dragon. Painted on the dome overhead, gods and goddesses reclined on clouds, attended by nymphs and other spirits.

Beyond the tingling on my arms, I'd come to recognize magic by a twinkling of light, as if the enchantment struggled with reality. This anteroom and its contents appeared awash in such light. All I surveyed, this new reality constructed and maintained by the will of its master, had not been well kept, with signs of decay everywhere.

The walkway led to a broad passage, though not as tall as the anteroom. Along its walls hung dusty paintings of children, each embellished by a gilded frame. Here, a portrait of a girl gazing to the horizon with vacant eyes and an ivy wreath in her hair. There, a boy browned by days in the sun, staring back with a crooked smile as if unsure whether to show joy or sorrow. Above the exit spread a tapestry of knights on armored horses crossing a moat, a striking image but for its having faded to the color of shadow.

Next came a circular foyer with a marble floor. Our bootsteps echoed off the walls, reflecting a somber tone. I slackened my stride, concerned about what lay ahead.

Mia stopped me short and held a finger to her lips. Murmurs emerged from the following chamber, words too soft to comprehend. As we approached, the sound became clearer — a man's voice.

We followed the voice into a shadowy hall, larger than any we had yet seen. This too had reached the limit of the sorcerer's attention. No arches graced the ceiling, and no suits of armor adorned it, as expected in such a castle. No stained-glass windows breached the solid stone. No windows brightened the space at all. At the far end, a fireplace provided warmth, and on its mantle, a clock with a pendulum ticked away. Light came from candles in sconces along the walls. Six tall mirrors hung opposite each other, enhancing their glow.

At the threshold, I hesitated, overcome by a sense of how naïve our mission had been. I had no measure of this wizard's power compared to our own, or of how malicious his intent might be. I'd been propelled forward by a desire to make right whatever evil he may have wrought, the quest of a fool.

I quieted my heart and peered into the chamber. In the far corner stood a square table, covered with a cloth of scarlet linen with a border of gold. A single candle lit its surface, and on the wall above it incense burned, its vapors further obscuring the view. Two chairs bracketed the table, with sculpted tiger paws to serve as arms. A still figure hunched in each of them. Between them lay a checkered board, and on it, elaborate carved pieces — knights on horseback and gryphons, fire-breathing dragons, and kings and queens.

In the chair facing us sat a man who had to be the lord of the castle. For such a regal setting, he appeared far from impressive, with no crown or curious hat upon his head, nor a scepter or wizard's staff nearby. Slight of stature with a pointy nose and sunken cheeks, he wore a black waistcoat too big for him. In the candlelight, his skin took on a pallid tone, as of moonlight filtering through clouds. A pair of spectacles clung to the bridge of his nose, magnifying close-set eyes as he studied the board.

When we approached, he held up a finger, urging us to wait as he contemplated his next move.

We glanced at each other, not daring to say a word. Like in a dream where the most extraordinary events arrive complete without explanation, I found nothing to be surprised at... until I recognized the second person.

In the chair opposite the lord of the castle sat a young boy, looking remarkably like his brother.

We'd located the missing Isaac.

Chapter 14 – The Lord of the Castle

The scene remained hushed, as if the two figures were shadows cast by the flames from the fireplace.

The lord of the castle's hand hovered over a piece, uncertain despite his apparent powers. After a halting breath, he lifted a dragon and moved it two spaces to the diagonal. The piece landed so hard it sounded like an additional tick of the clock.

While the boy studied his next move, his captor glanced up for the first time. "Ah, new guests. It's not often I encounter a fellow traveler, not to mention two. Do either of you play?"

Before I answered, Isaac's laughter broke the silence. He grabbed a knight and scurried it across the board, knocking over his opponent's king.

The loser sighed and spoke in a whisper, yet I had the notion his words, though soft, would pass through stone.

"Our young man has mastered the game in little time. If he continues to thrash me like this, I may have to send him home and gather a new companion to mentor. Well, Isaac, that's it for today. Shall I conjure a banquet to welcome our guests?"

The boy nodded, beaming as if he'd witnessed such an event before and relished the thought. He appeared neither oppressed nor abused.

"Then a grand banquet it shall be."

Though his magic required no gesture, our host rose on tiptoes and whirled about, waving his hands at the four corners of the chamber, causing the room to transform. Candles swelled into torches, their flames doubling—no, tripling—in size. In the middle, an enormous table materialized, surrounded by cushioned chairs sufficient for fifty or more.

A silken cloth with a fringed edge covered it, and every few feet, a brass candelabra graced its surface. Before each seat rested a setting with a porcelain plate edged in gold, a crystal goblet, and silverware on a folded napkin.

He clapped his hands as if summoning servants, and a stream of these arrived, all dressed in royal livery and bearing a tray of food or drink—roasted ham and glazed duckling, ample servings of mushrooms, peas, and beans, and pitchers frothing with mead.

The parade made my eyes water, a feat of magic beyond my imagination, but something was wrong.

Why do their footsteps make no sound? Why are their forms so faint as to be translucent?

Then I realized it. The food simmering on serving trays was real, but those who bore them were phantoms, illusions of the light.

Once the table had been set, the lord of the castle raised his right arm and twirled it around, and in a voice lacking the drama of the moment, not much more than a nasal whine, he called out, "Welcome, honored guests."

I'd hoped for villagers, but instead, well-dressed lords and ladies paraded into the hall and took their places behind assigned chairs, but these were no more real than the servants. Their feet floated above the floor, and the light from the torches flickered through them so they appeared to be dissolving in a dazzling, golden glow. At his command, they sat down as one.

I recalled the words of the custodian and Lyra, who had both cautioned us about the limits of magic. Even this sorcerer, after years of practice, could not conjure people.

Mia and I settled at the head of the table, opposite our host and the boy. The ghostly attendees pretended to partake of food and drink from their goblets, but their motions made no sound—no clink of crystal and no clicking of cutlery on plates. Their mouths opened and closed as they made merry gestures, but no voices emerged.

Mia's hand rested on my arm, her fingers squeezing tighter as she tried to keep her anger in check. When she could hold back no more, she spoke. "With so abundant a feast, why not invite the villagers instead to join the child? Such kindness would not only satisfy their hunger but calm their fears."

He set down his goblet without drinking, lowered his chin, and stared at his plate. His features tightened. "How long have you been here? From your paltry powers, I would guess no more than a few days. A time will come when you'll understand. These people may worship you or hate you, but always, they will fear you.

"Over the years, I've met a few travelers like yourselves—one learns to sense their magic. Some like you hope to be kind at first, trying to win the villagers over. Others never care and do as they please, using whatever means necessary to lord over them, but always, we remain apart and alone."

Mia rose so fast her chair scraped on the stone floor, and the blood rushed to her cheeks. "What you do is wrong, stealing children in the dark of night. It's no wonder they fear you. You may mean no harm, but what you do devastates the families. Why not admit your need and ask for their permission?"

He listened with lips pressed tight as if to contain unwanted words. When she finished, he sprung up and slashed an arm overhead. The ghostly guests vanished, leaving us confronting our host alone across the long table.

"You think you're so wise. Wait until you've been here months or years. I came through a portal as you did because I'd suffered at the hands of my neighbors, shunned in my town, an outcast as too small and too weak. After the custodian explained the rules of this world, I had the best of intentions. Here I might make life better for all and be embraced. The newfound powers would make up for my appearance.

"My first year, I wandered from village to village, performing what they perceived to be miracles. I mended fences and made crops grow, but did they welcome me into their homes? Not willingly. Unlike the more nefarious wizards, I abhorred doing them harm. After months of rejection, sometimes driven off with torches and pitchforks, I retired to this castle, but it's not much of a home. It's vast and cold, and my voice echoes through its halls, so I schemed to bring a companion to ease my boredom. I meant no malice so long as they left me alone, yet they came in anger to burn my creation down. In my one fit of vengeance, I hurled lightning at their temple, and that has kept them at bay."

I stood as well, less to confront my host than to keep Mia from rushing toward him. "What if you explained to them why you do--"

"The only thing worse than having power over them," he said, his shoulders slumped and the corners of his eyes drooped, "is having power and showing weakness."

I cast my gaze down to the table, unable to meet his.

He spoke with a trace of bitterness in his voice. "How fortunate to have two of you. It's lonely, being a sorcerer amongst these people. The magic forms a barrier between us, one our powers cannot cross."

He ceased talking and resumed savoring his meal. The ticking of the mantle clock grew louder.

Beside me, Mia trembled. "We won't let you keep the boy. We'll bring him back with us, return him to his parents as promised."

The lord of the castle smirked at the boy and ruffled his hair. "Do you wish to stay with me, Isaac, or do you prefer to go home with these strangers.?"

He'd caught the child in mid bite. Isaac chewed and swallowed, and lifted his goblet and drank his fill before answering. "Stay with you."

Mia grasped her knife and rushed toward him.

Her adversary never moved. No dramatic gesture required this time.

She startled as the knife in her hand transformed into a sparrow, which wriggled free and flew out the door.

"Now, my friends," he said, "I'm afraid your visit is at an end."

At once, we found ourselves standing outside the black door, closed and locked behind us.

I'd learned the first lesson of the enchanted land, one I needed Lyra to explain. Our host had conjured a castle and a giant feast. He had mesmerized young boys to come play his game, and expelled us without twitching a finger.

Yet he had no power to banish loneliness.

Chapter 15 – The Thorny Parts

We fled from the castle and staggered down the hill, not stopping until we reached the cave. Mia squatted on the ground by its mouth, fiddling with the totems in the adjacent shrine, while I paced ten steps up and ten back, stomping on the underlying moss.

How had this wizard conjured such an elaborate structure? Had he also made the clouds billow as well, and the wind blow in our face? How had he banished us from his presence without so much as a twitch of his finger? Would we ever attain such powers, and if so, would we be doomed to become like him or worse, seduced to lord over others?

Mia glanced up at me and laughed, but it was a bitter laugh. "What worth is this enchanted land? We thought to find meaning but found meanness instead. Sorrow has followed us here. This world is no better than the last."

I paused my pacing, glared once more at the castle turrets looming above the treetops, and whirled on her. "I came here to rediscover hope, and I won't let a deranged sorcerer steal it from me. Years wielding power have corrupted his mind. Our fate can be different. He showed us how much is possible. We need to learn from this experience, to become powerful like him but, unlike him, to stay kind as well. Only then will we make this world our home."

She scrambled to her feet and challenged me. "Yes, hope. I hunger for it, but where do you propose to find it? Not in the castle, not in the village below, and not in these blasted woods. We have no more chance to find hope than to discover a wise man emerging from this spider-infested cave."

"There'll be other villages. Some might embrace us when they realize we mean no harm. Or we'll find a different wizard, not so disillusioned, who will share his knowledge with us."

Her fury faded, and she slowly shook her head. "You're a dreamer, Lucas. You and I have no home. Our old lives are gone, and we're unlikely to find new ones here."

I pictured my cottage above the lake, its barren rooms filled with sad memories. I'd left it behind, hoping for a new life, but what did I find? Magic I could barely control and people who'd hate me if I used it.

Am I to wilt at this first storm, or be resilient like the first crocuses of spring, to grow stronger in the sunlight and flourish?

I grasped her by the arms, noting her eyes were brimming. "Enough! Would you prefer quitting this so-called enchanted land and returning home? Are you ready to go back to searching the dunes, waiting for a boat that never comes? Better to search here with even a trace of hope. Better to search together."

She brushed away a tear and rested her cheek against my shoulder. "I want to believe, but hope's a fickle friend. Remember what Lyra said: 'No hope without the chance for despair.'"

I glanced at the shadows beginning to darken the trail. "We'll learn nothing more in these woods. Let's go down to the road and choose what to do when we get there."

Hand in hand, we trudged along as if to delay the decision as long as possible, but sooner than we'd have liked, we were forced to decide. To one side and around the next bend lay the village; to the other, the unknown.

Mia spun about, taking stock of each direction, but I focused on the village. "I hate going back and confessing our failure to Isaac's parents, but we found their son safe, and he should be returned to them soon. They deserve to know."

She turned to face me, her lips drawn tight and her hands balled into fists. "What use to know if it changes nothing? We have no power to help."

I took two breaths and spoke in a measured tone. "You and I came into this world desperate for a new life. Can the way to a new life start with the way of the coward?"

A calm came over her, the triumph of an inner strength I had just begun to appreciate. She nodded, took my hand, and led me to the village.

When we reached the cottage, we were shocked to discover an open door and the echo of laughter within. I eased past the door jamb and peeked inside.

I'd encountered many odd happenings since passing through the maelstrom, but what I found now made my eyes water. I blinked three times to confirm what they revealed.

Around the table sat mother and father, and their two sons, Caleb and Isaac, the latter poking his younger brother and grinning as if nothing had happened.

Mia and I attacked the road, setting a frantic pace until we'd gone far from the village. In a grove of aspens, we settled on a fallen log.

The custodian had described magic as creating one's own reality. I'd been amazed at the lord of the castle's powers, but what I'd witnessed went beyond amazement to awe at his ability to bend the world to his will.

The scene we'd witnessed played out in my mind like a bad dream.

Unable to control myself, I'd blurted out, "Isaac, you've come back."

The father stood to greet us, but his welcome turned to puzzlement. "Come back from where? Just last evening, you shared a meal with the four of us, and our son has never left us since."

Mia leaned in and mouthed the word, 'Magic.'

Magic indeed. The sorcerer had managed to transport the boy home ahead of our arrival, erasing his memories and those of his family. While I wondered at such a feat, I understood why. He feared we'd reveal his secret, and rather than lose the dread in which the villagers held him, he'd changed the world.

Next to him, we were children playing with magic.

What choice did we have? No one would believe our story now, so like two fools we mumbled agreement and lied, claiming we'd come to make our goodbyes. The mother urged us to stay for another meal, but we declined, citing obligations in the neighboring village.

Since leaving them, Mia and I had spoken not a word. I stared at a knot in the log, while she plucked a daisy from the edge of the woods and proceeded to yank off its petals one at a time. When the stem was bare, she tossed the flower away, stood, and glared down at me with fire in her eyes.

"You're right. We have to stop being cheap magicians and learn proper magic. We need to become as skilled a sorcerer as him, so we're never humiliated again."

"How? Not by building cottages or gardens. Not by conjuring shelter and food."

She stared up at the treetops with knitted brow and brightened. "Let's find out how much we can manage if we stretch our minds together, now that we've seen what's possible."

"Now?"

"Yes, here and now. We'll change this log into a miniature model of a castle, complete with tiny servants, lords and ladies, and a fairy or two."

I agreed, anything to lift my spirits.

The two of us hovered over the log and gathered our will but had failed to agree upon the changes. Stone battlements sprouted on my end, and pennant-topped turrets sprung up at the other. On the parapet between them scurried grotesque figures. As I gaped, the entire structure shimmered and its unreality spread to the trees, making the earth spin around me.

I groped for something solid to hold on to, nearly tumbling to the ground, until a voice called out from behind.

"What a mess you two have made."

I turned to catch movement, in my flustered state expecting a demon to appear. Instead, I caught what I perceived to be a wraith slipping through the branches. Images of those departed passed in my mind, a parade of ghosts, but as this ghost approached, it took on a more familiar form.

Lyra.

She waved her hand. Reality firmed, and the log resumed its former shape.

Mia rushed toward her, pleading, "We need your help. Can you teach us how to do better?"

Lyra laughed. "So now you want more magic, not less. No, I cannot teach you. That's not my role. I can only guide you in the direction you want to go."

I stood and confronted her. "Then guide us to someone who *can* teach us."

She picked up the discarded daisy and returned it to the soft soil, where it took root before our eyes. "You're not the first to ask such a question. Of those who have entered this world, countless have given up and gone back to their old lives, some after days, others after years. Of those who stayed, only a few have found the right balance, for magic alone does not bring contentment, but there is one who might help: the healer."

"Healer?"

"That's what the villagers call him. He's another who passed through the portal like you. Over many years, he's mastered his power, but he hides it in the guise of potions and spells. Though he keeps apart, people come to him. Sometimes, he uses real magic to soothe their sorrows and heal their pains, but often, hearing his blessing is enough, because they've come to have faith in him."

Mia knelt and wondered at the flower, whose mangled petals had begun to grow back. "Can you take us to him?"

"I can, but it's a long day's trek, and you've had a difficult time. Rest tonight, and in the morning, I'll take you there."

She checked one last time to make sure all the shimmering had settled, and then resumed her wraith-like form and faded away.

We continued along the road, confident Lyra would find us wherever we landed. By late afternoon, we located a clearing by a stream, an appropriate place to camp for the night. As the sun set, flaring like a single red jewel, we used our crude magic to conjure another shelter. After the long day, Mia lay down and mumbled, "Goodnight, my —." She bit her lip, and after a pause, closed her eyes and rolled over.

In seconds, her breathing slowed into its nightly rhythm, but I remained restless. I crawled outside and squatted by the water, intent on recording the day's events in my journal, lest some future sorcerer erase *my* memories.

After making a lighted candle appear with an unnecessary flick of my wrist, I recorded these words in its glow:

> *Lessons after a painful day. No meaning comes without a struggle, for only through hardship do we discover what we're made of. It's in the thorny parts that we come alive. Magic alone makes life too easy and is therefore insufficient to create meaning. Magic needs challenge. Tomorrow, we'll follow Lyra and learn from this healer, and only after, will be tested.*

After I finished writing, I tucked the journal away in its waterproof case and blew out the candle. The night air enveloped me with warmth, and as I sat unmoving, the sky turned from red to deep blue and then to black. When a crescent moon arose, I determined to forego the shelter and sleep outside.

Within minutes, the heavens were ablaze, the stars emerging all at once as if some cosmic magician had ordered it so. One moment, a single star; the next, a million points of light—constellations and planets, brighter and nearer than in my former home.

I lay on my back, searching for old friends: the big dipper, and the archer whose stars formed a belt, bow, and arrow. In my youth, I'd gaze at them on a summer evening, tipping my head back to make the dipper's cup slant, wishing stardust to pour upon me and change the course of my life.

Now, as I gazed at the night sky, I spotted no familiar sight. The dome above was as alien as this world, a different reality. I wished to use magic to restore my favored constellations to their rightful spots, but doing so would be creating a phantom from memory. Instead, I tried imagining new ones, until under a canopy of stars too numerous to count, I drifted off to sleep.

I returned to the shelter. A heavy cloud had floated across the moon, dimming its glow. In the lesser light, I eyed the sleeper inside, for a moment hoping she was Addy.

In Addy's final days, an elderly neighbor came to sit with us, one who had already buried her husband and two children. As Addy began to fade, the woman told me, "She's begun her journey."

After Addy died, she invited me in for tea and shared her comfort and wisdom.

She stared into her cup, as if the rising steam was imbued with memories, and spoke more to herself than to me. "When you've lived as long as I have, you watch many friends and those you loved die. With each, you die a little yourself, so now I approach my own death with less fear, not because I expect to see them soon — though finding a real heaven would be lovely — but because I have so little of me left alive. No sense clinging to life when so little of you remains."

She shifted her gaze and fixed me with moistened eyes. "But you're a young man. While your loss will never go away, you will move on. You have time remaining to add other friends, and if you're lucky, a new love."

Was it possible Addy's journey had also brought her here at last, somehow joining me in this strange world? Had my magic attained conviction sufficient to break the rules and revive her from memory.

A rising wind swept the cloud from the sky, exposing the moon. Its light streamed over the shelter, and I realized the sleeper was Mia. A strand of hair had fallen across her cheek, caressing it, and she bore a look as if dreaming of hope.

The memory of my dream lingered upon waking the next morning. I stirred in a fog, and through closed eyelids perceived a red glare. I heard a voice too, speaking as if carried from a distance. A hand stroked my cheek, encouraging me to awaken. I nestled my face against that hand and felt comforted by its warmth.

At last, the cloud of confusion cleared, and I recalled where I was: the red glare was a warming campfire, and the voice was Mia's.

Chapter 16 – Enchanted Forest

Our quest to find the healer started pleasantly enough with Lyra setting a leisurely pace. The day stayed mild, with a warming sun slipping in and out of the clouds. The road never grew so steep as to challenge our breathing and was lined with a delightful variety of trees—spruce and birches, lindens and oaks and rows of flowering dogwoods.

Around midday, both the weather and terrain changed. A dark cloud drifted across the sun and stuck, and of the trees, only the naked trunks of oaks remained. Soon the darkness deepened, a prelude to what lay ahead, for on the horizon, the path ended at an impenetrable wall of murky woods.

We might have lost our way again without Lyra, but she steered us through the overgrown thicket until we found an opening. She insisted we rest before entering, since travel would become harder once inside. This, she explained, was the healer's forest, where we may encounter resistance more confounding than trees.

As Mia and I hunkered on the ground and conjured food and drink, my mood rose. If the healer had created this forest, he'd have to be nearby. Soon he'd favor us with his wisdom.

While we ate, Lyra told us more about the enchanted land, a place more complex than I'd imagined.

"Most of the sorcerers of this world, those who stayed and developed their skills, have carved out domains, controlling a single village or two or three. These they rule with various degrees of cruelty, sometimes going to war with others to extend their territory, transforming peaceful villagers into soldiers for their armies. Over time, only those with sufficient strength survive, but even they need to defend their turf."

Mia knitted her brows. "Why do so many become cruel?"

"Because magic will exploit flaws in your character, leading to a lust for power. The healer possesses a more noble nature. He also has his domain—the villages of Narthwick, Pontybridge by the river, and Montvale at the base of the mountain—but he hides his sorcery from the people he serves, except to protect them from other would-be lords. He has imbued this forest with an extraordinary enchantment to keep out trespassers."

"So how are we to pass?" Mia said.

She laughed. "You're no threat to him. Your magic is too weak."

As soon as we entered, the hairs on the back of my neck rose. I'd learned to detect the presence of magic but not how to distinguish the benign from the brutal. The healer had conjured these woods to protect from intruders. What if he'd lost the battle? What if bloodthirsty creatures lurked within or bedeviled villagers raged nearby? If a breeze rustled the overhanging branches, I feared a predatory bird; if a gust whistled from the shadows, I fancied a squad of men with axes and swords.

The overhead canopy grew so thick it blocked out most light. Rare glimpses of the sun's angle signaled dusk, though only a few hours had passed since dawn. Soon clouds swept in to block the remaining rays, and a violent wind arose in the west. The leaves showed their undersides, and heavy rain followed. The woods took on a spirit of their own, old and full of malice, causing a traveler to fear as much from the trees as from an attacker hidden within.

With limited visibility, we trudged along in single file, my eyes fixed on Lyra's flaxen hair, and Mia tracking so close behind, her fingertips brushed my back when she swung her arms.

Then, as if we'd passed a test, reality bent. The rain stopped, the wind calmed, and the world shifted. A blinding light appeared before us, as if a flight of angels had descended through the dark to guide us. I could almost imagine their wings white as swans, and the whir of those wings making the air around me tremble. They flew ahead through the trees, showing us the way.

As we followed the light, my mind calmed and my confidence returned. Until now, I had no thoughts, had only stayed close to Lyra and dreaded. Now, I regained the faculty of reflection.

A few days ago, I'd brooded in my cottage over the lake and wondered if I should chance the maelstrom, never suspecting entry into such a strange world. Now, I'd discovered a place more distressing than my prior home. Yet for all those years before Addy passed, my nature had tended to the positive, and now the journey to this healer promised a better future.

At last, the time of day arrived that my father called the gloaming, when nothing was as it appeared, an appropriate time for magic. Sure enough, a change came. The trees thinned in front of us and the trail began to rise. The bright light vanished, and the switch from light to dusk became disorienting. I tried to focus, afraid the intensity of my circumstance would confound my senses and invest illusory visions. Minutes later, we came out under the open sky and found ourselves looking up at a fine sight.

In the center of a clearing arose a round tower, so wreathed in ivy it may have sprouted from the ground. In its shadow, a feathered creature lurked, emitting an emphatic caw. A few steps more and the creature became clear — a black bird as tall as my waist guarding the door. It twisted its head around and regarded me with one of its button eyes. Once satisfied, it hopped aside and let out three more caws in an irregular cadence.

At this signal, the oaken door swung open and a man appeared, framed by the light from within.

Lyra approached and made a small bow, an uncharacteristic sign of respect from our mystical guide.

The man stepped out from the door frame and nodded to her. He had a mop of tussled white hair and a full beard curling down below his chest. For someone his age, he possessed a stocky build obscured by a loose-fitting brown robe secured with a rope. In his left hand, he grasped a wooden staff capped with a brass knob, which he leaned on as he limped toward us. He projected an unassuming presence that belied his powers, except for his eyes, which burned like coals in the darkness.

He approached within an arm's length, and those eyes bore into us until we wilted under their glare.

After too long a moment, he turned back to Lyra. "New apprentices?"

She nodded.

"We'll see if they're worthy." Shifting his gaze to us, he snapped, "Don't stand like scarecrows. Come inside."

This then was to be our mentor.

This then was the healer.

Chapter 17 – First Test

Like the man, the abode appeared modest, lacking the grandeur of the wizard's castle. A spiral staircase arose at the rear, leading to the private quarters, leaving the lower chamber as a place where villagers in need might visit. Books lined shelves on the wall, interspersed with rows of jars and vials containing odd concoctions. The setting bore the markings of a scholar, a wise man whose powers came from years of study in harnessing nature's cures, but I knew better. This man's power came from within.

In the center stood a high-backed chair behind a simple wooden desk laden with ink bottles, pens, and sealing wax on top. Two visitor chairs lay in front, where the sick and needy might wait as the healer treated their ills. A single stained-glass window breached the wall above, likely casting an ethereal glow on his ministrations in daylight, though now only candles in brass candlesticks illuminated the area.

I shuffled toward the desk like a supplicant approaching what might have been an altar in another world.

Now inside, the healer's demeaner eased. "I apologize for my rude greeting, but I don't receive many fellow travelers, and of those who come, too often their visit ends in shambles. They arrive with such misconceptions, and I forever lament their ignorance. They beg me to show them fairy-spirits, unicorns, and other nonsense. The utility of my teaching is lost on them. Nothing but the most frivolous activities excite their interest. Of course, Lyra recognizes my quirks and would not have brought such fools here. For your sake, I pray she's right.

"First lesson: magic is simple. Magic is everywhere, even in your old world, if people would believe. It exists in all creatures, in the wild thought of a bird as it casts itself into the wind. No other creature has so much potential, perhaps flying each night between this and other worlds."

As he spoke, he gestured in the air and paced until he left not a patch of floor uncovered. He became breathless; his powers aside, he was not a young man.

He settled onto the high-backed chair, and when he caught his breath, continued. "The bird succeeds because it accepts magic without a shred of doubt, knowing only hope and never despair, a perspective harder for us thinking beings. That's why most humans fail, that and flaws in their character."

I leaned in and rested my hands upon the desk. "We've witnessed such flaws before and intend our fate to be different."

His eyes narrowed and he lowered his voice. "That's for *me* to decide. If I sense such a flaw, I'll withhold my teaching and you will regret seeking my counsel." He blew out a stream of air, almost extinguishing one of the desktop candles, and his smile returned. "I grow so excited when speaking about what I've learned and the benefits it can bring, once mastered by the right temperament, yet I have so few chances to expound. Most of my visitors are villagers, from whom I mask my powers. Let me demonstrate how I would deal with a farmer whose crops had failed."

He extracted what appeared to be a pumpkin seed from a jar and laid it at our feet. After poking through the shelves, he chose a book, opened it to a page marked with a folded parchment and placed it on the desktop so we might follow. After we gathered around, he began to chant. An enchantment swirled, stronger than any I'd ever conjured. Mia and I turned to stare at the seed. Though I understood it only for show, I held my breath, waiting for him to speak the final word that would seal the spell.

Almost at once, a speck of green sprouted where none had been, and the fresh odor of planted sod wafted through the air. From the shoot, a pumpkin appeared, and within seconds grew to a size that would have won awards at our harvest festival back home.

As we gaped, the healer confronted us. "Tell me what you observed."

I took three breaths before responding, buying time to consider what answer he was seeking. "Impressive magic, a season's worth of growth in the blink of an eye."

"Yes, of course, but what else did you see?"

Mia stepped between us. "A show intended to deceive the farmer—you disguised your powers by casting a spell, when you could have accomplished the same with no effort."

"Guilty, but my deception reveals nothing about its essence."

He slipped behind the desk and settled into the high-backed chair. With an unnecessary wave of his hand, the pumpkin disappeared. Then he waited, with a glare more disconcerting than his sorcery, judging our every movement.

Each trick I'd performed or witnessed in the past few days played in my mind, those minor ones we'd managed and the more complex feats of the lord of the castle.

How does this one differ?

Mia glanced at me with a half-smile and a knowing tip of her head. I nodded back, encouraging her.

She cleared her throat and answered with only the slightest quiver in her voice. "You performed more than magic, something the farmer would perceive as a miracle, because your kindness allowed him to save his family from hunger."

The healer squeezed his eyes shut while we waited. Seconds ticked away, measured by my heart straining at my ribs, beating loud and fast.

He looked up at last and sighed. "So often those who come to me miss this simple fact, that magic may be used for the benefit of others rather than serving one's own needs. The urge for power is seductive and can corrupt the strongest character. You have done well... for now, but your power is too weak to tempt you. The test will come as it grows. Only then will your true character be revealed." He turned to Lyra, who'd been lurking in the shadows, watching a scene she'd likely experienced many times before. "Very well. I will take them on."

After he closed the book of made-up spells and replaced it on its shelf, he bid farewell to our guide and resumed the role of cordial host. What followed might have transpired at a mountain inn back home.

He took us up the spiral staircase to a wood-paneled dining area with walls lined with hams set out to cure, and strings of fresh mushrooms and onions. The round table in the middle lay bare when we entered, but with a wave of the old man's hand, a tablecloth appeared with wooden bowls and earthenware cups upon it.

He served up a meal more appetizing than any we'd managed to summon ourselves. Without the pomp of the castle's lord, a pleasant aroma filled the air, and trays spread before us, with mutton and roasted fowl soaked in gravy surrounded by mounds of peas and slices of yams.

I gaped at the conjured meal and scanned the surrounding walls crammed with fresh produce.

"Why store food when you can make it appear at will?"

He laughed. "Not knowing my abilities, the villagers are afraid I'll starve with no cultivated land or animals to raise. They bring me gifts from their farms, often cooked with tasty spices I couldn't name. I'm most grateful to them, but admit I sometimes use their generosity to feed the nearby creatures."

We served ourselves—no servants here—filling our bowls and eating our fill. While we ate, he continued to expound on his premise: magic pervades and is simple once you learn how to access it, but it seemed anything but simple to me.

I interrupted his lecture to ask a question that had puzzled me since experiencing the enchantment of the forest. "Today, we trekked half the day through your woods. We passed not a pumpkin patch but thousands of trees. The entire time, I sensed each one judging me. How is magic on such a scale possible? How can a single person command so much?"

He lowered the piece of mutton he was about to consume, returning it to its plate, and folded his hands on the table. "I did not command them, nor would I presume to do so. I approached them with humility, accepting that their combined powers dwarfed those of this humble sorcerer. I earned their trust, and they became my partners."

He resumed his eating, his demeaner showing he was done teaching for the day.

Mia's features expressed the same confusion as mine. We'd learned little from him, only how much we still had to learn.

I reviewed all I'd experienced since coming to this world. Though I struggled to accept it, I'd witnessed extraordinary exploits, wizardry beyond my imagining.

After we finished, he led us up to the third-floor guest quarters and urged us to get a good night's sleep, so we'd be ready for a more challenging day in the morning.

As he began to close the door, Mia stopped him and made a small bow like Lyra. "Thank you for taking us on. We understood little of what you taught us so far, but we're eager to learn since we have no other choice and nowhere else to go. We'll try our best not to disappoint."

Chapter 18 – Lessons

Not much past dawn the next morning, Mia and I awoke to a pleasant sound. We staggered down the spiral stairs to discover its source and found the healer seated at the table serenaded by phantom musicians playing a soothing tune, one with a flute and one with a harp.

He winked at us as we stumbled in, eyeing the ghostly pair. "I considered waking you with a brass horn and kettle drum but remembered my vow of kindness and relented. Come join me."

Breakfast consisted of a plate stacked high with biscuits, a crock of strawberry preserves, and a jug of milk, a satisfactory way to start the morning but short of a feast. The festivities had ended the night before. This day was meant for work.

He gave us sufficient time to finish our meal without gulping it down but not much more. No sooner had we cleared our plates than he ushered us outside.

Under the shadow of the tower and surrounded by enchanted trees, he lined us up like soldiers in formation, inspecting us head to toe while waving his walking stick at us. "I can measure the strength of your power, but I cannot sense the direction it has taken. Give me examples of the magic you've performed."

We took turns answering, Mia first. "We made food and drink appear as needed...."

I chimed in. "...and shelter to protect us from the rain."

"Lucas created a lovely cottage with a fireplace...."

"...That she landscaped with lilacs and rhododendrons."

"A sparkling pool with a waterfall...."

"...And a vegetable garden we designed together."

"But nothing like the other wizard's castle...."

I winced. "Or him bending reality and controlling villagers' minds."

He gazed up to the clouds as if organizing his thoughts before facing us again.

"So you've experienced much but accomplished little. That will serve you well. Humility will aid in your learning. Now, both of you, stretch out your right hand, palm up, and hold it steady. No flinching."

We did as he asked.

"What do you see?"

Mia answered first. "My hand, my fingers."

"What else?"

I added, "Some lines, a few peaks and valleys."

"Are the lines straight or rounded? Are the valleys deep or shallow?"

I grew frustrated. "What does it matter?"

He sighed and turned to Mia. "What does it matter, he asks." Then back to me. "What does magic matter? Shall I tell you or are you too impatient to learn what has taken me many years?"

My throat went dry, and I wondered if he could stop my heart with a thought.

His dark eyes bore into me. "Keep your hand still, and we'll have you make a leaf appear. First, consider the tree it fell from. In your mind, regard its bark. Is it reddish, brown, or black? Imagine your fingertips brushing its surface. Is it rough or smooth? If rough, follow its whorls like canyons dug into the soil by long gone rivers. And now the leaf itself...."

My hand began to cramp, and I let it relax. "Why do this? What's the purpose?"

His thick brows rose. "The purpose? What do think magic is? It's the purest form of imagination, a vision vivid enough to challenge reality. Add a smidge of faith and a pinch of conviction, and the scale tips. What you've imagined becomes real."

He grasped my hand in both of his, his gnarled fingers massaging until mine straightened.

"Now, try again. Imagine the leaf. Is it rounded or oval. Are its edges smooth or prickled with tiny thorns. Does it have points? How many? Five or seven or nine? Is it green like grass or dark like the forest at night, or has it already turned to the yellows and reds of fall? Perceive not just the surface but its depth as well. Is it spongy or firm. Can you track the veins as they spiral out from the stem, for it's through the stem the leaf takes its life, which in turn draws life from the branch, the branch from the trunk, the trunk from the roots, and the roots from the earth. See it all. Believe it." His voice crashed down upon me, a striking command. "Now make it real."

As I bit my lip trying to ensure I was awake, a leaf formed in my hand exactly as I'd imagined it. I stared at it for a count of ten and checked with Mia.

She held in her hand one different from mine, a deeper green and more oval-shaped with only one point, but a leaf nonetheless.

I gaped at our mentor, open mouthed, but no words emerged.

He smiled back. "You asked about the forest, about magic on such a massive scale. This is how it begins, leaf by leaf, branch by branch, and tree by tree."

For the rest of the day, we performed minor miracles, almost like the learning games small children play at school. He taught us until my eyelids drooped, and I squeezed my lips together to suppress a yawn.

As the sun touched the top of the trees, he relented. "Enough for the first day. I sometimes forget how long it took me to attain my powers."

After a modest dinner and before heading to bed, I stopped him at the foot of the stairs, seeking an answer to a problem that had gnawed at me. Lyra claimed less principled wizards were always fighting to expand their rule. How did this kind old man protect his three villages? Not by sprouting pumpkins or healing their ills. Those who sought more power were unlikely to be appeased by kindness.

"I have a question that will bother me as I try to sleep. You say you use your powers to help others but never explained how you keep the more wicked sorcerers at bay. Are you not sometimes forced to employ the more... sinister side of magic?"

His lips formed a bloodless line, and his features darkened. "Yes. Magic has a meaner side. When you're ready, I'll teach you how to control it, but only as a last resort. You'll learn to restrict it to the proper time, or I will banish you from my sight. I will not be party to unleashing more sorrow on this world. Now get some sleep."

That night, I dreamed the hills rumbled and the sky wept. The blackbird from the tower steps flew by and whispered an incantation in my ear. Trees too came forward and spoke to me. They insisted my fate lay inside rocks and crumpled leaves, that everything—stones and rivers, wind and fire—had a will of their own, but my magic could persuade them to a different purpose.

What that might be, they did not say. I'd met a man corrupted by magic's power, who had abused it to place his needs above others.

As my own powers grow, what purpose will I choose?

I startled awake in the dark with a single thought reverberating in my mind.

Magic, like life, possessed two sides—one brought hope, and the other despair.

Chapter 19 – Phantoms

Our apprenticeship stretched out for weeks on end with little rest, except for intervals when the healer had to minister to villagers or replenish herbs. While he proved a strict taskmaster, he was a superb teacher with a splendid way of making the complex simple and the magic less mysterious.

Take the trick with the pumpkin seed. The seed, he noted, had always contained the capacity to grow, a miracle of nature. As long as one respected that nature—one could not expect it to become an ear of corn—one could embolden it to show off its ability. It already knew how to grow. Treat it with respect, and you could convince it to grow faster.

The same held for all plants, as we had discovered by accident with our flowerpots and garden. Those had reacted to our desperation with a response that now hardly seemed magical.

Phantoms were different. Possessing no essence of their own, they were nothing more than a trick of the light. How to control their appearance and behavior was a more complex matter.

We started with musicians like those who serenaded us over breakfast. The healer asked each of us to conjure a single form.

"Envision their gender and stature, their face, round or drawn. Is their skin taut and smooth like youth or weathered like mine? Do they have thick lips or thin, long hair or short, curled or straight, and of what color? Picture every detail of their clothing, smart and stylish or the dust-covered wool of the farmer. At last, what instruments do they embrace, and what tune do they play?"

Mia and I worked on opposite sides of the tower so as not to corrupt each other's efforts. I envisioned an old woman playing a harp, trying to avoid recreating the likeness of Addy. Where Addy's golden locks flowed down to her waist, I chose instead gray hair in a bun. Where she had been tall and slender, I made my creation squat and stout. My sole concession to the past was the melody she liked to hum while puttering about her garden. I wondered if Mia's vision somehow reflected *her* past.

Once we'd mastered basic phantoms, our mentor encouraged us to experiment while he attended to a farmer with a sprained ankle. The man arrived in a wheelbarrow pushed by his son and left walking without a limp. The healer had conjured a wrap of ice but also used magic to repair the injury.

In the meantime, we practiced our newfound skills. At first, our visions clashed. Figures cropped up with three arms or eyes of different colors on the same side of the nose. After some negotiation, we came up with a knight on horseback and angels with wings, a flowered maypole with children dancing around it, and a wizard with rotten teeth. Without our mentor's critical gaze, we even conjured unicorns and fairies. We played at phantoms until the sun settled to the tops of the trees, and the healer emerged.

He staggered down the few steps, looking older and more tired, but he was not finished with our day's training. He led us down a narrow path on the far side of the tower and urged us to hurry along before the light faded.

As I walked from behind, I noticed his limp had become more pronounced.

Always curious about the limits of magic, I blurted out, "If you healed the farmer's leg, why not your own?"

He stopped and whirled on me. "Because we're sorcerers, not gods. We cannot create life from nothing or revive the dead. And though I can speed up the healing of flesh that would one day heal on its own, I cannot reverse the effects of aging."

Having left me chastened, he stomped off, while I slunk two paces behind.

At last, we came to a small opening where the trail diverged.

"Can you tell me what this is?" he said.

"A crossroads?"

"Aye, and by their nature crossroads are enchanted. Do you know why?"

Mia, who always seemed more in step with him, responded. "Because the path you choose may lead to a different life."

I toed the entrances, peering down each, hoping for some hint of where they led, but they refused to yield their secrets. They appeared identical, nondescript tunnels through the trees, tapering into darkness.

I turned to the healer. "What lies at their end?"

"That's for you to decide, you and the magic, for as you have already discovered, the magic comes not just from your conscious self but from a place inside beyond your control."

He positioned us at the start of the paths, me on the left and Mia on the right, and ordered us to conjure not only phantom characters but a complete scene, something beyond what we'd attempted before.

"Imagine the terrain. Is it pastureland or hills? If high ground, what is the shape, rounded or with sheer cliffs? Does it taper in front or roll down to foothills? Is the slope scarred with ravines or gullies? What of the vegetation? Treed or rich with wildflowers... or barren? Underfoot, is it grass, dirt, or sand? Is water nearby, ponds, lakes, or ocean? One more condition: allow the vision to flow, not only from your fondest desires but also from your deepest fears."

Mia shuddered at the mention of an ocean.

What would *my* deepest fears reveal?

We lingered at the head of our respective trails, hoping to fulfill our mentor's directive but wary of what fantasies we might unleash.

He gave us a few minutes to complete our vision, but before we set off, he surprised us with an unexpected command. "Now switch sides. Each of you go down the other's path."

I checked with Mia, uncertain. Her widened eyes must have reflected my own, but the healer's order was unyielding. We switched sides and started on our way.

I lurched forward, hands outstretched like a blind man, though plenty of sunshine remained. The trees on either side blurred, and the trail narrowed, converging to a pinpoint of light. Time lost its meaning, and in what might have been a moment or an hour, the familiar tingling returned, and I spotted a shimmering ahead.

The trees vanished, and I stumbled onto loose sand, with little pools of salt water and the brackish smell of the sea. As my eyesight cleared, I beheld on my left an expanse of bluish green, with waves breaking forever on the beach. To my right, towering dunes arose with no exit in sight. Overhead a lonesome seagull screeched. Above the bird's cries and the crash of the surf, I detected a gentle keening.

Around a bend, I found its source, a girl with raven hair, squatting so close to the incoming tide that it lapped her bare feet. I turned to a roar from offshore and winced as a swell approached, so high it threatened to wash the child away. I dove forward to save her, forgetting she was a phantom.

The swell broke and engulfed the girl, leaving her soaked with seaweed. Before I could reach her, the subsequent undertow sucked her into the sea. But this vision hadn't finished tormenting me. She reappeared and cried out again. The wave crashed, and once more she disappeared under its fury.

I cursed the healer and his magic. Helpless to change anything, I spun around and raced back to where he awaited, with Mia arriving at the same instant. The blood had drained from her face, and from her expression, my appearance was no better.

Seeing our sorry state, our mentor relented and conjured drinks of cold water for us.

When I grasped my cup, my hand shook so much that the liquid sloshed over the edge.

Alone in our room, Mia and I rested opposite each other, holding hands, while I told her what I'd seen of her vision.

In turn, she shared mine. "I came to a cottage on a cliff overlooking a lake. Inside, my footsteps were muffled, but a different sound emerged from the next room, someone struggling to breathe. I followed the sound but found the room empty. Another doorway appeared. More gasps came from the next room and the next, an endless sequence of rooms, but with each came a new cry of desperation, and I was powerless to help."

Her eyes misted, staring into the distance as if still viewing the phantom vision.

I squeezed her hands to recapture her gaze. "These phantoms are a curse, a source of pain we cannot ease."

"Like our old lives," she said.

I reached across and brushed a vagrant tear from her cheek, and she did the same to mine.

That night, for the first time, we fell asleep in each other's arms.

Chapter 20 – Wind, Rain, and Fire

As our proficiency grew, the healer drummed into us that with enhanced power comes increased responsibility. If we dared to celebrate a new skill, he chastised us for our pride, asserting arrogance begets abuse. Despite his warnings, we became giddy, like young eagles spreading their wings. In our free time, we conjured phantoms at will, even replicating the lord of the castle's feast, though with fewer guests and servants.

After three days of lessons on manipulating the elements, we managed to cause water to freeze or boil on command, and organize wood, sand, or stone into complex structures. Where before we'd struggled to create a simple cottage, now we cobbled together a two-story building with soaring spires and an ornate façade. While not as advanced as our former adversary, we'd progressed enough to imagine someday matching his abilities.

Yet our apprenticeship remained incomplete, with many questions unanswered. How had that misguided sorcerer made a gate impervious to assault? With what power had he induced lightning to shatter the temple door? How had he compelled children to leave in the dead of night and return with their memories altered? How had he cast us from his presence, and transported Isaac home ahead of us? Most confounding, how had he convinced the grieving parents their son had never left?

When we raised such questions, our mentor deflected the discussion, urging patience and mumbling words like wielding the wind, shaping the clouds, and controlling the flow of time, all lessons yet to come.

One evening, after another long day, he told us the time had arrived to make his monthly pilgrimage to his neighbors.

"I go to help those too old or ill to travel but also to maintain friendly relations. I used to trek to each village on foot, departing early in the morning and returning at night, but in recent years, I tire too easily. First thing tomorrow, a stone mason from Pontybridge will lend me his horse and wagon. I'll visit Montvale first, followed by Narthwick and the mason's home last, after which he'll escort us back to the tower."

I perked up. "Us?"

He pressed so close his breath warmed my cheeks. "I expect you to accompany me. This too will be part of your training, how to serve villagers, a lesson you must learn if you hope to make a proper life in this world. Leave behind your fancy belt and Mia's pendant, and your emerging pride as well. I'll present you as humble apprentices, so no using magic while there."

The next morning, he asked me to help gather supplies for the outing—a few books and jars of herbs, which he had me stow in a satchel. I noted some were the same as my grandmother administered to me as a child—coneflower to treat upset stomach, elderberry for toothaches, ginger for nausea, and others. I asked about them.

"Yes, you're right. Over the years, I've found plants that display healing power on their own. By combining them with the faith the villagers have shown in me, I can help much of the time without using my powers. As I've taught you, magic is everywhere. I suspect a few in the village possess some measure of their own—helpful because my sorcery can be fickle at times and not guaranteed."

By the time we emerged from the tower, the mason had pulled up in a four-wheeled wagon, drawn by a solid bay mare with a white star on her forehead. She ignored Mia and me but whinnied a greeting when she spotted the healer.

"This is Fara," he said, as he patted her mane. "She's been my steady companion on my outings, and this stout man is my dear friend William, who has saved these old bones now going on two years."

The mason stood a head taller than me, with square shoulders and a face he himself might have chiseled from stone.

He eyed the two of us. "Who might these be?"

"My new apprentices, here to pick up some of the healing arts to bring back to their own villages. They're eager and well-intentioned but have a lot to learn. I'm hoping this trip will add to their knowledge."

William shook hands with each of us, wished us well, and begged off without more pleasantries.

"It's an hour's trek back," he said, "and I have a full day's work to do."

As he strode off down the trail, the healer marveled at his pace. "He'll be home in an hour as I would have been in my youth. Now, I'd take more than double that or more if not for Farah and the wagon."

He proffered the mare an apple, which she devoured with gusto, then climbed onto the front seat and grabbed the reins, while we hopped in the back. Before we could utter a question, we found ourselves on the dirt road to Montvale.

The seating arrangement did not prevent our mentor from continuing his teaching, adding to our knowledge as we trundled along.

"Montvale lies to the east, Narthwick to the north, and Pontybridge to the west, all connected to each other and to my home by these roads. All three villages are contained within the enchanted forest, which protects them from intruders with malicious intent."

"So we'll encounter no danger?" Mia inquired.

He remained silent for an unsettled moment. With his back to us, his reaction was hidden, though I sensed a tightening in his shoulders. When he answered, his response was measured.

"Likely not. Montvale is protected by the mountain and Pontybridge by the river, but on the trip to Narthwick the woods thin, coming close to the village of Ironforge. That cursed place resides outside my control, its people ruled by the tyrant, Malik. Free lands bordering a tyrant's realm are hateful to the tyrant, who will forever long to gobble them up. It's at that point where he likes to make mischief. Those travelling that way have reported frightening phenomena—violent storms, bloodthirsty monsters, or bands of villagers frothing under Malik's spell—but that worry is for tomorrow."

The healer went silent, as did we, contemplating threats to come. The lord of the castle's solitude had driven him to abuse his magic, but his intent, though ill-advised, stopped short of malice. Lyra had warned of crueler sorcerers more corrupted by their power. Tomorrow, our days of innocence might end, with our training less than complete. I pondered the possibility of our first brush with evil and was relieved to be traveling under the healer's protection.

The people of Montvale greeted us not as lords or visiting dignitaries, but like family, contrasting with our earlier village encounter. No castle loomed above this place, and no fear filled the air. Far from cowering behind locked doors, everyone burst from their cottages to welcome us with bowls of fruit and sprays of flowers. More than one child hopped onto the wagon for the chance to sit beside the healer, an opportunity he embraced with a broad smile. To our delight, a girl with flowing curls jumped in the back and nestled between Mia and me.

Throughout the day, the healer greeted villagers by name, asked after their wellbeing, and when requested, catered to their ills—a sick goat here, a nasty case of the gout there. In each instance, he hemmed and hawed, remarking on the challenge their problem presented. He took more time than needed, fumbling with his book of spells or puzzling over which of several jars to extract from the satchel. In the end, he cured the patient, but perhaps with more drama than necessary.

For a time as a boy, I trusted in magic, never considering it a chance for wealth or power but as a pathway to a better life. I believed a boat crafted of paper tiny enough to hold in my hand could transport me to the land of dreams. As I grew older, I gave up on such fantasies... until the bad times struck. Then, in desperation, I resurrected my faith, only to have it dashed once more. Now, I marveled at this man. He made the world better with his kindness, more so than with his magic.

The next day at Narthwick brought more proof of his neighbors' high regard for him. They once again poured out to greet us, led by a woman, whom the healer introduced as Susanna, their village elder. The tiny woman appeared ageless, with a spark in her eyes, a puckish nose, and fiery red hair tied up in a bun.

After embracing the healer, she handed the reins to a strapping young man to tend to the mare. "This is Seth, our newly trained blacksmith, who will give Fara a new set of shoes. Don't let his scowl frighten you. He's a well-meaning fellow but impulsive. I expect gentle Fara will keep him in line."

In the morning, our mentor went about his duties as usual, but as the shadows lengthened, he became anxious, rushing his cures and insisting we leave before dusk. As we loaded the wagon preparing to depart, a boy with ruffled hair came running up. Not much more than seven, he clutched the healer's hand and begged him to help his mother. The healer checked the angle of the sun, calculating the remaining daylight, and with a sigh, dismounted and followed the child.

At the boy's cottage, we found his mother in bed propped up with pillows, her face flushed with fever and her sheets soaked with sweat.

"Fetch me a glass of water," he ordered the boy.

While he waited, he rummaged through his satchel and selected two jars. To the water the boy retrieved, he added a powder made of white willow bark mixed in with garlic and had the mother drink. After she emptied the glass, he grasped her hand and mumbled a spell without bothering to consult any book.

Once certain the fever had broken, he accepted the family's gratitude with a nod and hurried us back to the wagon as fast as his limp allowed.

On the road back, Mia and I rested beside each other, relishing the travel sounds, the clip-clop of Fara's hooves and the rattling of the wheels. We recounted the day's events, whispering how we might have found a purpose in this world. With every sway of the wagon, our shoulders touched, and a sense of peace surrounded us... until halfway home, a sudden wind kicked up.

The healer cursed and slapped at the reins, urging the horse to a trot.

The sun, which had shone the whole day, had just kissed the treetops when a dragon-shaped cloud swallowed it whole, followed by a swirling fog.

Fara's ears perked up, her nostrils flared, and unhappy with what she sensed, she tossed her head and snorted. The wind swelled to a gust blowing from the south, and bringing with it shouts from the forest.

Mia pointed, and I caught smoke rising in the distance. Through the trees, I spotted shadowy figures, villagers wearing masks, some waving swords and others brandishing torches, setting the dry brush on fire. The small fires merged into a blaze, creating a firestorm. Its heat stung my face as it surged north toward our wagon and beyond it to the village of Narthwick.

I longed for our mentor to speed up, to flee from the attackers, but he did the opposite, yanking on the reins and pulling Fara to a stop.

Gazing skyward, he concentrated until fresh clouds billowed dark and menacing. The wind shifted to the south, away from the village, and thunder rumbled, followed by rain strong enough to extinguish the flames.

Those with swords rushed at us, but he transformed their weapons into harmless stalks of wheat and, for good measure, cast a single bolt of lightning to block their way. Confronted with these otherworldly events, the masked intruders turned and fled.

The smoke cleared, and the sky became bluer but for a few fair-weather clouds scurrying past. A gentle breeze replaced the wind, scattering drops of moisture from the swaying trees and carrying cool, delicious scents our way.

"Evil men," Mia said when our heartbeats had settled.

The healer twisted around to face us, his cheeks flushed, and his breath coming in bursts. "Not evil. Deluded."

"But how—"

He shifted his eyes to the road ahead, and clucked to urge Fara to a canter, sitting with a posture that screamed no more questions.

Back at the tower, he slipped from the wagon and slumped onto the steps, elbows on knees and chin in hands. His magic had saved us and the village but had taken its toll.

"How often does this happen," I said when I dared to ask.

He glanced up with a weak smile. "Oh, my friend, Malik keeps coming up with a new approach, hoping I'll be unable to counter. It's like a game. He attacks, I defend. This time, he assumed my enchanted trees would resist an unnatural fire, so he sent his minions with torches to burn the woods."

"Why do they follow?"

"He conjures a phantasm of lies that casts a veil over their mind, with visions so often repeated they become like memories. Imagine if you believed your grandfather's tale of awakening in the middle of the night to screams. He draws the curtain aside, but not so much as to be spotted. Outside rages the stuff of nightmares, rampaging men from the neighboring village, running through the street with torches and setting fire to cottages. No matter if these are lies. They condition the people to regard their neighbors as enemies, and so they follow the call for revenge."

"Why limit yourself to extinguishing fires and disabling swords? Why not attack back?"

"They know not what they do, so how can I harm them?"

Mia dropped down from the wagon and nestled next to him like a daughter comforting her father. "It must be hard, having such enemies."

"Yes, hard, but be thankful for your enemies. They make you strong. You'll find no better teacher than your enemy."

A tense silence settled over us as I climbed down to join them. My mind raced with visions of villagers made crazed by a mad sorcerer, with no healer to protect us. How would we ever go out on our own to build a new life here?

"If an attack happened to us," I said, "without you, what should we have done? How would we have defended?"

"You'll learn. Elements can be transformed, the wind itself can be a weapon, and as you've seen, a sudden storm comes in handy to dissuade a band of marauders. You'll discover many other ways to defend."

"But how—"

"That's a lesson for another day." The blood drained from his face. He grasped his walking stick in both hands and with trembling arms, forced himself to stand. "Soon, I'll teach you to control the weather and other tricks, but for now, I need to rest. We're done."

Chapter 21 – A Veil over the Mind

Our next excursion went without incident. On the way back from Pontybridge, William drove, and with her owner at the reins, Fara stepped out with head held high. Our mentor rode alongside the driver, leaving his two apprentices in back to eavesdrop on their conversation.

"I caught smoke on the horizon yesterday," the mason said. "More mischief from Ironforge. Rumor has it luck was on our side, the raid foiled when a storm out of nowhere snuffed out the fire."

He cast a glance at his friend, his statement more a question left hanging in the air.

"Malik playing his games."

The mason turned his head and spat on the road. "The people of my village grow weary of these games. Before our luck runs out, you should lead us to put an end to this scourge. Along with our neighbors, we're strong and brave, and eager to right this wrong. We can't always rely on timely fortune that happens to follow you around."

The healer twisted about in his seat to face William. "Have I taught you nothing? Violence begets violence."

The mason stayed silent for a while. When he answered, his tone reflected the grit apparent in his features. "Nevertheless, if those madmen attacked *my* village, I'd fight them with hammer and chisel. What else would you have me do?"

"What of Malik?"

"Better to die than live as slaves. We're not like those who bow under the tyrant's rule."

The healer had no retort, no words of wisdom to offset the mason's rage.

What would I do in his place? I'd only begun to appreciate the power of a seasoned sorcerer devoid of the healer's scruples. These people would have no chance without a similar ally on their side. Despite our mentor's righteous preachings, my rage rose as well.

In my old world, we had experienced no war in my lifetime, although my father told of one they fought before I was born. He never spoke of heroes or enemies, only of the dead and maimed on both sides, but among my childhood friends, many played at war. They reveled in its thrill, feigning courage and fighting for make-believe noble causes. I imagined the little boy with the sickly mother fleeing from flames engulfing his home. What I had witnessed the prior day was no game.

In the following days, the healer taught us to whip up the air into a whirlwind, to cluster moisture in the heavens until it billowed into clouds, and to coax rain and lightning from them. He emphasized ways to escape a tense situation without violence by mustering a combination of weather, the elements, and phantoms, insisting creativity and judgement mattered more than magic.

"Above all," he stressed again, "strive to do no harm."

Do no harm? My head spun, still wondering what I'd do if confronted by a horde of crazed villagers under the spell of a mad sorcerer.

Mia challenged the healer, quicker to question than me. "What if we met someone like Malik, whose skill far exceeded ours? What if his minions attacked in force? Would these tricks be enough to fight them off?"

He shook his head and sighed, showing all his years, and signaled the day's lesson had ended though two hours of daylight remained. Instead, he brought us to the tower and had us sit with him upon the steps, now more father than teacher.

He rubbed his beard and stared at the ground for a long time before forming an answer to Mia's question. "You've mastered more magic than you realize, but much depends on how you apply it. Nature detests using your gift in immoral ways. You must not use it to kill another — such an attempt would violate the natural order, and as a result, you'd lose your power — but applied in a more subtle fashion, you can still cause harm. I've shown how to bring the wind, but wind might blow down a tree, which falls on an unsuspecting child. I've taught you how to cast lightning, but lightning might strike an innocent farmer in the field. Aren't these actions as wrong as killing outright? Yet you've witnessed me using weather to defend without doing harm."

I recalled the lord of the castle. He might have struck down the mob gathered to storm his home but chose instead to make the entrance impervious to assault and scare them off by shattering their temple door.

I recounted his exploits to the healer, to illustrate the limits of our power.

"Limits?" he said. "Such feats are well within your ability. He created the gate from a slab of stone and conjured a phantom to make it appear like wood, so when the villagers set fire to it, it did not burn. As for lightning, he picked a time and place when they were safe from its fury."

"But he also cast us outside the castle without so much as a wave of his hand and transported the boy home ahead of us."

"Yes, it's true. A lesson you've yet to learn—to adjust the flow of time. Your sorcerer sped up travel just as I healed the farmer's ankle by speeding up his recovery. He assumed the two of you would rush back to the village to tell the parents their son would return soon and drove that inevitable event to happen a bit faster. But he could never transport someone to an indefinite place in a vague future. Too many conflicting possibilities. To do so would counter nature, a misguided attempt to alter fate."

I struggled to digest his words. Was so much of a sorcerer's skill in how to apply the magic? Still our former adversary had performed one feat hard to explain.

Mia raised it first. "What about controlling minds, how he altered memories?"

He placed a fatherly arm around her. "He never controlled minds. He used phantoms to muddle their memories."

She stared up at him with knitted brows. "I don't understand."

"Have you ever had a dream so vivid that when you awoke, you struggled to distinguish dream from memory?"

We both nodded. Sometimes our past seemed more like a dream.

"An experienced enchanter can conjure visions so realistic they become like a waking dream. The illusion takes over, and what had once been real fades. The boy became convinced he'd imagined his time in the castle. The parents, so terrified he'd be taken, accepted his captivity as a nasty nightmare."

I went silent, kicking at the dirt and questioning whether the earth beneath my feet was solid. What if my home world had been nothing more than memories manipulated by some cosmic sorcerer?

No. My love for Addy was beyond question, the pain of her passing real, though the time since had been cloaked in fog. I longed now for firm ground, for a new reality to build on.

I glanced at Mia, wondering if the healer's words had stirred similar concerns in her. She reached across, grasped my hand, and squeezed.

Her touch was no dream.

Chapter 22 – Trial and Error

The next day, we focused on how to accelerate time, a skill our mentor claimed was invaluable but complex to manage.

"The pace of time is relative, but its direction is not. You may alter its speed but not change the future. Employ this technique only when certain of what's to come. The farmer's sprain was going to heal in a few days. After adding a bit of ice and a pinch of turmeric, I used my gift to nudge the healing along. Your adversary in the castle told you he'd return the boy soon, and any fool would realize you'd race back to the village to expose what you'd found."

Mia scrunched her nose and shook her head. "How are we to know what will happen. Every morning brings new surprises. This power requires foresight beyond what we possess."

"Correct, but in a real confrontation — not puttering with games — you'll find none of your powers provide perfect foresight. What makes a master sorcerer has less to do with the depth of his magic but rather with the wisdom in how to apply it. What I teach you is but a fraction of what you'll become. Little is what you're taught. Much is what you must learn on your own."

Doubt overwhelmed me. "What if we don't measure up? What if we fail?"

He paused, took a deep breath, and gazed at us as if we were soon to graduate, and he to make his final farewell. "Do you think after my long years in this world, I chose you as apprentices on a whim? No. I recognized the goodness in you at once — innocent, yes, well-intentioned for sure. Don't forget, I came here as you did, cynical, confused, and doubting myself, but at my core, I discovered an untapped strength, as both of you will one day. You must tap that strength to grow, for I will not always be with you."

With that, he announced we were done with the basics. Time to practice applying our magic.

In the following weeks, the healer continued testing our resolve. He'd present a challenge—sometimes benign but often terrifying—and let us cope as best we could, rescuing us from harm only when necessary, and critiquing us afterwards.

On the first day, he sent us out on the trail that had led to the crossroad, but this time, it dead-ended into a glade surrounded by pines so dense they almost appeared black. As we left the woods to cross, the ground shuddered beneath us and turned into a sea of mud. We began to sink.

"Run for the trees," Mia cried.

We twisted around to discover the opening from which we'd entered had vanished. We had nowhere to go.

Just an illusion.

We sank to our ankles and then to our knees.

I reached for Mia as she sank to her waist.

Just an illusion. Just an illusion!

The mud tugged at me as if the earth meant to swallow me up.

I conjured a phantom of a broad meadow seeded with thick grass and clusters of daisies to firm up the soil.

No difference.

Mia cried out, almost to her neck.

"No, no!" the healer's shout echoed from the forest. "Not everything's a phantom."

At last, I realized it. He'd used his control of the elements to flood the glade. We were drowning in actual muck. Now how to combat it?

With weather? A wind to dry out the land?

Too slow.

I scanned the surrounding trees and recalled conjuring a castle. I closed my eyes and envisioned a wooden bridge, supported by a series of three arches, starting below us and rising to a peak above the mud before descending into the tree line. To make it more convincing, I added ornate balustrades on the sides and carvings of lions to mark the exit.

The earth groaned beneath my feet, and the ground firmed.

I grabbed Mia by the wrist and shouted, "Climb!"

We battled to escape, one step at a time. In moments, we reached the top of the bridge. After we caught our breath, we peered back at our near failure. The mud receded and the glade resumed its natural form. At the edge of the woods in a now reopened path, the healer waited, hands on hips and a grimace on his face.

"You did well once you regained your wits. Learn to control your panic. A calm mind is required to understand the challenge, to differentiate what's real, what's phantom, and whether the elements have been manipulated. You need a clear vision to devise a plan."

As we trudged back to the tower, our boots caked with mud, Mia whispered to me. "What if he wasn't with us? What if the earth had swallowed us up?"

I drew in a breath, pursed my lips, and blew it out. "We'd die, I suppose."

"But would we die as well in our old world, or would we wake up as if from a dream and find ourselves back home?"

"You mean separate and apart, you lost in the dunes, and me grieving above the lake?"

She winced. "Then we should make sure not to die."

After that episode, our mentor drilled us with a new urgency, focusing on how to analyze the situation before reacting. "Determine if the looming threat is caused by the elements, weather, phantoms, or some combination. Don't guess, for as you've discovered, guessing may lead to disaster. An illusory weapon will pass through you, but conjured steel will kill. A phantom's edges always flicker. Learn to recognize this telltale sign."

I pictured raiders rushing at me with swords drawn while I tried to scan the weapons to distinguish illusion from reality. The price of error: life or death. But what if the attackers themselves were real?

"How can we know if the wielders of those weapons are phantoms or innocent villagers with clouded minds? How can we tell an evil sorcerer from a projection of himself?"

"An important question. Check the face. Do the eyes have a human spark? Seek defects in the features? The most skilled illusionist cannot replicate reality."

To sharpen our skills, he'd cloak an animal with an illusion to make it appear fierce or send a ghost warrior wielding an axe conjured from actual wood and stone. For each, he'd give us seconds to call out the correct answer before coming to our rescue.

Once we mastered the simple tests, he made them more complex, combining all elements of magic as weaved by a true master.

Late one day, as we relaxed by the tower believing our lessons done, we were surprised by a rustling in the trees. A dozen men burst from forest wearing grotesque masks, like those who had attacked us on the road from Narthwick. These too brandished swords, but in addition, they were led by a pack of giant wolves. The animals raced ahead of them, snarling and frothing at the mouth.

A week earlier, I would have fled inside and barred the door, but this time I calmed my mind and studied the attackers. The masks shimmered at the edges, as did the swords, and the eyes visible through the mask holes lacked spark, not the eyes of those embarking on a life-or-death struggle.

What about the wolves? They appeared oversized for real life, and their rage was missing the fire of a pack on the hunt, but something about the illusion was wrong.

Mia nudged me. "Their paws kick up dust."

The paws were solid, but the cloak of rabid terror was not—dogs made up to appear like wolves.

Phantoms may frighten or confound the mind but can do no harm, but the dogs....

I conjured slabs of meat in front of them.

The wolf veneer vanished as the dogs skidded to a halt to savor their treat, and the attacking horde raced on, passing through us like a cold wind before fading away.

The healer clapped his hands. "Well read, well done."

Mia wrinkled her brow. "Why did the wolves disappear? We did nothing to drive them away."

"But you did. Reality will always transcend magic. Once the dogs reverted to their nature, the phantoms disappeared."

My mind moved beyond this latest test.

"What if those attackers had been villagers from Ironforge? You insist we do no harm. Can you teach us a way to remove the false memories muddling their minds?"

He rubbed his beard and smiled, pleased by the question. "Yes, by creating a counter illusion showing them true scenes to awaken them from their dream. But a warning: such a phantom must be convincing, conjured with an intensity that can only come from the heart."

After a few more weeks of practice, a time came when he combined all we'd learned into a masterpiece. The ground shook as a rampaging horde of ghouls, ogres, and goblins attacked, some wielding swords, some spears. The sky darkened overhead with a flurry of foul wings and a blackness of giant vultures and bats, a gathering of creatures to haunt a child's dreams.

But we were no longer children.

His training had conditioned us to think before reacting and evaluate the scene.

First, no such creatures exist in nature. These are either phantoms or living things cloaked to make them appear as monsters. Yes. I spot the shimmering aura surrounding them, a distinct sign, and when I inspect them further, I detect the imperfections. Phantoms for sure, but if so, why does the ground shake, and why does the flapping of wings make the air tremble?

Of course, if he can raise a storm, he can make the earth shake and the wind blow to make the vision feel more real.

What of their weapons? The creatures may lack flesh and bone, but their weapons may be fatal. Even I can conjure a sword or spear and make it fly — a possibility too dangerous to dismiss. No shimmering on the sharp edges of the blades. I glance at the woods where a willow grows. In my home village, neighbors put up willow branches to ward off evil. I have a better use. When the spears launch in our direction, I transform them into delicate, weeping branches.

The vision vanished. The healer emerged from the tower grinning, a proud mentor. We had passed.

Mia and I rushed him, the blood pumping in our veins.

"Such a grand scene," she said.

"A masterpiece of magic," I added.

"Beyond what we could ever do."

"So many choices."

"The form of the phantoms."

"The force of the wind."

"So little time to react...."

"... and find the right response."

"But what if the next time...."

"... it's not a test...."

"... and you're not with us..."

"Will we still prevail?"

He settled on the steps and invited us to sit on either side, wrapping an arm around each of us.

"When I first arrived, I viewed this world much as you do. My past had been marred with pain, scars I still bare, and I longed for the chance to start anew. Soon, like you, I realized where I had landed was less than heaven. Both good and evil dwell here. I vowed to not be corrupted, to strive to do what's right, but the choice of right and wrong is rarely straightforward. As my power grew, I found it necessary to make choices with less than perfect knowledge, so I came to terms with picking the best available plan. You ask me how to distinguish between right and wrong. I have no answer to give you, but in the weeks since you've stayed with me, I've come to know your hearts. When the time comes, you'll find a way."

Chapter 23 – Final Test

The next morning, we descended the spiral stairs to silence. No phantom musicians played, and no healer appeared. We searched for him outside on the tower steps and down the path he liked to take when gathering herbs. At last, we climbed to his private quarters. When no one answered our knock, we entered.

He lay in his bed, looking pale and wan, as if the effort to train us had drained him.

"I'm so proud of you," he said in a weak voice. "You've mastered enough to practice on your own, and now I need to rest."

He stayed like that for two days, while we practiced our skills as requested. Both morning and afternoon, we'd return to his bedchamber and beg him to clear up a question as an excuse to check on him. We brought him food, but he ate little.

On the third day, we found him hunched in his favorite chair with a blanket wrapped around his shoulders. Mia ran downstairs to fetch him breakfast while I kept watch.

After a few bites and a sip of tea, he rallied and the light returned to his eyes, though without the spark we'd come to expect.

After a second sip, he spoke in a voice ragged from disuse. "The time has come to determine whether you're ready to be on your own. Until now, I've hovered over you, correcting your mistakes. Tomorrow, I'll conjure for you a new challenge, but I will not be nearby to help. In the morning, you'll find a different path, one that will take you far from me. On it, you'll encounter events aimed to confuse, visions to frighten, and choices to test your judgment. Unlike your prior encounters, these will attempt to thwart your responses, as they would if you confronted an enemy." He paused for a cough to settle, took a long drink, and leaned in with all the intensity he could muster. "Do not return until you've conquered your fear."

We emerged from the tower at first light. As promised, the healer was nowhere to be found—not on the steps, not at breakfast, nor in his bedchamber, but our objective was clear. A striking new opening had appeared through the trees.

Though a powerful wizard, our mentor possessed an artist's heart, and the gateway he'd crafted to start us on our way may have been one of his finest works. He had woven together vines to form an arch and embellished its surface with a silken web that sparkled in the sun like fairy lace. It led to a path charming enough to be a portal to an elven kingdom, but its intent was as clear as if a sign above it read: *Final Challenge, This Way.*

I hesitated, gaping at the dappled sunlight filtering through the leaves, lending it the aura of the unknown. We'd grown reliant on our mentor. One more step, and we'd be on our own.

We started off in no rush, eyeing the edges of the forest and prepared at any moment for a surprise, but no surprise came. We trudged along all day without incident until the light faded, pausing only for a bite to eat. An hour before sunset, we stopped to camp for the night.

As we readied for sleep, I rested my head on Mia's shoulder, and she wrapped an arm around me, drawing me closer. An unwarranted calm settled over us but not for long. A rising wind swept the clouds from the sky, revealing a blood moon that cast pale shadows from the overhead branches, making them dance about us like demons. Expecting the healer's test to come at any moment, we spent a restless night, always on alert.

We woke at dawn or something close to dawn. The light was watery, dim and sad, spreading a pall over a scene we'd missed the night before. Grey, gloomy cliffs rose up on either side of where we slept, thick with menacing trees and offering no opportunity to deviate from the path. I thought I'd never viewed a landscape so bleak, as if created to reduce us to despair. I might have turned back if not for Mia's urging.

She flashed the sort of we-must-be-brave smile people use when trying to pretend something awful isn't about to happen. "If we hope to complete this test, we have to go on."

The path led through a narrow valley where spongy moss gave way to jagged rocks, forcing us to pick our steps carefully lest we turn an ankle. By midday, the skyline expanded, revealing snow-capped mountains ahead. The trail began to rise in sharp switchbacks. The temperature dropped and a chill wind followed. Tiny flakes fell at first but soon came down hard enough to make the footing slippery. The terrain left us exposed, not just to the weather but to would-be attackers.

We 'd be easy to find. With the covering of snow, our tracks were plain to follow.

"We're not safe here!" I shouted over the wind.

Mia gave a shiver, nodded, and quickened her pace.

At last, we arrived at a treeless summit. We relaxed for a moment to catch our breath, until we realized the dilemma at hand. Not one but seven paths spiraled downhill, each snow-covered for a stretch before warming to brown earth and pine needles. None but the one we came from bore any markings. No other feature differentiated them. No sign showed the way.

Despite all he'd done for us, I cursed the healer for leaving us freezing on the exposed mountaintop with no hint of which way to go.

Mia paced from path to path hoping to find a clue, but I stood still for a long time, thinking, remembering, listening to the whispers of my past and trying to pierce the fog of my future.

As I pondered the unknowable, I caught a sound so faint it might have been imagined. I held my breath. In the distance, something like a flute played a haunting tune that recalled the bleak moors of the borderlands, a tune conceived with magic for sure.

I turned to Mia. "Do you hear it?"

She nodded, came to my side and, hand in hand, we circled the summit, pausing at each trailhead to listen. We halted at the fifth one.

While I struggled to identify its meaning, the melody changed to a murmur, sounding more than the sighing of the wind and less than the crackle of fire consuming dead leaves. My skin tingled from the top of my ears to the tips of my toes.

The tune turned to a voice in my head, a single word repeated: follow.

The trail descended for several hours. Lower down, the mountain eased into a more pleasant setting, a wooded gorge with a bubbling stream running alongside it. A variety of wildflowers filled the open places near the water's edge, and the air buzzed with the sound of bees collecting nectar. Still no surprises, no attack from phantoms, no violent weather, nothing as dire as what the healer had foretold. As the shadows lengthened on this second day, doubt crept in.

I stopped in mid-stride and turned to Mia. "What if he'd become too ill to finish devising the test?"

"Or what if he decided we'd never be strong enough and used the test as a ruse to send us away?"

"Far from the enchanted forest...."

"...and beyond Malik's grasp?"

We glanced back from whence we came but only for a moment. The healer's voice echoed in our ears: *'Do not return until you've conquered your fear.'*

Our doubts did not last long. As the sun dipped below the treetops, we spotted our first surprise—a chestnut tree blocking the way, with a trunk so broad and canopy so thick as if placed to hide what lay behind.

No phantom, this. No shimmer flickered about its edges. I shuffled forward and brushed its bark with my fingertips. Perhaps a marvel of nature; more likely the work of a master sorcerer.

Bramble and brush clustered around the tree, leaving scant space for us to pass. We turned sideways and slipped by, one at a time, too absorbed in the passage to peek ahead. Once through, we froze in our tracks, too shocked to speak, too stunned to move.

At another time and circumstance, I would have considered what I found a fairyland glade, surrounded by blossoming trees. At its center rose a cottage that might have been made of gingerbread, like in the old fairytales, but the scene was too familiar. Before us stood what appeared to be the thatched-roof cottage I had conjured in the borderland.

Has he cast us out of his enchanted world and back to the borderland?

On closer inspection, I spotted differences. We had described our cottage to the healer but not in precise detail, and discrepancies showed. The pond we had created lay down a short path out of sight from the cottage, but this waterfall flowed to the right of the glade. The fence we'd built to protect the garden had been post and wire, but this one was split rail. Mia had added many details missing from this scene, a sure telltale. Our mentor may be wise but was unable to read our minds.

What does he mean by this near replica? In what way is this a test?

I stared until my eyes watered, trying to penetrate beyond the walls to discover what lay within. When no insight came, I crept forward and extended a finger to touch the door. Solid oak. I reached for the latch.

Mia grabbed my wrist and held me back. "It looks innocent enough, but given the healer's warning, I expect a gang of ghouls or man-eating vultures lurking."

I pulled my arm away. "Whatever awaits, he trained us well and believed in us. Time to believe in ourselves."

I drew in a long breath and blew it out, pushed the door open, and stepped inside.

Chapter 24 – A Cottage in the Woods

Much like the rest of our journey, we were surprised by the lack of surprise. The inside appeared like a normal country home, decorated not with Mia's flair but with the humdrum tastes of the healer — a plain round table with no rug underneath, curtains a shade darker than amber, and a bed of straw. No pictures lined the walls, no bowl of flowers graced the table, and the feature closest to our former dwelling was the fireplace, made of stone like mine.

Mia gazed at the empty fireplace and hugged herself, still damp from our trek through the snow. "Did you notice the rack by the door stacked with firewood?"

Not all surprises were unpleasant. I slipped outside still wary, glancing from side to side and up at the giant chestnut, now shadowed in the dusk. Convinced I was alone, I fetched an armful of logs. Minutes later, with the help of some basic magic, a fire roared in the hearth.

We plopped down before the flames, the sight of them reviving me as the fire in my old home had done on a cold winter night. The wood crackled and glowed as we stared in silence at the tongues of yellow and red, and followed the sparks flying up the chimney and into the night.

Mia spoke without looking away. "I wonder why we're here. What if he's testing to determine if we'd prefer a life of peace rather than the world of demons and ghouls?"

"...or of mad sorcerers."

"Is he tempting us with a simpler life?"

"Like the one we left behind...."

"Before the bad times struck."

"Or is the test yet to come?"

My question hung in the air.

Unable to answer, Mia staggered to her feet and stumbled to bed, worn out from two days of hiking and the strain of anticipation.

I went to secure the door, shifting the slide bolt into place and checking it twice, though the creator of this cottage would have no problem breaking in. Given our mentor's power, nowhere was safe.

With that happy thought, I went to sleep.

That night, I tossed and turned — too much talk of vultures, demons, and ghouls; too much waiting for the test to come. I listened to the wind gusting and calming. I counted Mia's soft breathing and my own. Above the roof, I imagined dark clouds massing, but one thought resounded.

My powers have grown strong enough to meet any challenge, but to what end?

Staying in this cottage, albeit the healer's poor copy, had stirred in me memories of tragedy but also of better times. And I wondered what I feared the most — the claws of the vulture or the wings of the dove?

As I pondered, exhaustion took over and I lapsed into a dream.

I stood in a clearing in front of a cottage, though I could not tell which one — my home above the lake, the one Mia and I had conjured, or this product of our mentor's fancy. From this spot, four roads diverged, to the north and south, and to the east and west. An odd wind swirled, not a breeze or a gust but a wind of possibilities. I spun around, hoping the wind would point the way, but in each direction, it blew in my face.

Four black birds circled overhead, enchanted birds like the one that guarded the healer's tower. I spoke to them, begging them to show me the way. They separated, each flying in a different track off into the night.

Every direction was magical; every direction was real.

Why had I come here? Why had I chanced the leap through the maelstrom? I was running away from my old life but to what? A question magic could not answer.

We awoke to a loud bang and the stench of wood burning. I opened the curtain a crack and peeked out. The chestnut blocking the clearing lay struck in half by lightning, its exposed trunk still smoldering. Above it, a band of thunderheads darkened the sky.

Through the split in the tree, a marauding horde emerged, parading single file before forming a line ten paces in front of our cottage. Each warrior was naked from the waist up and bore streaks of blood-red paint on their cheeks. At a signal from their leader, they brandished swords and spears and began marching towards us.

Wake up, Lucas. The test is upon you.

Mia joined me, peering out through the second window. "Phantoms, I believe."

I spotted as she did the telltale shimmering, but what of their weapons. With my newfound skill, I scanned these as well. Nothing but an impressive illusion, sufficient to make villagers run away.

She came to my side to await the approaching horde. We clutched hands and held our breath as they passed through the wall and vanished.

"Too easy," she said.

"But why would he--?"

"Because it's not done. Look!"

A black cloud formed behind the chestnut tree, racing toward us. As it came closer, we realized the cloud was a flock of real birds, but how did he make them attack? Several screeches provided the answer—six red-tailed hawks in pursuit, shimmering in the dim light.

These phantom hawks, under their master's control, flew with a purpose, driving the frightened birds down to our windows.

Mia reacted before me, and iron bars, less than a hands width apart, protected the windows in time. The first birds smashed into them at full speed, leaving a mess of blood and feathers outside the wall.

Those surviving veered off, while the phantoms disappeared.

We took a long breath but stayed alert, knowing the method of our mentor.

For a minute or two, nothing more happened, but then a growling sounded in the distance, followed by the earth shaking. A frantic water buffalo lumbered through the opening in the fractured tree, pursued by five ghostly lions. One chased from behind, while the others herded the larger animal to our front door. Eyeing the upcoming collision, the beast lowered its massive horns.

No time to think. Not a moment to imagine an elaborate response. I pictured the impenetrable door of the lord of the castle.

The cottage door transformed into the castle's gate, twice my height and three times my girth. Though coated with a black illusion, its core was of enchanted stone.

A deafening crash. We peered through the bars of the window as the stunned animal staggered away. Its pursuers, like the hawks, dissipated into thin air.

We waited, staying silent enough to detect the squeaking of a mouse or the buzzing of a bee. Nothing. My heartbeat slowed, and I embraced Mia, but our mentor's test was not yet done.

This time, no screech sounded from the sky, no roar from the forest. The ground stayed still and the wind calm. Instead, emerging amidst the smoke surrounding the tree came a lone child, too indistinct at first to identify. As he approached, I recognized him as the boy from Narthwick who'd begged the healer to help his fevered mother. He shuffled toward the cottage with a shy smile on his face and a sprig of daisies in his hand. Beyond the improbability of his being there, the shimmering gave him away.

Believing this a peace offering signifying the end of the test, we let our guard down, but tensed when the flowers transformed into a single metal rod. The boy's image faded, but the rod remained. Before we could react, it floated up and embedded itself in our thatched roof.

An instant later, thunder rumbled, and a bolt of lightning struck the metal, setting the roof ablaze.

I understand. He's lulled us into inaction, and now we'll pay the price.

The flames spread, racing through the dry straw. Clumps of burning thatch plopped into the cottage. The bed caught fire, and the table and chairs. A choking smoke filtered into the room.

I grabbed Mia by the hand. "We have to get out... now."

We raced to the door, forgetting I had transformed it into an impenetrable gate. I closed my eyes, struggling to concentrate, and pictured the original door.

Nothing happened.

With the distractions, not enough conviction? I urged Mia to join me.

No change.

"The windows," she said.

No chance to pass through, as the bars she'd conjured blocked the way.

Again, we concentrated. Again, we failed.

The smoke thickened and we struggled to breathe.

"The healer's final words," Mia said. "'Unlike your prior encounters, these will attempt to thwart you, as they would if you were confronted by an enemy.' He's taken over. The changes we made are now under his control. We have no way out."

"Not his final words," I managed between breaths. "Those were, 'Do not return until you've... conquered your fear.'"

My conviction stiffened. I'd find a way, but how to save us? No chance of reversing his enchantments—they were too strong—but what if....

The crackling of the flames grew louder, the heat from them becoming unbearable.

Too late for rain. The fire was in our space.

What should I do? At once, it came to me. Like with the garden fence, I needed a combination of magic, muscle, and will.

I conjured an axe with a sturdy handle and a metal head imbued with all the enchantment I could muster. The rest was up to me.

I swung the axe. The gate withstood my blow as the past had blocked my future.

The past was who I am, but the future is who I will be if I can conquer my fear. I will not leave us trapped in this burning cottage.

I swung again. The stone creaked at the next blow, cracked at the second, and shivered at the third. One more and the door collapsed into rubble.

A surge of triumph came over me, a sense I could dash up mountains and glide over snow, battle demons and prevail over tyrants.

No need, for all these visions—the cottage, the chestnut tree, and the storm clouds—had floated off like wreaths of smoke and vanished. We were met instead by a blaze of sunlight that made drops of water on the grass glitter like beads. Best of all, in place of the cottage, a comforting sight arose—the tower that had been our refuge these past months.

And on its steps, a frail but smiling healer.

Chapter 25 – No Teaching Today

Though we'd passed our final test, the healer resumed his training as best he could in his weakened state. Sometimes, he managed to instruct us while slumped on the tower steps. Other times, he'd bring us into his healing chamber, have us fetch a book or two from the shelves, and teach us what he called nature's magic.

"These books hold my learnings over many years," he said. "Sometimes, I believe they hold more wisdom than I do. Learn from them."

As we continued to improve our powers, our mentor's lessons grew shorter. On his poorer days, he'd quit well before noon and retreat to his bedchamber. Mia, less inclined to books than me, would use the time to practice at phantoms or go for long walks in the woods while I studied the healing arts.

I'd climb the ladder, select a book, and immerse myself in it. Though I'd only glanced at the single spell on the day we'd first entered the tower, I marveled at them now. He'd written his notes in a clear and steady hand, with dramatic downstrokes and thin upstrokes, so exquisite I admired them for a while and almost forgot about reading them. In the margins, he'd scrawled pictures of the various spices and herbs, as well as diagrams for their preparation.

I read about garlic for infections, colic, or fever, prepared either cooked or raw; ginger for stomach upset and pain, with a drawing of the leafy stem and yellow-green flowers from whose underground root the spice derived; lavender for treating insect bites and burns, and promoting better sleep; and so many others. I would need months to master them all.

One morning, the healer failed to join us for breakfast. We ate our meal—now conjured by ourselves—in silence, and left the tower on the off chance he'd slipped out before we awoke. To our surprise, he appeared on the steps, or seemed to appear. Even such a seasoned sorcerer as him could not perfect human expression. This phantom had a forced smile revealing more sadness than joy.

The healer's phantom beckoned us inside, and we followed.

Mia and I raced up to his bedchamber, taking two steps at a time.

He rested on his bed with eyes half shut and head propped up on a pillow. "I was too tired this morning to navigate the spiral stairs, so I conjured a messenger to summon you, a simple test you passed with ease. I shall not teach today, but I've scrawled out a list for you to practice."

He handed us a piece of parchment with writing upon it, and proceeded to close his eyes as if asleep.

We lingered awhile, hoping for more, wishing for him to be well again. After a time, we turned to leave, but stopped when he began to speak in a muffled voice, eyes still closed.

"I've led a long life and have no regrets in this world, but memories from my younger days still haunt me, visiting me in dreams." His eyes opened but took on a faraway gaze, as if seeing what he'd left behind. "You've both told me the story of why you came here, but I've never told you mine. This may be my last opportunity, a confession of sorts.

"Nothing matters more than the quest for love, and I had my chance when I was young, but youthful pride ruined it. I wished for magic to undo what I had done, wished with all my heart, but no magic came. That's why I fled through the portal.

"Why do so few from our old lives find their way here? I've come to think this is the reason — to pass through, you must believe in magic with all your being, enough to will it into existence. People like us are driven to abandon reality in order to create a world as we'd prefer it to be.

"I've made the most of my time here, honed my skills while never giving in to the corruption of power. I've based this life on helping others. That's the meaning I created for myself, real or not.

"So know this: your old lives accompany you wherever you go — you can never escape them — but don't let them own you lest they visit you on your final days."

With that, he closed his eyes again and drifted off to sleep.

The pattern continued for another week. His phantom would summon us, and we'd respond. Sometimes, he'd have the strength to answer our questions, explaining in his usual patient fashion what we did right and wrong. Other times, he'd ask us to come closer, squeeze our hands, and murmur how glad he was Lyra had brought us to his doorstep.

One day, no more phantom came. We rushed upstairs to find him at peace.

Mia and I waited like supplicants, praying at least his phantom would rise like his soul and continue teaching, but his days were finished.

We made a grave for him, conjuring only the shovels but digging by hand, as we had with our garden fence so long ago, needing to experience the pain in our muscles and the ache in our hearts.

After burying him, we stuck his walking staff in the ground above him as a simple memorial, the kind he would have preferred. Then we bowed our heads in respect and shed tears as we embraced to comfort each other. In an enchanted world where anything seemed possible, one truth stood out.

He was gone, and we were on our own.

PART 3 – PILGRIMS

"Pilgrims are persons in motion – passing through territories not their own – seeking something we might call completion, or perhaps the word 'clarity' will do as well, a goal to which only the spirit's compass points the way."
~ Richard R. Niebuhr

Chapter 26 – Omens

I awoke the next morning to a changed world. The tingling on my skin diminished, and my mood, which had pulsed with possibility, now throbbed with doubt. Most striking were the trees surrounding the tower. These no longer vibrated with a consciousness of their own, but appeared as trees back home, alive only when a breeze ruffled their leaves or a bird nestled on their branches.

We wandered about the healer's bedchamber, searching for any note he might have left and touching his belongings, as if to further fix his memory in our minds.

After a few hours, we descended below and commenced poring through his books and herbs. No magic would bring him back, but we could at least preserve what he'd discovered about nature through a lifetime of learning.

Mia gathered the containers while I sat at the desk, finding matching descriptions in his books and cataloguing them in my journal.

By late afternoon, with our ears sensitive to unusual sounds, we caught the clip-clop of hooves approaching. We raced outside to find William, the mason from Pontybridge, at our doorstep. He dismounted from a sweating and winded Fara, his face drawn and haggard, so different from our prior meeting.

"The healer—?" was all he could say.

We shook our heads.

"I knew last night. The clouds billowed in the strangest way and hovered over our village, and the trees lost their enchantment. No longer did they whisper warnings to our enemies, and already the raids have begun. This morning, we received a message from Narthwick saying they'd awoken to fences shattered and goats and sheep missing. I rode here in haste, hoping for guidance but fearing the worst."

Fara swung her head about, searching for the healer, and let out a mournful whinny when he was nowhere to be found. William patted her mane to calm her and asked for water to quench her thirst after such a hard ride.

"As soon as she's rested, I need to return. The villagers are gathering to organize our defense. We're not warriors, but each farmer and craftsman has been tasked with bringing whatever tools they possess that might be used as weapons—axes and pitchforks, hammers, knives, and scythes."

Mia grimaced. "What of his directive to do no harm?"

He winced when he swallowed, as if his next words brought a bitter taste. "The healer's gone, and we must defend our homes. What other choice do we have?"

Can the peace our mentor had maintained be shattered so soon?

I approached the mason, still grasping the journal I held when we'd rushed from the tower. I showed it to him now. "What about his healing art? His herbs and spells? We've spent the day cataloguing them. They might be of value to your villagers."

He accepted the journal, thumbed through the pages, and handed it back. "You realize we humored him all these years. One can't live in a world with sorcerers and not perceive their power."

Mia rested a hand on his arm. "Many of his cures work without magic. If you trust them, they can become their own miracles."

He sighed, glanced up to the top of the tower and back to us. "Yes, I agree it's possible. We have stories from before he arrived of neighbors blessed with the healing arts, those with knowledge of herbs and spices. Some believed these folks had a touch of fairy blood in them. Perhaps with your help, they might relearn the ancient ways." He grimaced. "We may soon need these to heal our wounded. Prepare them in boxes, and if I survive the battle, I'll come back with the wagon and retrieve the healer's wisdom. For now, I must return to be with my people."

I recalled the humiliation when the lord of the castle banished us from his presence.

It can't end like this.

He mounted Fara to ride back, but I grabbed the reins. "What if we can help, not just with healing but with the defense?"

"I appreciate the offer, but you're mere apprentices, and this is not your fight."

He yanked the reins free, swung Fara's head around, and rode off at a gallop.

As he vanished down the road with the mare's hoofbeats trailing into silence, our shoulders slumped, and we bowed our heads.

Mere apprentices.

Is this what it's come to, that we become pilgrims again, not of this world but searching for our place in it? Are we doomed to wander until we find another healer who will grant us wisdom or another Malik who will show us the void?

Mia and I trudged back to the tower to continue our labors, this time adding the task of packing-up jugs, jars, and books, to be ready when and if the mason returned. This kept our hands busy but not our minds.

As I filled the last box, she grabbed my arm and turned me to her. "For the first time since the darkness descended, a new purpose lay within my grasp. How can I let it slip away?"

I set down the vial I'd been packing and led her outside. We settled on the tower steps and gazed at the trees, wishing our limited skill could enchant them again. After a time, I rose, trudged to the start of the road, and stared down it.

I spoke without facing her. "Malik may be content to send his underlings to fight for him, but if the villagers begin to prevail, he'll use his powers against them, magic unconstrained by the scruples of the healer. William and his friends may defeat the horde, but they'll stand no chance against a seasoned sorcerer."

Mia came up beside me and wrapped her arm around mine. "Would we? Suppose he'd trained us for this very purpose, realizing the challenge to come, knowing his days were short."

"But what if the training ended before we were ready?"

Her eyes flared. "What else can we do? Leave this no-longer-enchanted forest and set out to who-knows-where? Are we likely to find a less cruel wizard or villagers more in need?"

"He *did* teach us that cunning mattered more than magic, conviction more than power...."

"... if used for a righteous cause."

"What if Malik is more cunning?"

She took a deep breath and repeated Lyra's words. "No meaning without the void."

With the decision made, we adjourned inside to prepare. First, we gathered those herbs most useful in a battle: garlic, ginger and goldenseal for infections; nettle juice, blackberry tea, and loosestrife for bleeding; and an assortment of cloths and cords to bind wounds. Next, we conjured provisions for two days, fearing we might lack time to summon them amid chaos. All these we stowed in packs.

Before leaving, we paused at the healer's grave as if hoping he'd bless our venture.

Mia spoke through tears. "Is this what you want us to do?"

No answer, but his words echoed in our ears.

'Do not return until you've conquered your fear.'

The path we'd chosen was righteous; the path we'd chosen was true. At its end, we would find either meaning or the void, because the one could not exist without the other.

The healer had claimed the mason would reach his village on foot in less than an hour. Though not as hardy, we maintained a brisk pace, while still managing to appreciate all we'd missed on our wagon rides.

The road traveled through a mix of trees. Though enchanted no more, each spoke to us in its own way. A stand of birches evoked ghosts from ancient battles, and a row of willows wept for the fallen. Now and then, we passed brambles ripe with berries, tempting us to stop and conjure a basket to collect them, but we kept going, having vowed to abstain from magic lest we alert Malik to our presence.

At the first farm on the outskirts of Narthwick, we slowed our pace, not from exhaustion but out of caution. Beyond chickens clucking in a coop and a few curious goats, the place appeared deserted. The same eerie calm pervaded the second farm and the third. At the fourth, almost to the village center, we paused to listen. Voices carried on the breeze remained indistinct, more of a murmur indicating a crowd.

We jogged ahead but hesitated as a rise loomed, blocking our view.

The murmur became words, the villagers calling out to each other. "Form your lines. Hold your ground."

We took off, lengthening our stride until we reached the crest of the hill.

Below, dozens had gathered, forming a ragged line three deep, everyone grasping some implement of their trade now converted to makeshift weapons. All stared to the east.

In the distance, visible only by the dust they stirred up, the horde from Ironforge approached.

Chapter 27 – Violent Visions

The healer had claimed the best teacher was one's enemy. Perhaps now, despite his loss, we were about to learn more, not so much in the realm of magic but in the depth of our character.

We rounded the hill and stopped by the edge of a barn, concealed from the people below. As the intruders emerged from the trees, I counted no more than a couple dozen. While they bore razor-sharp weapons, they seemed more like a raiding party than an army, sent to probe the village defenses before attacking in force. They hesitated when realizing how many defenders awaited, armed and ready and outnumbering them several times to one.

A few of the less brave turned to flee but froze at a screeching from behind.

We crept from the side of the barn, anxious to find out what had frightened them. What we discovered made me blink twice, my eyes unwilling to accept what they saw.

Above the trees on the far end of the clearing, a pair of gloomy shadows glided toward the village. At first glance, I might have mistaken them for wisps of smoke but for the foul stench they gave off. An instant later, instead of billowing and curling, the mist took shape in the form of two hideous creatures.

Each had the head of a bird of prey with a cruel, curved beak, and the body of a man so gaunt the rib bones showing through yellowed skin. Black wings twice the length of an eagle's clung to the top two of their six arms, sending forth a chilling breeze as they flapped overhead. A second pair of hands grasped flaming swords, and the last two ended in sharp claws, extended as if to snatch the whole village in their grasp. The expression on their faces made white-hot anger seem benign—no mercy to be found there.

The ghastly creatures flew past the invaders and hovered before the terrified villagers like generals leading the attack. Where they floated above the ground, the grass beneath them withered.

My heart thumped in my chest, and my breath came in short bursts, but our mentor had trained us well. I calmed my mind and focused on their beaks and wings, their talons and flaming swords. All shimmered at the edges.

These phantoms may cause no harm, but they would drive the frantic marauders into the panicked villagers. Whatever the outcome, blood would be shed.

Mia stepped closer, also too trained to be fooled. "An impressive illusion by Malik—the foul stench, the chill wind from their wings, the grass withering beneath them."

"And the build-up," I added. "Floating in like storm cloud before reforming as monsters. Theater at its best, but how should we respond?"

Her face turned red, and she balled her hands into fists. "Strike the invaders down with lightning."

"If we offend the natural order, our magic may fade. When more enemies come, we'd be powerless to help."

"Then scatter them with a whirlwind."

"What if a tree or a stray branch hit one of the villagers. The sides are too close to each other."

A devilish smile curled her lips. "I know. We respond with theater of our own."

She faced the enemy and waved her arms, an unnecessary gesture, and a milk white unicorn appeared above our friends as if to defend them. After so much time together, I at once grasped her plan. Despite a pounding heart, I conjured a unicorn of my own.

Mine pranced across the sky, a lordly beast, with the creamy whiteness of his flank and a glowing silver horn. Hers was daintier, a mare with a silken mane but a horn as sharp. Both bore grim expressions, as if the tyrant's phantoms had offended them. Their horns glistened as they glided through the air toward the two demons.

"Mommy," a child called out from below. "I thought you said there's no such thing as unicorns."

Mia spun around to the nervous crowd, shouting in a confident voice, "And no such thing as monsters. These are Malik's illusions made to frighten you."

As the free folk gaped, our unicorns charged the creatures. When they clashed, each passed through the other, and with the illusion shattered, all vanished.

With their master's demons vanquished and still faced with superior odds, the Ironforge horde turned and fled.

Now all eyes shifted to us, and foremost amongst them William, who viewed us anew. He motioned for us to come down and join them.

"I'm humbled," he said when we stood beside him. "You *do* possess some sorcerer skills, but what you've witnessed is a just a ploy to test our mettle. Thanks to your help, we've driven them off, but this temporary rout will only feed Malik's fury. This is not his first attack. He's sent visions to give us nightmares, but always before, we were protected by the enchanted forest. No more."

I spoke to the assembled, hoping to learn more. "What kind of visions? Have you seen Malik?"

The villagers tried to answer all at once.

"Twice at midnight."

"He appeared in my dreams."

"A ghastly figure."

"Tall as the trees."

"Shooting flames from his fingertips."

"And fire from his eyes."

People shuffled their feet, and children buried their faces in their parents' hips.

Mia whispered to me, "They've never seen him, but the thought of him terrifies them. Unless we dispel this myth, they've already lost the battle."

William separated from the crowd, along with Susanna, the leader of Narthwick, and a man we'd never met. The man, though much older than the other two, had a straight back and square shoulders, holding himself like one who would exude calm in crisis. The woman appeared as before, except the spark in her eyes had turned to fire.

"I believe you know this fine lady, and this proud elder is Joseph of Montvale. Let us retire to Susanna's home to continue our discussion lest we upset the people further."

He led us to a cottage situated on the commons, larger than the others but less prominent than might be expected of a village elder. Its lone distinguishing feature was four window boxes filled with geraniums so bright they put those Mia and I had conjured to shame.

Once inside, Susanna hung a kettle over the fire to boil, and we settled around her kitchen table.

Joseph spoke first. "We're thankful for your help, but now an angered Malik will send far more troops, better armed with weapons he's forced his blacksmiths to forge. Like us, the people of Ironfrorge are simple folk, but they're terrified of him. We've seen it in their eyes. They'll do his bidding... not out of loyalty, but fear. The next attack will be no illusion. Is your sorcery enough to counter it?"

Susanna stood and gathered cups from a shelf on the wall as his question hung in the air. The clink of stoneware on the wooden table echoed in the silence.

I glanced around at all the faces—decent people and brave but no more accustomed to war than we were. Now they sat with hands folded in front of them and lips stretched into thin pale lines.

Can we help or is this a fool's errand? Are we deluding them into believing they can prevail, only to have the battle end in disaster? Are we better off quitting them as we did with the first village, abandoning Caleb, Isaac, and the others to the whims of the lord of the castle?

The kettle began to steam, and Susanna rose to fetch it. As she poured water for tea, she responded as if she'd read my thoughts. "Our people are brave and are defending their homes and families. None want to live under the tyrant's yoke, but though his magic may be illusion as you claim, it strikes terror into their hearts. They will not stand their ground against such an onslaught."

I took a sip and set it down, still too hot to drink. "We can teach them how to recognize illusions, so they'll no longer be afraid."

Mia stood, circled the cottage, and stopped at the head of the table, her hands splayed out on its surface. If troubled by the same doubts as me, she hid them well.

"With your help, we can begin at once. We can conjure phantoms as we did with the unicorns, show them in such a manner they'll laugh in their face."

Joseph gazed into his cup. "Not all magic is illusion. We've seen windstorms rattle the shutters of our cottages, and lightning strike nearby trees. Today, we felt the wind from the monster's wings, smelled their foul stench, and witnessed the grass beneath them wither. Our cheeks burned from the heat of their flaming swords."

William rose from his chair and confronted Mia. "Wind can destroy, lightning can kill, fire can burn. Can you counter these as well?"

She stared back unblinking. "Magic is ruled by the laws of nature, with limits all sorcerers must obey, including Malik."

I came to her side, feeding off her strength to hide a false bravado. "If he tries such devices, we have ways to defend just as the healer did."

The mason, who knew our mentor best, whirled on me. "The healer was more than Malik's match, but neither of you are the healer, yet you ask us to believe you can defeat him, even at the risk of our lives."

Susanna stepped between us and gazed first into my eyes and then Mia's. When she'd seen enough, she confronted the mason with all the power of her ancestors, fairy or otherwise.

"Our choice is to submit to Malik or fight, but we cannot prevail alone. These two have offered their help. I can't measure the extent of their abilities, but I sense the goodness in their hearts. I for one will never become his slave. We should accept their help and pray they are up to the task."

Chapter 28 – Hope and Fear

What had we done? We'd convinced these desperate people to believe in us, but did we believe in ourselves? And if so, was such a belief the greatest illusion of all?

Suppressing our doubts, we stood aside as the leaders concocted a plan. William sent the fastest runners out to the north, the east, and the west, each armed with a ram's horn and ordered to climb the tallest tree. When the first scout spotted the enemy approaching, he would sound the alarm, and the others would pass on the warning, giving the defenders time to muster.

While the horns stayed silent, we assembled the remaining villagers for training, allowing them the rest of the day to learn how to distinguish the real from the phantom. We invited children to participate as well as their parents.

Mia approached an eight-year-old boy with freckles and a mop of curly hair. "Have you ever played with soap bubbles?"

He nodded.

"How big were they?"

He spread his thumb and forefinger apart, as far as they could go.

"Would you like me to make one this big?" She stretched her arms to the limit.

The boy beamed, and his eyes sparkled, a pleasing sight after the earlier scare.

"Let's see what we can do."

She waved her hands in the shape of a circle and mumbled a nonsense incantation. At once, a huge bubble appeared.

"Now, do you think you can burst it?"

The boy grinned, took a half step forward, and poked at the phantom with his finger.

His hand passed all the way through to his shoulder, but the sphere remained intact. Perplexed, he tried again and again, and then other children joined in, none with any success.

I raised a hand to silence the crowd. "You cannot burst it because it doesn't exist. It's an illusion, a trick of the light." I surveyed the assembled, spotted a girl clutching a floppy-eared puppy, and signaled to her. "Can you bring your pet to me? It's all right. I won't hurt him."

The child shuffled forward and set him down at my feet. With Mia at my side, we blocked the pet from view, and with more unnecessary gestures, I conjured an identical phantom.

Turning back to the villagers and revealing what I had done, I challenged them. "Without touching them, can you tell me which one is real?"

A murmur rippled through the crowd. After a moment, the girl's mother cried out. "The one on your left."

"How can you tell?"

She knitted her brow, certain of her choice but not knowing why. At last, she brightened. "The other one, something about its fur is wrong. The air around it ripples like heat rising from the ground on a summer day."

Mia nodded approval. "That's right. The other dog is an illusion, and the shimmering gives it away. Now come and fetch both."

The mother stepped forward with her daughter. The little girl snuggled the real pet in her arms as if finding it again after it had run away, but when the mother tried the same with the phantom, her hands passed through it.

I gave the crowd a moment to settle before completing the lesson. "The monsters you witnessed today were no different than the bubble and the dog. Had you regarded them with what you learned just now, you would have recognized them for what they were—harmless illusions, not to be feared."

A man shouted from the back. "Can you make this morning's creatures reappear?"

A hint of worry crossed Mia's face. Our skills had grown sufficient to conjure most of what we imagined, but Malik's elaborate creations exceeded our abilities. Given a proper canvas, paint, and brush, anyone can draw a picture, but only a master can create a masterpiece.

Susanna came forward to rescue us. "You've seen the tricks the tyrant presents. They may be nothing to fear, but the enemy is real. Go home now and rest. We'll need all our strength to defend ourselves when they come again."

As the crowd dispersed, she led us back to her cottage, offering us a place to sleep for the night. When we were alone, she confronted us, a concerned but composed leader who recognized the danger but remained in command.

"You did well today to calm their fears, but that alone will not save us. Malik's people are no different from ours. We all cherish our children, savor the first day of spring when the crocuses pop out of the snowy ground, and recall the moment we met our first love, but their master has planted hatred in their hearts. If you cannot reverse that hatred, they will do his bidding and attack with more vengeance the next time. We're not warriors but will defend our homes and families. Our people will fight back because they have no other choice. With luck, we might prevail, but at what cost?"

She left the question hanging. She had to trust us but realized the challenge ahead, perhaps more than we realized it ourselves.

After night fell and the village quieted, neither of us could sleep, so we slipped outside to contemplate the moon and stars.

"Do you think they're real?" Mia said.

"The stars? They *do* shimmer like phantoms."

She stared at me with an odd expression, as if viewing me for the first time.

"Why are you staring?"

"To see if you shimmer too."

I laughed, but my grin turned into a frown. "You know I'm real, but we may have spun the biggest illusion of all for these villagers, making them believe they can defeat a better armed force and a more seasoned sorcerer."

A chill breeze blew through the commons, causing the surrounding branches to creak and groan.

Mia hugged herself and rubbed her arms for warmth, but her expression hardened. "They will have to defend themselves with or without us. Malik has instilled in his people false visions, bitter memories that make them hate their neighbors. To avoid the fight, we need to offset those visions. The healer claimed an experienced enchanter can conjure phantoms vivid enough to restore true memories."

My chin drooped to my chest. "Yes, an experienced enchanter. Even if we were to succeed, would it be sufficient?"

"What would?"

"Exposing illusions. That skill would not have saved us from sinking in the mud or burning in the fire or being trampled by a buffalo driven to madness by phantom lions. The enemy will attack like a beast crazed with fear. If we manage to remove the veil over their minds, we'd next be challenged by the magic of a sorcerer far more skilled than us."

Uncertain and filled with doubt, we stared at our boot tops as if tottering on the brink of an abyss, until a welcome voice sounded from the shadows.

Lyra.

I rushed toward her, hoping for answers before she vanished again, leaving us to our own devices. "Can you help us? Will you stand by our side when the tyrant comes?"

She frowned and shook her head. "I've witnessed good and evil in this world and prefer good, but unless the rules are broken, I'm not allowed to interfere."

"Can you at least advise us on how to fight him? From his reputation, his abilities are beyond ours."

"Beyond yours, yes, but don't forget that he's still a pilgrim like you, another lost soul who stumbled through the portal. The difference? You seek meaning, while he's found his by lording over his people. Now corrupted by such power, he's become a cruel and seasoned sorcerer who can work around the rules to do harm. How he will wield it, I cannot say, but you'll need more than mere magic. You'll need your wits about you and all your inner strength."

Mia heaved a sigh. "At his command, his people will attack. We've trained the villagers to scoff at his illusions, but their enemy's weapons are real. Susanna claims they're decent people driven by hate and fear. How can we heal their hatred? How can we banish their fear?"

"It's not only fear and hatred driving them. He's cast them into the void. Restore hope to those poor people, and they will refuse to fight."

Lyra often spoke in riddles, but I needed more than riddles now. "I don't understand. What sorcery can return hope to lost souls?"

"Remind them how to hope again by conjuring happier visions. Show them what might be."

She'd had her say and turned to leave, her image already thinning, but paused to offer one last piece of advice. "A final warning: be certain those visions are true or else they will fail."

As before, she disappeared, leaving us gaping at the space where she stood.

We trudged back to our room in Susanna's cottage, still frustrated and confused. Mia fell asleep at once, but I lay awake, staring at her. In the dim light, I made out the curve of her neck and her raven hair falling about her shoulders. Would she too be at risk in the coming battle? I watched over her until darkness turned her to shadow, and only then did I doze off.

I dreamed I awoke at midnight to the sound of a ram's horn. Everyone raced from their cottages, old and young, men, women, and children, startled by a horrible noise. From the tree line came the entire Ironforge horde made rabid By Malik's twisted memories. Each wore a frightful mask and brandished a sword and shield. They banged swords against shields as they marched toward us. No phantoms, these.

Susanna appeared at my side along with Mia. "Are you wizard enough to drive them off, or must we fight to defend our homes?"

As she spoke, two spears flew from behind the enemy lines. I deflected the one headed for Mia with a gust of wind, but before I could react, the second struck the little girl who'd brought me the dog hours before. As she lay bleeding on the ground, her mother rushed out to comfort her, and a keening arose from the villagers.

"No time to mourn," I shouted. "Time to fight."

Despite the absence of terrifying monsters, the mourners ignored my plea.

My blood rose. I summoned all my anger at injustice everywhere, in this world and the last, and stretched out my arms toward the horde. Lightning shot from my fingers as I whirled to the left and right, striking the enemy. Many screamed, their clothing on fire, and the stench of burning flesh filled the air. Those still standing fled back to the trees.

Then, in this dream, the healer appeared to me, wagging his finger. "I taught you to do no harm."

"They would have killed everyone — father, mother, and child."

His eyes flared, furious at the demon I had let possess me.

The scene grew deathly still, so his whisper resounded as he pointed at the vanquished. "They're fathers and mothers too."

The next morning at first light, the village stirred to the sound of a distant ram's horn, followed by another and another, ominous echoes foretelling doom.

Chapter 29 – Battle

The able-bodied assembled at the commons, while the elderly and infirm hustled frightened children to cottages on the outskirts of the village. Behind us, doors locked, and windows shuttered. Moments later came the sound of tramping boots as allies from the other two villages joined in the defense.

The would-be army mustered into a ragtag formation, feet shuffling, and eyes probing the tree line for any sign of activity. Men and women clutched their makeshift weapons, the young waving them about in a show of bravado and the older ones conserving energy. I counted axes and wood splitters, pitchforks and scythes, hammers and kitchen knives, and broom handles honed to a point—anything sharp or that could be swung with force.

As they waited, scouts burst into the commons, returning from their posts. Last among them came the boy who had first spotted the enemy, his cheeks flushed with the color born of the urgency of his mission.

William rushed toward him. "How many? How close?"

Breathless and red-faced, he replied in gasps. "Too many... to count... marching to drums... moving fast... driven by giants... not far behind."

William's eyes narrowed as he turned to face the woods.

At first, the sound came like a throbbing, not much louder than my heart pounding in my chest, but soon the drumbeat grew distinct. *Thrum, tha-thrum, THA-RUM!*

What had been a light breeze became a tempest. Enchanted no more, the forest groaned in protest as if trying to flee the approaching horde. Next came a crash. Several trees fell to the right and left, parting ways to open a path for the invaders.

The heads of two giants came into view, towering above the trees. Each had an oversized skull covered in matted black hair, bloodshot eyes, and rotting teeth, and carried a huge, spiked club on his shoulder. Soon after, Malik's army burst through.

The villagers held their ground; we had trained them well. A woman in front pointed out at once how the air shimmered about the giants and their clubs—illusions, nothing to fear.

Except for the rabid horde racing terrified before them.

The intruders formed ranks at the edge of the clearing, their numbers this time matching those of the defenders. Each wore body armor and clutched a variety of weapons fashioned by their blacksmiths. Those on the flanks brandished swords, archers in the rear bore crossbows, and the squad in the center hefted spears with tips glowing like white hot metal. The glowing tips were phantoms, but the rest was deadly real.

A man emerged from their midst to the no-man's land between the two sides. Taller than the others, he possessed the bearing of a leader, like a younger and more muscled Joseph. His armor differed from his comrades by a spiked helmet lined with silver, and a breastplate embossed with an image of the creatures from the day before.

He spoke with a voice accustomed to command.

"To our neighbors, I bring you a generous offer from my master. Lay down your arms and vow allegiance, and he will leave you in peace. He has three simple requests: at the end of each harvest, provide tribute, a fifth of your crops and goods; at the start of the new year, deliver thirty young men to augment his army; and set aside festivals at the equinox and solstices, to pay homage to his glory. This he demands as penance." He stepped closer, his armor rattling in the hush of the crowd. "Should you decline, we will wreak vengeance for your ancient transgressions."

I turned and surveyed the villagers. A few bowed their heads and stared at the ground, but most had defiance in their eyes.

Out of the silence, William strode forward unafraid, stopping three paces from the man.

He shouted loud enough for those hunkering in cottages to hear. "Your so-called master lies. Before he arrived and clouded your minds, our people lived as friends. Now go home and leave us in peace."

The enemy leader sneered. "Our master warned us to expect such attempts at deception. Now prepare to pay the price."

He unsheathed his sword and raised it overhead, a signal to his troops. They lowered their spears pointing at us. Archers notched their arrows.

Is this my moment? Is this the time to unleash my anger like in my dream, to lash out at the evil before me.

Mia rested a hand on my arm, holding me back, and repeated Lyra's words: *"They know only the void. Show them hope."*

She conjured a vision of the healer's last visit. In the gap between the warring sides, parents accompanied children who skipped and laughed as they presented bowls of flowers to the attackers.

I followed, this time with a scene from the joyous reunion of Natty and John, and their sons, Caleb and Isaac. Shouldn't happy families be preferable to war?

Uncertainty seeped through the enemy ranks but not enough. A few spears lowered, but most stayed pointed at us. Archers raised their bows.

Why isn't it working?

Mia whispered encouraging words in my ear. *"Be certain the visions are true."*

In our recent lives, we'd both faced the void, but our younger days had brimmed with hope.

Show it to them now.

She focused, and a new scene spread before me. A boat ploughing through the waves on a clear day, a fisherman with a weathered face beaming at his daughter as she reveled in the bobbing of the bow and the spray of seawater on her face.

I reached deep into my own memories, to a place of joy I'd suppressed too long. Alongside Mia's Ocean, a lake appeared, gentler than the open sea. By its shore knelt a boy and a girl with golden hair. The boy clutched a wooden boat no bigger than his hand, with a tiny mast made from stolen cloth and two stick figures on board. With a flourish, he launched it, and their hearts filled with hope.

A boat to sail away to the land of dreams, my love, to the land of dreams.

I glanced up at the thud of metal clattering to the ground. A few attackers held their ranks, but most thought to leave, until confronted by the giants looming behind them. These ogres scowled and raised their clubs, threatening any who would flee. The poor souls from Ironforge, who had for so long suppressed their joy under the tyrant's yoke, now picked up their weapons and reformed their lines.

A voice from the crowd shouted, "Sorcerers! Give us giants of our own."

"Yes, let's," Mia replied, the blood rising in her cheeks.

While we lacked the creative art of a master wizard, we had perfected mimicking the work of others. Before us arose near duplicates of Malik's creations with two important differences. Instead of a cruel grimace, ours wore smiles, and in place of spiked clubs, they carried a bouquet of geraniums as bright as those adorning Susanna's cottage.

True magic ensued. Our giants floated past the stunned attackers like wisps of air, and approached the enemy phantoms, offering them flowers.

Unable to reconcile conflicting visions, the phantoms vanished.

A cheer went up from our villagers, while confusion reigned among the enemy warriors, who gaped like those awakened from a bad dream.

Joseph, William, and Susanna closed the gap and extended their hands in friendship. After a moment, a few on the opposite side began to respond in kind.

Then lightning flashed overhead, and a crack of thunder threatened to sunder the sky in two. The tyrant's servants let out a groan at the all too familiar sound. They scattered to the sides and fell to their knees, leaving a clear path lined with pillars of fire. Through the smoke and flame appeared the vision I'd dreaded since the day I'd first entered the enchanted forest.

Drops of sweat formed on my brow and dripped to the ground, while a chill ran through me, making me shiver from head to toe. I grew lightheaded as the wave of fear spread from the others to me. I grabbed hold of Mia's arm to keep the two of us from tumbling down.

After the thunder and lightning and pillars of fire, an imposing figure emerged from the trees, a masterpiece of power. Four white stallions hauled a golden chariot with glistening shields at its sides. In the carriage loomed a man who appeared ten feet tall, robed in red satin with wisps of silver and purple laced throughout, and wearing a crown embellished with precious stones of astonishing size. Around his neck hung a pendant in the shape of a dragon. Rays of light emanated from his person as bare-chested slaves spread rose petals before him.

The horses strutted forward with nostrils flaring, tossing their manes and letting out neighs that sounded more like screams, so different from the gentle Fara. No phantom, these—sparks flew up from their iron shoes with each stride.

I squinted, trying to filter out the illusion. Not all was magic. The gold and slaves, the horses and chariot, the bejeweled crown, the robe and pendant, were trappings of power to boost the image. But beyond the exaggerated height, the overstated thrust of his chin and the practiced sneer, stood one as Lyra had described, another lost soul who had stumbled through the maelstrom.

A lost soul pretending to be king.

Chapter 30 – Malik

The chariot stopped, the wind stilled, and the villagers froze, uncertain whether to be terrified or awed.

I assessed the scene, as calm as the situation allowed. A line of cowed warriors knelt on either side, their faces fearful in the flickering firelight, eyes averted, their reaction adding to the fabricated image of their god-king.

I'd imagined a wicked warrior complete with armor and helmet, bearing a flaming sword in one hand and a spiked mace in the other. Behind the face plate would be red wolf eyes, and lips curled into a permanent sneer, the face of a villain out of a childhood fairy tale. The man I now beheld belied my expectations.

Yes, the setting remained impressive, but anyone with enough wealth could surround themselves with horses and slaves, a satin robe and crown. Beneath the pomp, I recognized a lost soul who'd come through the maelstrom, too weak to seek meaning on his own, a little man who abused his gift to gain power over others.

He surveyed the crowd, taking measure of his adversaries, searching for the one who had thwarted his grand design. Perhaps because I used magic last, he settled his gaze on me.

I sought to stare him down, but my newfound confidence failed me.

His mouth spread into a horrible grin, and he cast a withering glare, the kind a predator shows when eyeing his prey. Without a word, he extended his right arm and twirled his hand, an imperious gesture. A spear appeared and took flight, headed for me.

Just a test. He knows he cannot kill.

I conjured a shield to block the spear.

Too easy.

He tried again, this time hurling one at me and another at Mia. I deflected mine, but she had a better idea, freezing the missile in mid-air, spinning it around, and sending it back to its source. Our adversary scowled, and both spears vanished without a trace.

Next came a ball of fire, targeting those assembled behind me. Though nothing but a feint—such a barbaric act would offend the natural order—I snuffed it out with a puff of air.

He glared at me for a minute before speaking. "You are no magician. You are only the servant of a now deceased magician." Then to the villagers, shouting this time, using magic to amplify his voice. "You're fools to place your faith in these two. They play with magic like mischievous children. I will show you real power."

In a fit of pique, he hurled a dozen fireballs, setting the surrounding forest ablaze. After the flames had consumed their fuel, he gestured at the woods, still smoldering from his rage. "Remember what you have seen. This is what happens to those who defy me."

To further terrify them, he conjured a champion, a massive warrior as tall as the trees, wielding a two-handed broad sword which he swung above his head, an illusion for sure but with the intent to intimidate the villagers, to make them run away.

The demon strode toward the crowd, causing the free folk to cry out and begin to flee, but as it came close, a second image appeared—Mia's idea. An old woman, gentle and kind and clasping a bouquet of daisies, shuffled forward, extending the flowers and offering them to the warrior. Like the unicorns and monsters, and the cruel and friendly giants, when the discordant phantoms clashed, they flickered and disappeared.

Malik's face flushed, and he gripped the rail of the chariot. How long would we be able to counter the efforts of this seasoned sorcerer? Yet as I worried, I detected a change in his demeanor. His shoulders slumped, and his eyes showed a hint of fear. I understood why. His authority was based not only on magic, but rather on an image he'd cultivated of an omnipotent ruler. Our powers concerned him less than our defiance, which threatened the awe in which he was held.

I braced for his next barrage, but he surprised me by dismounting and striding toward us, beckoning us to meet him in the middle. As I suspected, he'd been standing on a platform to enhance his height. This would-be king now stood a whole head shorter than me. Mia and I checked with each other and shuffled closer.

When we reached arm's length, he lowered his voice to a whisper, a negotiation to be conducted between pilgrims from another world.

"Why should we fight? These are not your people. Come and rule by my side, and I will grant you domain over a village or two. You will have comfort and riches beyond counting, and adoration beyond your dreams."

I answered first. "We have no interest in riches or adoration."

Mia added, "And your dreams are not our dreams."

I gestured toward his army. "Take your followers with you and leave your neighbors in peace."

He spun about to gloat over those cowering in fear of him, before glancing back at the confused villagers. "Don't you understand? I am their king. They are my people. As for your pathetic flock, they live their little lives without purpose, but you and I are different. Conquest is our destiny. Why else were we thrust into this world and given such powers? Why else place a sorcerer in the midst of the powerless if not to have them bow to our will?"

His words revealed the stark difference between us. Where he viewed the enchanted land as existing to serve him, the healer believed he had been brought here to serve others.

When we remained defiant, he hissed, "Very well. Have it your way."

He stomped back to his chariot and mounted his platform, so he towered above all again, and the rays of light emanating from him blinded us as if the sun had risen behind him. He spoke in a voice more amplified this time.

"People of Narthwick, Pontybridge, and Montvale. You have made a terrible mistake to place your trust in these charlatans, but Malik is merciful. I give you three days to accept the truth and yield to my demands. Three days before I return to destroy you and all you hold dear."

Having laid down his ultimatum, he raised his arms. The sky darkened, thunder rumbled, and lightning flashed across the heavens. A forbidding wall of mist rolled in from behind him, headed toward the village. The people cried out and scattered, retreating to the shelter of their homes. The fog crept forward until it blinded us all.

After it cleared, Malik and his army were gone.

Chapter 31 – Mountain View

In the following silence, I caught a moaning from the tree line. Mia and Susanna heard it as well, and we followed the sound. In the still smoldering woods, we discovered two victims of the enemy's hasty retreat. One was a graying man too old to be a warrior who had tripped on a root in the fog and injured his leg. The other, young enough to be his son, had stumbled in the rush into one of the pillars of fire and burned his arm. Their self-proclaimed merciful ruler had abandoned them without a thought.

Susanna called for help and had the two carried to her cottage, where we had the first opportunity to practice our newfound skills. I conjured ice to limit swelling in the ankle and used my limited magic to accelerate the healing. Mia applied a rag with cold water on the younger man's burns, followed by an application of a cream derived from the aloe vera plant.

The older man stared with terror as I approached but lapsed into amazement as the pain subsided. "He claimed you'd kill us in horrible ways if captured. That's why he insisted we fight to the death."

Susanna rested a gentle hand on his arm and smiled. "One of the many lies he told you."

While we ministered to the wounded, the villagers flocked to their leaders crying, "What shall we do?"

Willian and Joseph urged them to return to their homes with no immediate threat, but not before selecting a war council made up of representatives from each village. How to respond to Malik would be a communal decision.

They set up chairs on the Narthwick commons, with the leaders in front facing the others. William insisted that Mia and I join them.

With no obvious safe choice, the debate was chaotic. People shouted all at once, creating a clamor impossible to understand, until Susanna raised a hand for order and encouraged them to speak one at a time. Everyone would have their say.

A few favored surrender, but most preferred to fight, denying the harsh reality that many would be maimed, and some would die.

A grandmother from Montvale called out first. "Each village has blacksmiths. Have them make us weapons as deadly as theirs."

A man from Narthwick responded. "No time to make enough."

In response, Seth, the strapping young blacksmith addressed the crowd. "We'll ply the anvil day and night to make a lot more than we have now."

Another countered him. "They've trained for years as warriors. We're only farmers and craftsmen. Even if you forge us the best weapons, we'd still be no match."

Seth's face turned red, and the ample muscles around his neck and shoulders tensed. He rose to his full height, taller than all but William, jutted out his chin, and announced with the recklessness of youth, "We are free men. They are slaves. No matter how well trained they might be or how well armed, they fight under the tyrant's spell. We fight to defend our homes and families."

A young woman, expectant with child, spoke next. "Don't we teach our children to believe in what's right? We're in the right now, living at peace and minding our own business. They are in the wrong, driven by one man's greed. Goodness will prevail."

Someone in the back row called out, not waiting to be recognized. "What do our sorcerers think?"

I grimaced at Mia and she at me. With so much at stake, neither of us were eager to weigh in, but the healer had taught us that with power comes responsibility.

I stood and faced the crowd. "Malik's magic, like ours, has limits. Many of his threats are a ploy, but he can still drive his people to madness. We can try to temper their fear, to awaken them to the truth in time, but if we fall short a battle will follow. Yes, you're defending your homes and families. You may be brave enough to prevail, but in a battle, both sides bleed."

The blacksmith had remained standing and now whirled around to confront his neighbors, shouting, almost screaming. "What choice do we have? We either fight or become slaves. I, for one, would give my life to stay free."

As the crowd murmured its approval, Susanna cupped a hand over her mouth and whispered to me. "I've known Seth since birth—a splendid boy but headstrong. I'm so proud of him now. He's turned the crowd to the right path. It saddens me, but we have no other way."

An old man struggled to his feet, and all the assembled hushed, giving their elder due respect. "Let's say by some miracle we defeat them in battle.

Recall how the tyrant laid waste to the trees. He may not be able to harm us as our sorcerers claim, but he'd show no mercy. With a wave of his hand, he'd destroy our crops and homes. All will burn, and we'll starve."

I checked on the leaders sitting beside me, their faces grim. They'd had hoped to rally their people, but those gathered before them, representatives of the three villages who for so long had lived under the protection of the enchanted forest, now teetered on the verge of despair.

Amid the nervous murmur, William rose and called for quiet. When he had their attention, he spoke with the steel of a mason's hammer in his voice. "Then to protect our homes, we change the battlefield." As puzzled faces turned his way, he proclaimed, "In two days' time, when they least expect it, we take the fight to them."

After a pause to digest, heads began to nod.

Seth raised a fist and shouted, "To Ironforge."

The crowd responded as one. "To Ironforge."

The decision had been made. Before everyone settled in for the night, I cornered William out of earshot from the others. "What do you know of Ironforge? The name itself sounds ominous."

He shrugged. "Not much."

"What makes you think you can storm it?"

He rested a hand on my shoulder. "Because you two sorcerers will find us a way in."

I twisted away to keep from showing my surprise.

Mia caught my concern and offered silent encouragement.

I turned back to the mason. "Have you at least seen it?"

"Oh, yes."

"From inside."

"None of us would go near that awful place, but I've viewed it many times from the top of the mountain, a hike we often take on a fine spring day."

"A hike you'll lead us on first thing in the morning. I've had enough surprises for one day."

The next morning, William led us up the mountain for our first view of the enemy's lair. The trail lay behind Montvale village, at first glance, an easy stroll through the woods over well-trod ground. Soon, however, it began to climb until we encountered a series of switchbacks that challenged our breathing. After about an hour, as we struggled to keep up with the mason, the trees shrank to scrub, and then to rock. Moments later, we reached the bare summit.

When we first arrived, hot and breathless from the effort, a sea of mist obscured the valley below, but as we rested, partaking from our waterskins, the rising sun burned away the fog. Beyond the forest, the Pontybridge river divided into two streams, and on the land in between lay the village of Ironforge. Even from this distance, the sight sent a shiver down my spine.

Forbidding stone walls circled the place, so close to the river that its waves lapped against them. Battlements ran across their tops, tall enough to conceal those guarding them. Anyone hoping to breach these walls would have to cross open water exposed to the defenders, and be vulnerable to arrows fired from above. The sole entrance was a black barrier topped with spikes, more imposing than the lord of the castle's gate.

Why such frightful defenses? What was Malik afraid of? The nearest people resided in the three neighboring villages, peaceful folk who wanted nothing to do with him. Did he fear another greedy wizard like himself, or were these walls designed to keep his people in?

From the summit, I glimpsed what lay within, and the view saddened me. Rows of hovels clustered, all dust and gray with no flowers visible and no decoration, except for a striking structure upon a hill at the center. What had to be the tyrant's palace lorded over the village, with marble pillars, lavish carvings, and a gilded dome. As the sun rose higher, its rays reflected off the gold plate.

"You think we can storm that?" I said to William, gesturing to the fortress. "They'd slaughter us before we came close."

"Not if we surprise them at first light on the morning of the second day. We'll emerge from the trees in darkness while most of them still sleep, and in any case, they'd never imagine we'd attack."

"For a valid reason. I myself find it unimaginable."

He stared at the dark city and narrowed his eyes. "We'll cross the river from two sides and...." He paused, a would-be general weighing his next words. When he resumed, his voice reached me as if through a fog. "...and enter the walls through gaps you and Mia will create."

Has he gone mad, seeking miracles from a pair of apprentices? How can he expect so much of us?

I recalled Lyra's warning. *'You'll need your wits about you more than magic. Your wits and your inner strength.'*

What else could we do? If we refused to try, the battle would still rage without us. How could we commit to these people and, when their destiny turned bleak, abandon them?

No. When adversity strikes, you set one foot in front of the other and keep going, and when the thin voice inside cries out that you'll fail, you ignore it and go on.

These brave people deserved whatever help we could provide, and our wits and inner strength would be tested like never before.

That night, I dreamed I was standing in a fairytale village. Before me, at the base of a sheer cliff, a little girl played catch with her dog. Suddenly, the ground trembled and the land began to split open. This crack in the earth began at my feet and spread toward the child, threatening to swallow her up.

No time to rescue her, as the ever-widening chasm moved faster than I could run. No time to conjure a bridge. Magic would save her only if I had my wits about me and all my inner strength.

I focused on the abyss, hoping to move it away from the child, but to where?

Behind me lay the villagers comfortable in their cottages, oblivious to the danger.

No safe direction but the cliff, so with my fullest conviction, I willed the quake to shift. The ugly gap changed course, drifting toward what I believed to be an impenetrable wall of stone.

As I gaped, the cliff split in two, folding as if made of paper, and vanished into the earth.

The next morning, I leapt out of bed and woke Mia.

"What?" she muttered, still half asleep.

"We can conjure most anything Malik can, given enough practice and time."

She nodded, still confused. "So?"

"So don't plan on sleeping tonight. We have too much work to do."

Chapter 32 – Minor Magicians, Major Magic

We spent the day trying to come up with the needed miracles. First, we experimented with bridges. How long? Long enough to span the river but not run smack into the castle wall. How wide? Wide enough to let our army cross in force, but not so massive as to prevent our meager talents from moving the bridge into place. Plain or embellished? Should we add statues of eagles to inspire the troops?

After we converged on the design, we practiced floating it across the required distance, the stretch from concealment in the tree line to the fortress wall. Once we mastered the transfer, we tried on our own, needing one bridge for each branch of the river.

"Moving these may be silent," Mia said, "but penetrating dense stone will be noisy enough to wake the whole village. We'll need a signal to synchronize before we breach the walls.

"A raven," I suggested.

"Something more dramatic. How about the firebird from our childhood stories."

"The one that foretells a blessing or doom?"

"That's right."

I mulled it over. Blessing or doom... the symbolism fit.

To avoid confusion, we negotiated the appearance of the magical bird—made of fire with golden feathers and crystal eyes. I'd wait with Susanna, and Mia with William. At the Narthwick leader's order, I would launch this beacon into the pre-dawn light. If our plan worked, we'd breach both sides of the wall at the same time.

By now, the sun had risen past noon. I recalled the wagon ride when Malik's raiding party attacked us. In response, our mentor had opened the sky, and a fierce deluge had extinguished the wildfire, driving the attackers away. Afterwards, he'd been too tired to talk. Now, following a morning of intense magic, Mia and I were exhausted. We collapsed on a broad boulder at the edge of the woods.

After we caught our breath, she sighed. "We still need to figure out one last miracle—how to breach the wall."

I groaned. "A wall whose depth we can only surmise. What if our bridges succeed only to leave our friends trapped on the narrow bank beneath Malik's archers?"

She turned to me with fire in her eyes. "What choice do we have? Give up? If we do nothing to help, he'll still attack the next day. Do you think the tyrant unopposed will be kinder?" She stood and paced around the boulder twice before hovering over it. "Let's start small. Let's vent our frustration upon this rock."

I struggled to my feet, clasped hands with Mia, and channeled all my anger at the evils of this world and the last.

Nothing happened until I remembered my dream.

Focus on the earth beneath it. Make the ground quake.

The ground shuddered, and with an impressive crack, the rock split in two.

We worked for the rest of the day and well into the evening. Though not yet fully confident in our plan, we weighed practicing further against being too tired to execute when the time came. We had no choice—my eyes had begun to droop, and Mia struggled to stay upright.

Once the sun set, the free folk began to arrive in small groups. They marched with such stealth, I had to blink twice to distinguish between them and the fluttering of leaves. With Joseph too old to fight, William and Susanna led their neighbors, flitting among them and assigning positions for the battle. When everyone had been situated, they ordered the troops to rest in place but be prepared to spring into action when awakened.

Susanna had brought along the two wounded whom we'd helped heal. They approached us now, the boy with no hint of pain and the older man without a limp.

'They wanted to thank you," she said. "Until your kindness, they'd never thought magic could be used to help others."

The two men shuffled near and made small bows. The older one spoke first. "I am Samuel, and this is my nephew, Amos. I have lived for fifty-three years, twelve of them under the yoke of the tyrant. Poor Amos is almost too young to remember a different way. During this time, a fog has clouded our minds, a way of life we'd come to accept as impossible to change, but now the fog has been lifted, not only from your kindness, but from what we witnessed in the village—children laughing, men and women going about their day with courage and a smile, the warmth of their cottages, the glory in their gardens, and the fondness for their families. A life so much better than what we've lived these past years."

The young man, Amos, joined in. "Despite the risk of incurring Malik's wrath, we want to help. Perhaps our testimony can convince our neighbors you are friendly folk with whom we can live in peace. Perhaps we can avoid the battle."

After Susanna settled the two for the night and bedded down herself, the only ones left standing were me, Mia, and William.

I approached the mason as he paced like a caged animal. "Aren't you going to rest as well?"

"Not me. After tomorrow, I'll have time enough... one way or the other, but you both are too critical to be anything but at your best. Get some sleep. I'll be sure to wake you in time."

We lay down on the soft ground and closed our eyes but dozed no more than a few winks here and there. My mind kept churning, and judging by Mia's restlessness, hers churned as well.

After a while, she rolled over, raised up on one elbow, and gazed back at me. The stars were still out, and the grass was cold and wet with dew. The earliest glow of daybreak had yet to show on the horizon.

"Whatever happens," she whispered, "I'm glad I stumbled through the maelstrom and found you. We've now experienced sorrow in both worlds, but joy as well. No hope without the chance for despair. On this fateful day, I choose hope."

Moments later, the encampment stirred. The would-be warriors shook off their sleep, hefted their weapons, and began the trudge to Ironforge, their shadows marching with them like following wraiths. At the fork in the river, the villagers split, the half led by William to the left, and the rest with Susanna to the right.

Before we separated, Mia turned and embraced me. Her lips parted, but no words emerged.

I nodded. Nothing more to be said.

Across from the fortress, Susanna cautioned the assembled to hush, no matter what odd happenings they saw.

I took a deep breath and conjured the exact bridge we'd practiced. On my initial try, it hovered above the water but short of the far bank. I calmed myself and focused, and with the second effort, it floated into place. I had succeeded with the first phase of our plan and was confident Mia, a better sorcerer than me, had done the same.

I checked with my leader. The first rays of sunrise reflected in her eyes as she nodded.

I gestured to the sky, and my phantom appeared, a red and gold bird ablaze in the dim light. With a thought, I launched it high above the fortress, while the villagers held their collective breath.

Now comes the real test.

As the firebird cleared the dome of Malik's palace and flew to the far side, I felt Mia gathering her will. I did the same, dedicating this moment to all whom I'd loved, living and gone. I directed my hopes and fears at the ground underlying the wall.

If magic be a force for good as the healer claimed, conjure me now an act of violence, but also an act of love.

The earth beneath me trembled, resisting my command before yielding with a crack so fearsome I worried I'd be swallowed whole. I covered my ears and closed my eyes as dust and dirt flew. When the noise abated, in front of me lay a gap taller than the tallest man and broad enough for ten warriors to pass abreast. To my relief, from the far side of the village, light beamed through Mia's breach as well.

Through these two gaps, the army of the righteous poured through.

Inside Ironforge, misery pervaded, gloomier than I had observed from the mountain heights. Featureless hovels lined the streets, lacking embellishment of any kind — no flowerboxes, no floral curtains, no carved moldings over the doorways, and no color beyond gray and brown.

As William had planned, we'd taken them unprepared. We marched unopposed as the few sentries who had guarded the walls fled, and the handful of bleary-eyed souls who'd been awakened by the noise cowered behind shutters. All assumed anyone with magic strong enough to breach the walls must also be cruel.

Our surprise did not last long. No sooner had we mustered inside than the clanging of an alarm bell rang through the still morning air.

We quickened our pace, advancing through narrow streets until we joined with William's force, arrayed before the entrance to the palace.

A ragtag mix of Malik's horde had gathered, blocking our way, but these, startled awake at dawn, stumbled about in a daze. The worst part of being forced to act against your will is losing the ability to initiate action on your own. Those guarding their master's domain gaped at us confused, incapable of functioning without the tyrant's command.

William stepped forward and addressed them. "People of Ironforge, we are not your enemy. Join us and you too can be free."

Mia came to his side and to reinforce his offer, conjured a vision of what peace among villages might be like. In the space between the two sides, a springtime festival appeared, with laughing children bunched before a performance of puppets, while young men and maidens danced around a Maypole.

I supplemented the scene, creating phantom copies from several of the enemies, and adding the musicians the healer had provided to entertain us at breakfast. Malik's people gawked as peaceful neighbors swayed to the tune, celebrating together.

Those assembled on the steps wavered, but their tyrant had instilled in them too much fear. Despite the phantom frivolities, none of the real folk joined us.

Susanna emerged from the ranks, a small woman, dwarfed by the other warriors, but with fearless fire in her eyes. "It may be hard to believe after all you've been told, but what we offer you is—"

Before she could finish, a hush came over both sides. The golden doors above the marble stairs swung open, and out stepped Malik. At the sight of their tyrant, his soldiers turned pale, and some fell to their knees.

He'd arrived so late, I surmised, because he would never allow himself to appear in public without the accoutrements of power, his robe and crown, his accompanying slaves, and a bejeweled scepter with a glowing orb on top, but his arrival in haste showed. The robe hung askew off one shoulder.

"You'd believe this witch?" his amplified voice boomed. "Have I not taught you these demons are not to be trusted? They will lure you unsuspecting into their village and slaughter you, but only after days of torment."

He waved his scepter, and our festival scene was overwhelmed with visions of chaos and death, complete with the cries of the damned. To further incite his army, he replicated phantoms from among our numbers to represent the tormentors.

The impulsive young blacksmith, Seth, forced his way to the front, stopping beside Susanna, who rose just above his waist. His right hand gripped the hilt of his sheathed sword so hard his knuckles turned white. She restrained his hand lest he do harm but failed to prevent his accusing gesture toward the tyrant.

"He lies!" he shouted, his voice so loud it might have been amplified as well.

Malik pointed his scepter at the boy, his face reddening. "You believe these are lies? Are their weapons symbols of peace? No. They mean to destroy you."

He swept an arm at the false vision, The images grew bloodier, the screams more terrifying.

Despite this scene from hell, the two recovering men, abandoned by their peers and saved by us, pressed to the fore. Their neighbors gaped at them like ghosts, conditioned to think being left behind meant certain death.

The older one spoke first as before, pointing to a man his age who wielded a trembling spear. "Arthur, you recognize me, Samuel, your neighbor of many years. You know me to be an honest man. These kind folks have not only healed us but treated us as welcome guests. They are not the demons we've been told, and they offer us a better life than we have now."

As if overwhelmed by a cosmic force greater than us all, the tyrant's vision faded, and our more tranquil scene reasserted itself.

Now, at last, some of those long enslaved began to lower their weapons.

Sensing their weakness, Malik swung his scepter to the left and right, screaming at his troops. "Seize them! Seize these traitors! You've seen the price of defying me, and now they will pay."

Confusion reigned in their ranks, but a few cowardly souls edged toward the pair.

Before they could obey his command, Mia conjured a wall around the two men, a miniature fortress blocking the two of us and the tyrant from the others. We stepped forward in the brightening dawn, stopping so close I caught drops of sweat on his brow. In his rush to confront us, he'd foregone powdering his face and donning his wig. Here stood a little man with sunken cheeks and thinning hair, whose eyes lacked a royal spark.

"We might be minor magicians," I said, "but I need no magic to note the fear in your eyes. The veil has been lifted on your so-called army and they will fight no more. Now, at last, they realize what you are—someone who fled his homeland not for a better life, as we did, but for the pursuit of power. Free your people. Surrender your dominion over them. You can still live a content life as a revered sorcerer in this enchanted land."

He may have lost the spark in his eyes, but he retained the tongue of a snake.

"Yes, I come from the same place as you, but if you are so committed to saving a world, why not go back and save your old one? What if all this is a dream and only the home you left is real? What if all we perceive is a phantom manipulated to our own needs—me to rule my little kingdom, and you to be the heroes of a story of your own creation? If you long to be real heroes, go back and be heroes there.

"I understand why I stay. In my old life, I did the bidding of others, working as a menial laborer, bending to their will. 'Malik, do this, and Malik, do that, and you're too weak and clumsy.' Here, I can be king." He narrowed his eyes. "Why did you come here? What were you lacking? Oh wait. You've showed my people your visions from home."

Despite the lack of an audience, he twirled his scepter, and before us reappeared Mia's phantom—the child on the ocean with her father riding the waves. With a second gesture, mine unfolded as well, the two children with the boat of our dreams.

He sneered as we gaped. "Such a lovely fairytale, but if your past was so beautiful, why the need to escape? What dark secret drove you through the maelstrom to seek a better life? Did you despair of finding meaning there? Yes, I recall your world, and all was not beauty and light. Let me show you reality."

He raised the scepter once more, and the sky darkened. Above me shone my old friends, the hunter with his bow and the dipper poised to pour stardust upon me, but beneath them, grimmer scenes prevailed. On the dunes by the ocean, a bloated body drifted to shore. In a cottage by the lake, another in a shroud lay in state, while neighbors tore their clothing and wept.

Yes, sorrow abounded in our old lives as well.

With a thunderous crash, he shattered the wall Mia had conjured, as we stood stunned and silent, our magic for the moment impaired by the dark visions he'd shown.

"Seize the traitors," Malik ordered, "and show them the fate of all who disobey."

The more subservient soldiers now brushed past us and grabbed the men we'd healed. Fearing a similar punishment, the rest of his crew raised their weapons again.

As the two were being dragged away, the boy Seth burst from Susanna's side before she could stop him. He unsheathed his gleaming sword, a weapon he'd forged himself, and rushed at the tyrant.

I caught panic in Malik's eyes, but as a seasoned sorcerer, he might have stopped the young blacksmith in various ways—turn the steel into weeds or the ground into quicksand. Instead, flustered by this first challenge, the true Malik emerged, the weakling who'd come to this world to punish those who had mocked him. Cruelty overwhelmed his judgement as the corrupting power drove him to madness. He extended his scepter, and from it a bolt of lightning flashed, striking the boy in the chest.

Howls of anger erupted as the free folk surged forward, weapons drawn and seeking revenge. Malik's horde, witnessing the sorcery but oblivious to the sin, formed their ranks to defend.

In an instant, the tenuous reality of the enchanted land ruptured like an interrupted dream.

While Seth lay dead on the ground, the warring factions froze into a blurred tableau, leaving only the two minor magicians and the tyrant. The air rippled between us, and Lyra appeared, her gentle face now contorted in anger. As before, she was visible only to Mia and me.

And Malik, from the look of horror on his face.

She confronted him, pointing an accusing finger. "For too long, you have been a sore on our dear enchanted land, but now you have crossed the line, for here, unlike your old world, cruelty has its limits."

Malik's body began to splinter into ever smaller shards of light, until he became translucent. His mouth stayed open in a silent scream as the spell spread from his bejeweled crown down to the tips of his toes.

Moments later, he was gone.

I shuffled to the spot where he had stood and brushed the ground with my boot. "Is he dead?"

"No. He's been expelled to a place where he'll be unable to use magic to kill. He's been banished to the world from whence he came."

"Won't he be able to do more harm there?" Mia said.

"Perhaps, but he'll need to do so where decent folk still outnumber the bad. As for you two, you've done well. The healer would be proud."

With that, she disappeared, and the rupture repaired.

Susanna was first to grasp the new circumstance and dropped her weapon. Others soon followed.

The people of Ironforge, rid of their master, spun around toward each other confused, until the old man, Samuel, cried out, "We're free."

Enemies became neighbors again, with no need for weapons or seeking power over the other. Hints of smiles curled once tense lips, tempered by the realization that Seth was gone.

Susanna approached the blacksmith and cradled his head as tears flowed down her cheeks. Neither magic nor fairy blood would bring him back.

She signaled for some to carry the body. Two men from Narthwick came forward, and two from Ironbridge stepped in to help. Together they lifted the young warrior on their shoulders and, in somber silence, bore him home.

Chapter 33 – Rebirth

All victories come with a mix of joy and sorrow.

The villagers took one day to mourn the young blacksmith, and a second to prepare for the celebration. In the evening of the third, they balanced their sadness with relief at Malik's shadow being lifted after all these years.

They set up a feast in the Narthwick commons, with colorful lanterns strung to enhance the moonlight and wildflowers from the surrounding fields forming a glorious decoration. Dusk settled in, and Susanna called for quiet. The people bowed their heads as she dedicated that night to the boy. After a moment of silence, she introduced musicians with flute and fiddle joined by a strong tenor. Together, they performed a newly composed ballad recounting the battle and victory, including an embarrassing tribute to the two worthy sorcerers, praise that made us blush.

By the time they finished, the sun's rays had kissed the top of the horizon. The villagers turned their faces to the west, raised their arms before them, and began to chant a prayer to celebrate their newfound freedom. As they chanted, the gray clouds lifted, and the few remaining white patches took on a startling beauty. The sunset glowed so much orange and purple that the heavens seemed to have grown larger.

After the sun set, the elders lit a bonfire while young folks covered tables with sides of mutton and pork, bread with honey, ripe tomatoes, roasted chestnuts, and pyramids of fruit. Next came pitchers filled with mead and hot cider, and for dessert, baked apples spiced with cinnamon, and blueberry pies.

As everyone enjoyed their feast, a curly-haired lad approached us. I recognized him as the boy who had begged the healer to save his fevered mother. He shuffled up, hands tucked into his pockets, and asked the splendid sorcerers if they would please make a display of fireworks.

I grinned at Mia, and she winked back. We whirled about and waved our arms as a shower of daisy petals exploded into the air, bursting into streams of reds, yellows, and blues.

The assembled oohed and aahed at the show, and when it finished, clapped in appreciation. Afterwards, villagers streamed toward us, thanking us and patting us on the back. What a delight to use our magic, not to heal or defend, but to spread good cheer.

After the meal, the music resumed, this time not so somber but in a joyful reel. Men, women, and children joined together in circles. Once complete, they bounced on their toes for three beats and began to dance, spinning and twirling, lost in the rhythm.

As we soaked in the scene, Susanna wandered over to us and whispered, "This is not just any dance but our traditional ritual to welcome the spring. For these people, this year is different, more like the first day of creation, a rebirth of life."

The party continued until the sunset faded away, the stars came out, and the bonfire settled to embers that glowed like a beacon in the dark.

After the strain of the past few days, we wilted like old folks, too tired to stay and celebrate.

Sensing our exhaustion, Susanna turned to face us, a kind smile on her pixie face. "The spare room in my cottage is waiting to offer two heroes a well-deserved rest. Come. The villagers will understand."

She led the way, and we shuffled after.

Alone in our room, Mia had something to say. "I don't remember intending to be heroes. It seems like false magic."

I beheld her in the starlight filtering through the curtain. The faint glow hid her features, all but the eyes, which showed an innocent wonder.

"We intended nothing," I said. "We just stumbled about reacting to events."

"Yet in a way Malik never would have. He would have accepted the offer to be king."

"But we're not Malik."

"Yes, not Malik, but until now, we questioned what we were and, when the time came, whether we'd withstand the temptation. Not until this test, and in this time of testing, we passed, you and I, and we now know who we are." She rested a hand on my cheek, and her smile shone in the dimness.

We lingered in bed the next morning, long after the farmers had shaken off the prior night's revels and staggered to work. A yellow gleam filtered through the slats of the shutters, startling me awake. Finding the light too bright to bear, I rolled over, away from the sun, determined to lounge a bit longer.

When we finally emerged, Susanna and William were waiting at the kitchen table sipping tea. The Narthwick leader had her red hair untied so it drifted down over her shoulders, reinforcing her fairy appearance. She appeared tiny beside the stone mason.

I brightened at the aroma of a home-cooked breakfast, and came fully alert when I savored my first bite. The food, prepared without magic, tasted better than any meal the healer had conjured.

After we ate our fill, Mia thanked the leaders for being so kind to strangers, and promised we'd return to the tower this afternoon so as not to be a burden.

In response, the unpretentious village elder leaned in and placed her hand on Mia's arm. "Stay as long as you like, my dear." After checking with the mason, she took a deep breath to add import to her words. "William and I have discussed this at length. We wish for more, to have you come live with us, to become part of our community. Now that you've helped save us from the tyrant, you can take over as our healers. Your mentor was a saint who always used his powers for the benefit of others, but he was also an old curmudgeon who enjoyed living alone. You two are different—young, with your whole lives ahead of you. Don't go back to his musty old tower. Stay here and teach us the healing ways. Stay and make our village your home."

Home!

I'd almost forgotten the meaning of the word. The homes we'd abandoned held sad memories, and we'd been wanderers ever since.

I glanced at Mia. A lift of her brow told all, and she answered for the both of us. "A kind invitation, but we still have work to do. We brought only a few of his cures with us. Most are still to be retrieved. If you would loan us a horse and cart...?"

William rose from the table. "As I suspected. Come outside."

He swung open the cottage door. In the front yard stood a wagon, and munching on a bag of straw, our old friend, Fara.

When last in the tower, we'd almost completed the task of packing up the healer's lifetime of learning, though we'd need many months more to master their use. With William's help, we finished the job in a few hours, filled the wagon, and set out for what we were beginning to consider our new home, at least for a while.

After we unloaded our treasure and stowed it away, William turned to us and winked. "Since his legacy resides here now, you must stay to finish your apprenticeship. You wouldn't want his wisdom to go to waste."

Susanna came to his side. "We've identified a lovely plot of land for you at the edge of the village, situated on a gentle rise high enough to have a bit of a view. Several of your future neighbors have volunteered to build you a cottage on it."

We gaped open-mouthed, stunned to silence by the kind offer.

She encouraged us. "At least come see the setting."

By that time, the shadows had lengthened. A crowd of craftsmen, returning from their day's labor, joined in the conspiracy with so much enthusiasm we had to agree. They led us past a dozen cottages and three or four farms to the edge of the woods, where lay a clearing bordered by a bubbling brook and white dogwoods in flower. Their sweet fragrance filled the air.

Mia spun around and drew in a quick breath. "Look, Lucas."

The rise was less modest than Susanna had implied, overlooking the cottage rooftops, a fine sight with the stone chimneys puffing out smoke as the villagers prepared their dinner.

"How can you turn down such a beautiful spot?" William said.

"We can't," I said, "but don't trouble others to build our new home. We've conjured a cottage before and are more accomplished now. You've all been so kind. No need to impose on you further."

Mia stepped round the border of the plot as if measuring its size, brushing a blossom or two with her fingertips, pausing to savor their perfume, and kneeling to sample the ice-cold water. "Of course, nothing too fancy," she said at last, referring to the tyrant's palace and hoping to be a better neighbor. "We're too tired now but can start on it in the morning."

The two leaders glanced at each other and laughed.

"You're not the only ones who possess magic," the mason said.

To relieve our confusion, Susanna added, "You've done so much for us, and now it's our turn to make a gift for you. Get some rest and tomorrow, we'll show you how our craftsmen can make magic of their own."

The next morning dawned with a blue sky and the gentlest breeze, a proper day to start a new life. Six villagers waited for us outside, foremost among them Benjamin, a man of middle years who claimed to have designed many of the homes in the village. Under one arm, he grasped a yardstick and a scroll of parchment, and in the other, a piece of charcoal for writing. A second man carried stakes and a ball of twine.

The whole troop marched off to the homesite, which appeared more striking than the evening before. We spent the better part of the day negotiating the layout, with Mia taking the lead. In addition to a dining area and bedroom, we'd need a study to research the healer's cures, and a room in front to greet those needing our care.

Benjamin marked each wall, door and window with the stakes and twine.

Back at Susanna's cottage, we huddled around the dining table, where a sketch of our new home came to life on the parchment, a wonder beyond our limited artistic skills. We worked well into the night, by candlelight when necessary, and part of the next day.

When all were satisfied with the design, Benjamin rolled up the drawing and grinned at us. "Our magic doesn't happen with a wave of the hand like yours. Even with a hardy crew, we'll need more than a week, but you're not to peek until it's done. Trust us. I'll summon you when your new home is ready, and I swear you'll be pleased with the result."

To dampen our curiosity, we immersed ourselves in our mentor's notes, as well as making exploratory trips to the other villages. Despite skepticism about our healing powers, from time to time a stray villager would approach for help.

We awoke on the morning of the tenth day to the clamor of a crowd. In front of the cottage, most of Narthwick had come out, and some from Montvale and Pontybridg as well.

The tenor who'd sung at the celebration the prior week called for silence and started a traveling tune. The men and women, and the few children accompanying them, joined in, and thus, in joyous song we set off.

When we arrived at what had been nothing more than a pleasant setting, I had difficulty grasping the transformation and had to brush away a tear to appreciate the view. The home standing before me went beyond what Mia and I could conjure, imbued with a different kind of magic—the kindness of community and the generosity of neighbors.

Chapter 34 – Fairy Blood

The next day, we settled into our new cottage and a life more comfortable than what we thought possible weeks before. Our neighbors dropped off fresh baked goods daily, along with the ripest pickings of their farms. We welcomed their kindness, except for one bothersome quirk. They treated us with more respect than we deserved, insisting on calling us honorary terms like lord and lady. We rebuffed this practice, correcting them to our given names.

Using seeds they provided, we planted a small flower garden. For a couple of hours each morning, we'd tend to the greenery, and as the summer sun rose higher overhead, we'd settle by the brook and dip our feet in its cooling waters.

We spent afternoons studying our mentor's notes and cataloguing his cures. Despite our developing skill, few villagers came with their ills, unsure of what to make of the two apprentices who had helped defeat the tyrant but remained unproven as healers. Rather than depend on us, they reverted to old ways, remedies used generations before.

After several weeks, a smattering of the needy trickled in after traditional approaches had failed. As more sought help, we reserved time every afternoon for such visits. Following some trial and error, we learned what worked best, solving most problems with the right herbs and tender loving care, seldom needing magic. With each successful cure, the demand for our services grew, so we expanded our hours and added travel to the adjoining villages, as our mentor had done.

One day, as we strolled about the village, we encountered several dozen men marching two abreast and hefting heavy tools—splitting wedges and axes, sledgehammers and chisels. At first, we feared some distant sorcerer had emerged to threaten their lands, but their bearing belied such a notion—more work crew than army, laughing and joking as they went.

We stopped them to ask where they were headed.

A stocky man in the lead, carrying an oversized sledgehammer on his shoulder, grinned at us revealing two missing front teeth. "To

Ironforge, we go. Our new friends have asked for help in tearing down that dreadful wall, and we're happy to comply."

"They could've asked us," Mia said. "They've seen what we can do."

"Aye, they figured you'd offer, but sorcerers have brought them nothing but grief, and they've had their fill of them. We provide a different kind of enchantment, an old-time work party, sharing the labor with our neighbors."

I recalled conjuring our first cottage, how the most satisfaction had come from what we'd accomplished by hand.

I glanced at Mia, and she nodded. We had time to spare.

"Can we join you?" I asked. "We can heft tools as well."

"We promise to not use magic," she added.

He checked with the rest of the men, seeking their thoughts, and frowned. "Not the work for a lord and lady."

She stepped closer, with hands on hips. "Not lord and lady... Lucas and Mia. We're part of the village now."

So we joined the effort. For the next month, we spent a few hours of each day hacking and chiseling, bashing and banging at the awful symbol of Malik's tyranny. After the day's efforts, we returned home with tired muscles and slept as we hadn't slept in months.

After we finished, Ironforge remained short of rebirth. Much time would pass before it bore the charm of its neighbors, but it had started on the right path. Rebirth would come.

As summer turned to fall and the days shortened, our reputation as healers grew, and we now ministered to all four villages. Some afternoons, a line would form outside our cottage, and as the sun set, we'd have to ask less needy supplicants to return the next day.

One morning, William appeared at our doorstep. Despite no chance of anyone overhearing, he leaned in, rested a hand on my shoulder, and whispered in my ear.

"My wife is rumored to be one of those with fairy blood. Before the healer arrived, people would come to her, not only with their physical ills but with their troubled hearts. He recognized this quality in her and shared a few of his secrets. Perhaps you could pass on more of your knowledge, and she can help lighten your load."

The next day, he invited us to meet his wife, a slight woman with black button eyes and ears rising to a point like an elf. Over their fireplace hung a portrait of an older woman with a bonnet, who was the image of her daughter. On a table in front of her lay a mortar surrounded by vials, and she grasped a pestle in her right hand. A healer for sure.

With their children grown, she had time to join us in our ministrations and learn our ways. Each night, she'd leave with a few pages of my journal, which she'd study well into the evening before returning the next day. Within weeks, she had almost matched our skill. Word spread, and others came to learn as well, until each village had their own healer or two.

As more people cared for their neighbors, we found ourselves with less to do. To give back, we kept busy with various projects meant to ease the villagers' lives or enhance the villages themselves.

At first, we tried magic. We embellished the Narthwick commons with a fountain featuring a spouting angel at its center, but people insisted on something more whimsical, like a dragon. With no model to copy, our attempts struggled, until the local craftsmen conspired to help. Together, artisans and metal workers designed the perfect statue, with a forked tail, ample scales, and a formidable but not frightening head. Through its open mouth spewed not fire, but water fed from a nearby stream. The result—a work of art, surpassing anything we might have conjured.

We set out to do the same in Montvale, where streams flowed down the mountain into a rock basin, forming a shimmering pool. After a week of misguided efforts, the locals took over again, creating not a fountain, but a sequence of waterspouts that swirled and spiraled in a continuous ballet, a spectacle to enthrall adults and children alike.

At the ceremony to dedicate this marvel, everyone turned out, while Mia and I lingered in the background, proud of what the villagers had wrought without our help.

No magic needed.

Chapter 35 – Crossroads

The seasons turned. Leaves fell and soon the walkways glistened with white. Then, in what seemed like weeks rather than months, the snow melted, and the tips of crocuses peeked out from the soil. Buds popped on the dogwoods and flowered, but in no time, the petals blanketed the ground and new leaves replaced them, offering shade from the summer sun.

For a year now, we'd dwelled in our modest cottage, mostly refraining from magic. Moreso than adhering to the healer's warnings about corruption, we had little use for it. Our lives had settled into a simple, unhurried pattern. Like most ordinary, decent folk, we wanted a small, happy life at peace with one another. Now, at last, I had found the kind of contentment I'd hoped for, though for a long time I'd fought to suppress it—I'd been disappointed so often before.

More and more on our walks, Mia and I discussed how our time here had come full circle, now resembling the better times of our former lives. Yet always lurked the fear that with contentment loomed tragedy. It made me wonder: was this world we dwelled in so different from the other?

One summer day, we hiked to Montvale and took the trail to the mountaintop. We traipsed through slopes bordered with green pines and blue spruce, which opened into meadows thick with black-eyed Susans. Once, we followed a side path to the sound of rushing water and discovered a stunning waterfall. We nestled together and delighted in its roar, though our solitude puzzled us. Why wasn't such a lovely spot enjoyed by more villagers? Were the locals so accustomed to its presence they took it for granted?

At the top, the whole country lay before us—forest, hills, valleys and, winding away like a silver snake, the lower part of the river. The village of Ironforge was much improved. With the wall gone, planted gardens bloomed along its border, and the palace had been torn down, its parts scavenged to enhance the cottages, now painted in lively colors.

We stayed silent for a long time, me circling the summit for a better view, and Mia staring out in the distance.

"Do you see it?" she finally said.

"You mean the river?"

"What else?"

"Mountains to the north, jagged peaks covered with snow."

"No, to the east, past the notch between hills."

Far away, I caught a flash of reflected sunlight and realized I was gazing at the sea, and beyond it, a sky full of clouds soon to turn rose-colored with the sunset, like back home.

That night, I had trouble sleeping, so I slipped out of the cottage and shuffled outside. The moonlight cast its glow over a landscape silent except for the brook chattering over the rocks. I gazed into the water, imagining the lake of my youth and the fantasy boat sailing to the land of dreams. Around me spread a tranquil village with hard-working folks safe in their beds; above me stretched a sky sparkling with unfamiliar stars; and behind me lay the cottage where slept the person who had renewed my life.

Can this be the land of dreams?

No. This place fell short of my childhood aspirations. Like my old world, evil lurked with the good and death stalked the living. I'd found magic here, but it no longer felt magical, more like an illusion conjured by some cosmic sorcerer. For what is illusion but changing the way we perceive reality.

With such thoughts swirling in my mind, I returned to bed and drifted off.

A stream of nightmares followed — loved ones ravaged by disease; Mia's parents drowning in a storm; a legion of evil sorcerers sending innocent villagers fleeing from burning homes; and the young blacksmith, slaughtered under Malik's wrath. Then, the nightmare faded, replaced by a calmer scene — my old cottage on the bluff above the lake, and the bench where Addy and I viewed the sunset. I stared out at the village common below and at its center, the meeting house with its white wooden steeple poking at the sky.

As the view of my former home filled me with longing, a woman sang out behind me with a lilting tune, making me spin around. Where only dense forest had been before, two paths diverged into the dark woods, and at their intersection stood a half-dead oak, its branches pointing in either direction like bony fingers but revealing no preference.

I peered down the first path and the next to no avail; nothing but swirling fog. I took a step down each, trying to identify the source of the song. Mia's voice, perhaps, or more likely Lyra's. With the words too vague to understand, I struggled to grasp their meaning, but recognized it as a song of hope.

Though unclear of its purpose, I realized this dream mattered, and I would remember it all my life, and every night when I fell asleep, I would wish it to return.

After that, I became consumed by an ill-defined restlessness, unable to stay in the cottage for long. Driven by an unnamed yearning, I'd bring Mia for walks through the woods, seeking out obscure trails, those not created by people but carved out by rainwater.

One morning, as we meandered down one of our favorites, we discovered the path had undergone a baffling change. Where before, it had led to the river, now a crossroads blocked our way, and at its intersection, the oak tree from my dream.

"Did we wander onto a different path?" Mia said.

"Not likely."

"Then how did this fork in the trail appear?"

I edged to the oak and brushed my fingertips against its trunk. "I conjured this in a dream."

She stared at me, at the two paths, and back to me. "What does it mean?"

As her question hung in the air, a familiar voice provided the answer.

"A crossroads arises from uncertainty," Lyra said, 'a fork in your life where a choice has to be made. You have arrived at such a point, and the magic has granted you the way."

I recalled the healer's words: *Crossroads are by their nature magic, because the path you choose leads to a different life.*

Mia studied the tree, counting its branches and leaves. At last, she gave up. Both sides were identical. Her mind churned. "Where do they go?"

Lyra shuffled from one to the other, gazing down at each with a mystical vision incomprehensible to me. "This one on the right has you abandoning these villages where you've dwelled this past year. Likely, you'll encounter other sorcerers, some worse than Malik, few as wise as the healer, but you'd start this adventure with more skill than when you first arrived. As with all new lives, you may find joys and sorrows. More than that, I cannot say."

Truth be told, the villagers had replaced the need for our magic. By using the spices and herbs from the healer's tower and gathering their own, they had provided cures for most of their ills. Some healed from old-fashioned remedies and others perhaps from the touch of those with fairy blood. In any case, though our friends would miss us, they'd thrive on their own, and we were ready for a change.

I shifted to the second path. "What of this one?"

Lyra squeezed her eyes shut as if employing some supernatural sight, but when she opened them, she shook her head and sighed. "This one leads past the limits of my vision, a place beyond the enchanted lands."

Beyond the enchanted lands.

The healer believed magic existed everywhere, even in other worlds.

Mia approached it and attempted to step through, but was unable to enter, blocked by some invisible force.

She gaped at Lyra, questioning.

"I can't say whether it's another magical realm or not, but you cannot bring this world's totems with you. Your gold necklace, and for you, Lucas, the wizard's belt—you must leave these behind if that's your choice."

Mia fingered her amethyst while I stroked the eagle on my buckle. Were we ready to give them up for the unknown?

Passing through the maelstrom had been a leap of faith for both of us. The same held true for following Lyra into the enchanted land, for confronting the lord of the castle, for accepting the healer's teachings, and for battling the tyrant. Always, we'd chosen to move beyond our prior lives and bet on the future.

Mia's expression told all. Yes, we were ready. In each life, we can choose to stay behind or move on. In the morning, we'd choose to move on.

Chapter 36 – The Wood Between Worlds

We rose the next day before the village awoke, knowing our neighbors would beg us to stay, or at least make a long and sad goodbye. Better to let them imagine that sorcerers vanish at will to whatever magical realm sorcerers go.

We filled our packs with a few provisions, water skins and a selection of the snacks left at our doorstep the prior evening—apples, berries, and frosted sugar cookies. Though our destination lay shrouded in fog, these would serve us well on our journey. Last of all, I packed my journal, filled with memories of this world and our mentor's healing wisdom.

At the crossroads, Mia removed her necklace and hung it on a branch of the oak tree. I took off my belt and did the same. This time, the leftmost path let us through.

Deprived of sorcerer's attire, we expected a difference, yet the terrain remained unchanged. We traveled under a not unpleasant canopy of trees, which provided ample shade as the day grew warmer. After the sun passed its peak, the path began to rise. Eager to discover our destination, we kept going, until hunger and thirst forced us to rest.

We'd spoken little since setting out, each of us lost in our own thoughts. Now, as we settled on a log by a stream, we couldn't help but speculate on our future.

"Another world," I said.

"Where everyone's a sorcerer."

"Or where no healers are needed."

"Because no wars rage and no illness festers."

I gazed up to the sky where fair-weather clouds billowed and shook my head. "That would be the land of dreams, and no such place exists."

Mia nodded. "No hope without the possibility of despair."

We hoisted our packs and set off, this time not stopping until we reached the top of the rise where we could assess what lay ahead. Lofty mountains rose to jagged, snowcapped peaks on either side, and I realized the trail had taken us to the start of a highland pass.

From there, the going turned downhill. At the bottom of the slope spread an ancient wood, and beyond it, the vast body of water we'd viewed from the summit of Montvale Mountain. Lines of white foam ran up to a rocky shore, and at its edge glowed a swirling mist. What must have been substantial waves made no sound because we were too far away, but the sight, so familiar, caused my eyes to tear.

We reached the flatlands in less than an hour and paused to appreciate where we'd landed. No wagon ruts marked the way, and weeds grew wild to our ankles, untamed by the footsteps of others who had come before. We'd arrived at a secluded road through a wood between worlds.

We quickened our pace, and as the sun settled near the horizon, we reached the shore.

We'd come full circle. The healer had insisted magic lay everywhere, perhaps in our old world. Did I believe him? Maybe not, but I'd witnessed so much I'd never believed possible.

I held my breath and listened. The place was filled with the simplest pleasures—the chatter of water lapping the stony bank, the creaking of trees in the light breeze, and the warm aroma of sunbaked earth, grass, and flowers—just like my home.

Several paces offshore, we spotted it—the maelstrom.

Mia and I removed our boots, knotted the laces together and slung them round our necks, rolled up our trousers, and waded in.

I hesitated before the swirling mist, trying to pierce its mystery and decipher its intent. As with the first time, it refused to yield its secrets.

"When last we left, it held nothing but loss," I said.

"The loss was not by your lake or at my ocean's edge but within us, and will stay a part of us wherever we roam, but our time in the enchanted lands has changed us as well. We're different now from when we first entered, and that experience has made us who we've become today."

I stared, captivated by the maelstrom. "What awaits us on the other side? Will it be better than the life we built here?"

"Better, perhaps, but more real."

I nodded, then grimaced. "If we take this step, we'll lose our magic."

"Perhaps not. Are we so sure where magic may be found? Besides, we've already conjured the greatest magic in either world, never to be surpassed."

"What's that?"

"Finding each other."

The swirl in the mist calmed, and the portal became more inviting. I grasped her hand, and we stepped through.

THE END

**But... don't stop here. Please keep reading for our
Bonus Content, a Special Sneak Preview of:
THE TIME THAT'S GIVEN by David Litwack**

**Additionally, we'll provide a brief description of
David Litwack's 5 other books, each of them award winners.**

ACKNOWLEDGEMENTS

Writing a novel is itself an act of magic. The author imagines people and places that never existed in intense detail. If done with enough conviction, a new world comes into being. Add in the imagination of the reader, their life experiences, hopes and dreams, and the story comes to life.

I'd like to thank my editor, David Lane (aka Lane Diamond), for his help in polishing my rough gems over the years, and my cover artist, Kris Norris. I'd also like to thank my readers. Hopefully, I've served you well.

Most of all, I'd like to thank my family, living and gone, without whom I'd never have made it through these seven novels.

SPECIAL SNEAK PREVIEW

We are pleased to give a glimpse of another great book by this author. You'll find here the first three chapters, which we hope will entice you to examine this multiple award winner further.

THE TIME THAT'S GIVEN
By David Litwack

~~~

CHAPTER 1 – THE DIMMING

It came upon me one late winter evening as I waited for the call that never came. I'd been anxious to hear from Betty, but when the phone rang, Helen's voice sang out instead, too cheery for the circumstance.

Of course. How could she know?

Betty had been discreet, telling no one but me. No need to upset our expectant daughter needlessly.

A nor'easter of medium proportions had blown in that morning, leaving not much snow, but whipping the landscape with such stinging sleet that it forced me to cancel my walk and stay indoors. With little left to do but cook my customary meal of chicken and rice, and worry about my dear wife, I pondered how little value I added to the world.

Since retiring nine months before, I anchored my days with a trek to the Lexington green, site of the first battle of the revolutionary war and the shot heard round the world. There, I'd circle to the front, gaze into the eyes of the minuteman statue, and pat his patina-coated musket before returning home—a trip of four and a half miles. On the way back, I'd ignore the growing pain in my left hip and envision the minuteman confronting his fate with dignity and courage, awaiting the redcoats and the chance to change the world. Though no such opportunity loomed in
~~~

my future, I'd square my shoulders and jut out my chin, mimicking the statue, and quicken my pace as I conjured up heroic acts of my own.

Now, with the tree branches glazed and the driveway too slick to stand, I puttered about my kitchen, slotting dishes into the dishwasher and wiping down the tabletop with a sponge I should have replaced two weeks ago. Thanks to the storm, I spent the entire day still in my slippers and bathrobe, indulging my internet addiction. Around me, the cable TV blared, the laptop flashed, and my iPhone beeped. Every few minutes, I checked for messages, hoping for a surprise—a contact from an old friend, a text from Mark, or the much-awaited news from Betty. No such luck. Nothing but political solicitations and ads.

Yesterday, I stayed indoors as well, but not because of the weather. I'd awoken to a bulletin of another terror attack, this time at a nightclub in the wee hours of the morning. Young revelers celebrating their youth had been gunned down, with dozens killed and many more wounded. I sat glued to the story as it unfolded, positioning my computer screen so I could peer over it to the oversized TV on the wall. I poked around blogs for more details, trying to make sense of the senseless, until the sunlight dimmed and my eyelids drooped.

I'd slept fitfully last night and switched on my media first thing this morning, hoping for a glimmer of good news. A quick check, I promised myself, no more. Stories like yesterday's fed my addiction. Regardless of what I found today, I promised I'd tear myself away and escape to the fresh air for my walk, but the storm had thwarted my plan.

I'd lived alone since Betty went off to Ithaca in January. At college, she'd majored in art, and had taught the subject in middle school for twenty-five years, but always, she mused about reviving a career of her own.

When we both retired last June, we traveled the world and reveled in quiet moments together, but I was prone to darker moods and, with so much time on my hands, I began to grate on her otherwise sunny disposition.

On an unseasonably chilly day in September, she announced her intention to pursue her lifelong dream. While I preferred a less eventful retirement, my life partner of thirty-one years and mother of my children had different aspirations. How could I blame her? Despite her oncologist's assurance of an eighty-three percent survival rate at five years, her bout with breast cancer had left her mindful of her mortality. As the five years approached, and I worried about each mammogram, she grew more eager to take advantage of her remaining time on this earth. After thoughtful deliberation, she gathered her courage and a portfolio of her paintings, and applied to get her MFA. Though neither of us expected any school would accept this sixty-something former art teacher, Cornell responded that they'd love to have her.

When I grumbled about being left alone, she urged me to join her, reminding me I was retired and had nothing to tie me down. But I was in the midst of a reading of *The Lord of the Rings*, the fourth of my lifetime. The first had been as a thirteen-year-old newly addicted to fantasy, the second a marathon recitation conducted in my college dorm, and the third after my father died. Now, halfway through the Two Towers, I was not about to abandon Frodo on his trek to Mordor. Yet something more insidious was at play. In my brief retirement, I'd begun to retreat from the world, increasingly withdrawing to my study and losing myself in my backlog of books.

Betty refused to back down. The program only lasted two years, and a mere ten months per year at that, plus she could fly home for the occasional holiday weekend. She insisted time would pass quickly and I'd adapt. So, shortly after Christmas, she packed up her artwork and went off to study high above Cayuga's waters.

In the three months since she left, I failed to adapt at all. I missed sitting across the table from her at meals, as we shared the day's news and our innermost thoughts, and I slept poorly at night, unaccustomed to lying in bed alone.

Together, we'd raised Mark and Helen. Mark now resided on the west coast with his wife, the two of them busy with their careers in high tech, and with their self-absorbed decoration of their new home, a faux castle on a hillside overlooking San Francisco Bay.

Helen, our youngest, lived with her husband a mere half hour away. I adored Helen, though since Betty left, she fussed over me to no end, urging me to buy one of those bracelets to alert someone if I fell or became incapacitated. We'd developed a recurring routine. She'd nag, and I'd assure her I was healthy, fit, and not *that* old. I encouraged her to worry less, especially now that she was expecting my first grandchild.

With Helen's due date approaching, Betty decided to forego her final class before Easter and come home for the birth. She'd been scheduled to arrive today, but the storm had cancelled her flight, and with the whole east coast under a blizzard, she was unable to rebook for two more days.

I hoped Helen's baby didn't come early.

Now a new wrinkle: Betty's latest mammogram at the Cornell Medical Center had showed a cloudy mass—likely benign, the doctor had said, but he took a biopsy to be safe. As far as I knew, no results had come back.

After her flight was cancelled, why had she called Helen rather than me? Was she afraid to tell me over the phone?

A beeping from the TV interrupted my thoughts, along with a drumroll and sculpted logo heralding breaking news.

Now what?

I'd wasted yesterday watching coverage of the terror attack. How could I bear a new crisis? No crisis followed, but I winced nonetheless as a female anchor informed me that two hundred days remained until the next election.

An urge came over me, making my hands shake. If I were to remain in the dark about Betty's news, and helpless in the face of events, I could at least escape from the world, constrict my space, and be totally, utterly alone.

I silenced the talking head on the TV, shut down my computer, and powered off my iPhone. Then I double-knotted my bathrobe tie and retreated to the small study used to pay bills and read—the only room with no windows in my sprawling seven-room home.

In the past few years, I'd decorated the eight-by-eight with souvenirs from the trips Betty and I had taken abroad—after our nest had emptied and before she went off to school. A faded tapestry covered the left wall, one I bought in Carcassonne for nine-hundred and thirty-eight dollars despite Betty's objections. It depicted a castle complete with moat and drawbridge, and a knight on armored horse trotting across it. Opposite the tapestry, a glass case housed my collection of eclectic artifacts, Roman and Japanese swords, a steel breastplate, a plumed helmet, and several gypsy charms.

By the door stood the Ikea bookcase I'd assembled to store my fantasy novels. Though still half-empty, a few dozen covers blared at me with images of heroes and dragons, demons, sorceresses, and elves. I grabbed the latest, with the leather bookmark protruding midway through the pages, intending to lose myself in its prose.

After shutting the door, I cleared the clutter from the surface of the desk to make space for my elbows—and perhaps a place for my head, should I doze off—but before cracking open the book, I leaned in to admire the shelf above the desk that contained my collection of candles. I'd made a habit of buying a candle unique to every location we visited. Each had a story behind it.

Whereas Betty preferred art galleries with modern sculpture, my preference tended more to the obscure and occult. The trips became our first parting of the ways. She'd tour museums, while I'd wander off the beaten path, scavenging through cluttered alleyways in older sections of the city, searching for medieval weapons, figurines of knights, wizard's wands... and candles.

I eyed the candles one at a time: the tall one from Jerusalem with the blue and white braided wax, used to mark Sabbath's end; the elephant from Delhi with the wick sticking up from his rump; an Irish rose with the wick nestled between its petals; the tacky Stratford on Avon skull I couldn't resist buying—poor Yorick, etc.; a winged cherub from Rome bearing an urn upon its shoulder; two parakeets nuzzling; and my favorite, the one molded in the shape of a boy.

I picked up the last and fingered its surface, recalling how I'd discovered it in a dusty shop off an alley in the old city of Prague. The shopkeeper had urged me to handle it with care.

"A unique candle," he said. "It will provide light when nothing else can dispel the darkness."

I suppressed a grin. I liked the look of the candle but found the storekeeper odd. "Are you suggesting this candle is *magic*?"

The man drew closer. "Magic indeed."

"Will it grant my every wish?" I asked, playing along. The sandalwood incense pervading the shop must have dulled my skepticism.

He chortled, an unnerving sound. "Not wishes. It's not a genie in a bottle."

"Then will it provide answers to my hardest questions?"

His magnified eyes glistened through coke-bottle glasses as he whispered these words. "Not wishes, not answers, but this candle will light your way so you may find the answers you seek. Of course, its success depends on the questions you ask."

I struggled to maintain my manners, though a part of me wanted to believe—the reason I searched in these alleyways.

As I groped in my pocket to pay, he gripped my arm and squeezed until he commanded my attention. "A warning: don't light it frivolously."

I pulled out a twenty euro note and extended it to him, but he withdrew the candle.

"Not enough?" I said.

"I cannot sell this boy alone."

I smirked. These tourist shops were all the same. "How much more?"

"Nothing, but a second piece must accompany it."

"But *wait*, there's more," I mumbled under my breath, parroting a thousand commercials I'd seen on TV.

The shopkeeper released my arm and shuffled behind the counter. From beneath it, he pulled out something concealed in the palm of his hand. As he extended it to me, his fingers spread, revealing a thumb-sized vial that glowed with a purple iridescence, though it was unclear whether the color came from the glass or the liquid inside. The vial was capped by a black cork.

"Take this as well. No charge."

"Is this potion magic too?"

The shopkeeper's lip curled, a slight wrinkle, but less than a smile. "The candle will light your way, but in the moment of choosing, this will bring you peace."

I checked my watch. Betty would be waiting by now.

I reached for the vial, anxious to leave, but he pulled it back one last time. "Never open it until it's time to choose."

Now, smiling at the memory of that encounter, I fondled the candle and wondered. The wax had been sculpted with exquisite detail and dyed with subtle tones. The boy stood at attention on glistening black boots, with skin-tight gray pants tucked into them. A short red waistcoat fit tightly over slim hips, and gold epaulets made his shoulders more square. An ornamental belt girded his waist with what appeared to be a dagger hanging from it. On his head, he wore a tricorn hat like that of the minuteman, but this one had a gilded edge. A purple plume rose from its top and, although made of wax, it gave the illusion of waving in the breeze.

Most striking was the boy's face. The artisan who'd molded the piece had taken care with the features — a solid chin contrasted with a puckish nose; round cheeks displayed a flush so robust, blood might be flowing through them; and thin lips curled into a Mona Lisa smile. The figurine bore an impression of powerful innocence.

I nodded to myself, as I was wont to do when I'd made a decision. For the months since Betty left, I'd rattled about the house when not on my walk. I prepared and ate meals, showered and dressed, brushed my teeth, and kept the house clean. I watched football on weekends and read novels until my eyelids drooped.

I set up a Facebook profile, googled old colleagues and friends, and invited them to friend me. I joined groups for fantasy lovers and wikis for my favorite authors. I followed links from one to the next and bookmarked those I liked. My list grew so long that, by the time I followed them all, read their articles and scanned their comment sections, I could loop back to the top and find fresh content. The result: I spent entire mornings browsing, until my stomach growled and the clock on the screen showed noon, yet none of it made me wiser.

I fingered the candle. '...*you may find the answers you seek.*'

Now was the time

As I fumbled through the drawer for a book of matches, my hand brushed the vial, dusty from its exile in the dark. I pulled it out as well — the shopkeeper has made such a fuss about the two staying together — and placed it on the desk next to the candle.

After three breaths in and out, I struck a match and lit the wick.

The flame hissed and flickered, then settled into an even glow. A moment later, I rose on wobbly knees, shuffled to the door to switch off the light, wobbled back and plopped on the leather office chair to study the flame.

As the hat atop the boy's head began to melt, time slowed and the space narrowed — as I'd hoped — but the change continued beyond what I'd intended. A sinking feeling crept over me, as if some unseen hand was lowering me in a bucket down a deep well, and the circle of light overhead receded.

The flame flared — an event I oddly expected — and its yellow turned blood red as it rose a foot or more. Now angry and tall, it seemed more blow torch than candle. Fearing its heat, I rolled the chair back, but as I did so, I caught out of the corner of my eye a liquid shadow rolling across the floor, a dread encroaching like the onset of old age.

I turned to confront the shadow—just my imagination, nothing more. After a few seconds staring into the dark, I swiveled back to the candle, and the flame seemed to glow brighter than before. I held my breath and listened. In the silence, I imagined a muffled moan, like the sound fog might make as it dragged across the ground.

For the past months, I'd nurtured a fantasy worthy of my books, that an evil virus had infested the world and only I had discovered this, and that I would spend my latter years finding its source and destroying it. Now, dwelling on this delusion, I embellished it with details—a face conjured in the flame, a magical sword materializing in my grasp, perhaps a charmed amulet around my neck.

My reverie was interrupted by a hissing from behind, too loud to be imagined. When I searched the room for its source, I found the shadow had indeed taken substance. It flowed across the floor in waves, climbed to the foot of my chair, blackened the hem of my robe, and rose until my hands grayed as they fumbled for some means of defense. At last, the shadow reached the candle and spread from the boots of the boy to the plumed hat.

Then it touched the flame.

Poof.

The flame extinguished, and the room went dark.

I groped on the desktop for the matches, regretting I'd so casually tossed them aside, but as my fingertips swept the wooden surface, I knocked them to the floor. Over my sixty-two years, the floor had grown farther away; some mornings, I struggled to tie my shoes. Here, in total darkness, I had little chance of finding the matches, so I rose instead and hobbled to the door, my slippers slapping above the hiss of the shadow. I located the doorknob, but when I tried to turn it, it spun in my grasp, as if protected by one of those safety attachments parents use to keep toddlers in place. I patted the wall beside the door, found the jamb, and slid my fingers along it to where the light switch should be.

Nothing but polished wood.

Helen was right. I should have ordered one of those life alert buttons, though with the weirdness pervading this room, I suspect all technology would fail.

Before panic overwhelmed me, a glimmer of light flickered from behind.

I spun around.

A boy stood next to the desk, his face aglow as if illuminated by a spotlight from above. No... not quite a boy. Yes, he bore a slight stature with the slim hips and narrow shoulders of youth. Yes, his skin shone smooth as wax, with no furrow across his brow and no crow's feet about his eyes. Yet he carried himself like a more mature man, and those eyes... deep wells of brown that exuded a lifetime — or perhaps many lifetimes — of experience with a harsh world. Wisps of gray slipped out from beneath the brim of a familiar hat and tumbled about his ears.

I gasped when I recognized that hat, a tricorn with a gilded edge and a purple plume. Before me stood the boy from the candle, life-size and alive.

"Who are you?" A quiver invaded my voice, and it surprised me to be taking these events seriously. I'd slept poorly the night before, and this was surely a dream.

"I am the guide you summoned, Albert Higgins." The boy's pitch was more youthful than adult, but his tone sounded clipped and formal, like one accustomed to the ways of an Elizabethan court. His words bore a hint of an accent, Scottish perhaps, but from a highland village remote from the modern world.

Despite the situation, my lifelong aversion to my birth name sprang to the fore. "I didn't summon you, and don't call me Albert. No one has called me that since my mother died."

This so-called guide glanced at his boot tops and shuffled his feet like a grade-schooler chastised by his teacher. "Then what shall I call you?"

"Burt is what my friends call me... the few I have."

"I'm sorry. Burt it shall be from now on."

I wanted to give him a moment to collect himself, but I couldn't contain my curiosity. The two days stuck in the house had bored me, and if this were a dream, I intended to take full advantage of it. "Let's say I go along and pretend you're real. Where are you supposed to guide me to?"

"To wherever you seek."

I glanced at the floor where, in the glow cast by the boy, the murky shadow swirled around my ankles. "Where does this gloom come from?

"From the source of despair."

"Ah! And where is that?"

"A complex question with no single answer. I can bring you to a place where you may seek the answer yourself... assuming you wish to go."

I pictured the snow swirling outside. "I wish to go."

His eyes drooped at the corners, intense brown eyes that might have been a thousand years old, but still no crow's feet formed. "Are you certain?"

The question made me wary, but I determined to take the chance. It was, after all, a dream.

I nodded.

"Very well, but first, you've forgotten something—that which must accompany me on all my journeys." He gestured to the desk, where the shopkeeper's vial now throbbed purple.

I shuffled over, grasped it, and slipped it into my pocket, keeping my fingers wrapped around it. The glass felt hot to the touch.

I glanced back at my guide, and heaved my shoulders up and down. "I'm ready."

"Very well, Burt. Come with me."

"I'm still in my bathrobe and slippers. Can't I change first?"

"No need."

The boy slid one hand to his hip, where it rested on the pommel of his dagger, a clear crystal ball with a glowing spark within that mirrored the purple of the vial. He extended his other hand to me. When I demurred, he stepped closer and beckoned with such empathy that I could no longer resist.

I expected his hand to be cold and lifeless, like wax, but a pulse throbbed through his fingers as if blood rushed through the veins.

A flutter filled my stomach, and I swallowed hard. *What if this isn't a dream?*

"Come with me," he said, "if you hope to find the answers you seek." He led me toward the lone exit of the windowless room.

I hesitated, knowing the knob wouldn't turn.

Sensing my reluctance, he winked at me, and the Mona Lisa smile curled at the corners, a complex gesture beyond what the most accomplished artisan could mold from wax.

Entranced, I followed.

Then, without testing the knob, we stepped straight through the solid wooden door.

~~~

CHAPTER 2 – THE CHILDREN'S MARCH

We emerged not into the shelter of my living room, but to the fully exposed outdoors. A light wind brushed my cheeks, making me bunch my bathrobe around my neck. With no parka or hat, or scarf or gloves to protect me from the cold, I anticipated being buffeted by sleet, but I
~~~

needed no such protection. A bright sun shone overhead, and the breeze embraced me with warmth.

As my mind tried to grasp what I saw, my vision blurred, and what appeared to be heat waves rippled up from the ground. The earth undulated beneath my feet as if I stood on the deck of a ship in a storm. I stumbled and nearly fell.

My guide caught me by the elbow and gave a nod of assurance. "It's always this way for those who travel with me. Transition between worlds is hard, but the wooziness lasts only a few seconds."

I closed my eyes and counted to ten. True to his word, the unsettling sensation passed. Once the ground steadied, I glanced around to assess my new surroundings.

We stood at the edge of a dirt road on the side of a hill, up to our knees in a field of goldenrod. Far ahead, an impressive vista loomed. Mountains rose in the distance, their saw-toothed peaks jutting up to jab the sky. A ribbon of blue snaked along their base, what must have been a broad river. Downhill, to my right, nestled a shire-like village, a place that might have given birth to the heroes of my fantasy novels. Thatched-roof cottages clustered in a circle, forming a modest farming community situated by the banks of the river.

Uphill, the road rose to a craggy crest, on top of which stood a more forbidding structure, in circumference as broad as the village. A stone wall girded it with Arthurian-like battlements rising at intervals. The dirt road that wound toward it changed to cobblestones before a drawbridge, now lowered, allowing access through an arched gateway. Behind the walls, several turrets poked the clouds, tickling my fantasies, but this structure fell short of my expectations. No chain-mailed foot soldiers manned its parapets, and no knights in armor guarded its entrance. The turrets seemed more decorative than defensive, and black soot stained their tops. Looming above them rose the source of the soot: three smokestacks dwarfing the turrets and spewing ash. The structure seemed less a medieval castle than a factory, built with a storybook façade to embellish what lay within.

On the road before me, a parade of children trundled past, climbing to the structure on the hill. The girls pushed wheelbarrows covered with canvas, and the boys trudged alongside bearing wooden yolks on their shoulders, supporting buckets on either side. A few acknowledged my presence with a begrudging glance, but most stayed focused on the hilltop.

I turned to my guide and raised a brow. "Why do they ignore us?"

He pointed to their burden. "They labor under a heavy load."

As he spoke, a girl with raven hair strode by, no more than nine-years-old, so small she struggled to keep the barrow steady on its lone wheel.

As she passed, she peeked my way. Her dark eyes widened, and she twisted around to the boy who followed. "Look, Matty, a wizard."

The momentary distraction caused her to lose her balance enough to make the barrow totter and tip. Her knuckles whitened on the handles with the strain, and she bit her lower lip. Once she'd stabilized her load, she tossed me a look of resignation and resumed her march uphill.

The boy she'd called Matty trailed behind. He appeared older by a year or two, with tangled locks colored the same as the girl. He stumbled, not an arm's length from me, and dropped to one knee, his buckets thudding to the ground.

I peered inside. Each brimmed with a translucent gray muck, as if the fog from my study had taken solid form. I reached out to grasp his elbow and help him back up.

Matty scanned me head to toe, scrunched up his button nose and scowled, but he'd fallen behind the girl. He pushed off with a grunt and hastened to catch up.

"What is it they carry?" I whispered to my guide.

"Buckets of gloom, wheelbarrows of woe."

For the next five minutes, a dozen or more children shuffled past, eyes fixed on the structure ahead, laboring beneath their load.

When the last one passed, I queried my guide. "Why did you bring me to this horrible place?"

"You asked to find the source of despair."

I looked uphill and narrowed my gaze, mimicking the minuteman confronting his fate, and viewed the structure anew. I'd spent too many years worrying about my fate and doing nothing to change it.

Time to act.

"May I go there?"

The boy from the candle turned and swept a hand across the path, urging me to lead the way.

I hesitated. "What will I find inside?"

"That's for you to discover... I'm only your guide."

We fell in line behind the last of the children as they climbed to their goal. By the time we reached the archway, the first had begun to leave. Empty wheelbarrows now clattered along the cobblestones, and the buckets were stacked, one into the other, so the boys could carry them in one hand. As they put the moat behind them, faces that minutes before had borne the weight of the world returned to the innocence of youth. With their dark deed done, they skipped down the pathway to the village. The landscape rang with their laughter.

At the drawbridge, my guide motioned me inside.

I stepped across, slippers flapping on the wood, but on the far side of the archway, I hesitated. Despite the moat and battlements, the interior appeared more modern than medieval. No knights lined the passageway, and no guards blocked the way. No massive wheel drove a pulley to lower a spiked gate, and no torches in sconces flickered on the walls. Instead, recessed lighting revealed a three-story atrium, sterile but not unpleasant, like the reception area of the many corporate headquarters I'd visited in my former career.

A young man with closely cropped hair, wearing a blue button-down shirt and maroon necktie, sat at a desk, doodling away at a notebook and trying to appear busy while avoiding the eyes of the children. He ignored us as we approached.

Behind him, a row of three steel doors marked a bank of elevators. Those who had not yet unloaded their burden waited in well-ordered queues, six to each elevator. As a door slid open, they let the others exit, and filed in without coercion or fuss, as if performing an everyday chore.

When all had boarded, and we stood alone with the receptionist, I waved a hand to take in the white, sound-deadening panels in the ceiling, the potted plants and the elevators. "How can this be the source of despair?"

My guide glanced at his boot tops and shuffled in place, a gesture I'd come to know well. "You asked a hard question. I did my best to answer. Sources of despair are complicated things."

I checked above the nearest elevator, where two lights stuck out from the wall, one dark and marked "Lobby" and the other lit up with the letters "UZ."

"What is UZ?"

My guide shrugged and pointed to the ceiling three floors above us. "Unloading Zone."

Tiny black dots swam before my eyes, as if I were experiencing another transition. A bell dinged, the UZ light went dark, and the Lobby light flashed. The doors before me slid open, and more happy children emerged, leaving an empty elevator behind.

My guide motioned me toward the gaping doors.

I spoke more insistently this time. "What will I find?"

He stepped inside and waited for me to join him. "My role is to show you where to look. The answers are yours to find, as much as they might exist."

I stared at the gap between the floor and the elevator, which suddenly seemed a chasm. "Is it safe to go? I push no wheelbarrow and carry no bucket, and I'm certainly not a child."

"Safety is a relative term. Have you been safe in your life so far?"

I glared at him, recalling the old shopkeeper's words:

"Your questions will be well answered, but only if well asked."

I fumbled to phrase the question well. "Shouldn't I... have armor... or a weapon? I'm a bit exposed in my slippers and bathrobe."

He rolled his eyes as if questioning how he'd been saddled with such a fool, and shook his head.

I sighed and stepped inside. On the right panel, a single 'up' button protruded. I reached for it, a habit from a thousand elevators past, but my finger wavered in midair. "Should I press it?"

"It's your quest, not mine."

The shopkeeper in Prague had warned me. The guide from the candle possessed powerful magic, but would provide no answers without a struggle.

I drew in two breaths, buying time to formulate my next question. "Is there a reason... why I would *not* want to go?"

"Yes."

"Why?" My voice echoed off the metallic walls and faded to silence.

My guide squinted up to the topmost turrets where the smoke billowed, and his words billowed as well, no clearer than the smoke. "Because the source of despair may be different than what you seek."

<center>~~~</center>

CHAPTER 3 – THE FACTORY

I extended a finger and pressed.

The button lit up, the doors slid shut, and a motor hummed.

As the elevator lurched upward, I brushed my fingertips against my reflection on the polished metal wall. An aging man in a bathrobe stared back at me, but with a spark in his eyes and his legs spread wide, adopting the posture of the minuteman.

When the humming stopped, the doors opened, and I exited to a narrow corridor, the end of which opened up into a high-ceilinged chamber. Metal cauldrons filled the far side, each taller than a grown man and three times as broad, with a ramp leading up to them. Vents above them sucked up steam from their boiling contents, driven by pumps and gears that ground away with a dull drone—the source of the soot from the smokestacks. A fetid odor permeated the air like rotten eggs. The children who had not yet deposited their load waited in queues before a wooden desk.

I scanned the chamber, searching for a demonic figure, some winged creature or dark lord who directed this morality play, but found only a man who appeared more clerk than demon. Tufts of hair leaked out from the edges of a green visor, and a frayed tweed jacket with patches at the elbows cloaked a too small frame. He sat on a stool behind the desk, his feet not reaching the floor.

On the desktop lay a leather-bound ledger. As each child approached, the clerk asked their name and ordered them to place their load on an adjacent scale. Then he hopped off the stool to peer at the numbers on the scale through thick glasses, which emphasized his bug-like eyes. Once satisfied with the weight, he settled back down to record their delivery, scratching with a quill pen on the pages of the ledger before waving the child past.

Each boy or girl trundled up the ramp and dumped their load into the vat. As the gray liquid oozed from the barrows and buckets, the bearer's mood lightened as well. Once they'd emptied their containers, their grimaces curled into smiles. Childlike again, they skipped off to await their turn at the elevator.

I lingered in the shadows until only a half-dozen children remained, and then snuck in for a closer look, hoping to avoid notice. The flapping of my slippers on the tile floor alerted one child to my presence, the boy next in line. He turned, and I recognized him at once, the ten-year-old with the raven locks whom I'd tried to help on the road.

He took a step toward me and opened his mouth, but before he could speak, the clerk cleared his throat. The child's turn had come, so he hefted his yoke and set his buckets on the scale.

"And you name is...?" the clerk said.

"Matthias."

The clerk recorded the boy's name and the weight of his cargo, and motioned him past.

After discharging his load, Matthias headed toward the elevators with a lighter heart. As he passed me, he paused, set down his now empty buckets, and approached. With his tiny hand, he fingered the hem of my bathrobe and gaped up at me. "*Are* you a wizard?"

I ruffled the tuft of his hair. "Why would you think I'm a wizard?"

"Because you're wearing a wizard's robe."

"This? You think this is a wizard's robe?" I chuckled, but my attempt at humor became lost in the grinding of the gears.

The girl who had accompanied him came to his side. "Well," she whispered. "Is he?"

"I don't think so, Hannah."

"He might be, Matty. He *might* be. Sometimes the magic hides."

The boy stared up at me, unable to face her, his eyes glistening. "My sister hoped you could help."

I determined to hedge my reply. After all, my presence here defied reason, and I had a magical guide accompanying me. Perhaps I *could* help. "If I *were* a wizard, what would you ask of me?"

"Candy, for a start," the little girl said.

"Candy?"

"Yes. Sweet jelly beans in fruity colors, made with a wizard's touch."

A bell behind me rang, and the elevator doors slid open. She and her brother joined the others, leaving me alone with my guide.

When all had departed, I stepped up to the desk as I'd seen the children do, though I bore no burden.

The clerk glanced up from his ledger, took me in, and raised a brow, unimpressed by my wizard's robe. "What may I do for you?"

I rose as tall as my old bones allowed and rocked back and forth on the balls of my feet. "What is it you do to these children?"

"Oh, that tired old question." He went back to his accounting, drawing a solid line beneath the column, and began tallying up the numbers.

I leaned on the desk to regain his attention. "Why do you force them to come here with such a burden?"

He raised a finger, motioning for me to wait as he double-checked his figures. When satisfied all balanced, he met my gaze. "My job is to sum up the input and total the output, but I don't force them to come. I'd be happy to have them stop, but I don't know how."

When I refused to budge, he set down his quill, took off his glasses and wiped his brow. No longer magnified, his eyes narrowed. "If you believe you can stop them, please try. I'll go off into a peaceful retirement and be forever in your debt. Now if you'll excuse me, if I take time to chat, I fall behind. They keep coming, you know."

I hovered over him for a minute or more to no avail. The conversation had ended.

I glanced at my guide, whose bemused expression implied I'd made a fool of myself.

He whispered to be certain no one but me could hear. "Time to go."

I trudged back to the elevator, beginning to wish I'd never lit the candle. Once inside, I refused to push the button, staring instead at my image in the polished brass doors. An old man stared back, disillusioned—no sign of the minuteman now.

Outside, where the cobblestones met the dirt, I found the two children, Matthias and Hannah, sitting cross-legged on a flat rock at the side of the road. Matthias's empty buckets lay on the ground before him, next to Hannah's wheelbarrow.

The little girl spotted me first and scrambled to her feet. "I knew you'd come. I told Matty you were a wizard, but he laughed at me."

Matthias stood to join her, and placed his hands on his hips. "Well, are you?"

Time to change my approach. In this world, I had no idea what role I played, so I mimicked my guide. "Being a wizard is a complicated thing. I may or may not be able to help, but first you must answer my questions. Why do you come here?"

The boy shrugged. "The gloom needs to go somewhere."

"But why can't you just play and be happy?"

Hannah's hands fidgeted, and she kept turning to me and back to the boy. At last she poked him on the arm. "Tell him, Matty."

The boy's back straightened, and he tried to appear older than his years. "They say a war rages, and so the gloom lies over the land. The say—"

"And the boatman," the girl interrupted. "Tell him."

Mathias whirled on her. "Hush, Hannah." Then back to me. "My sister's little and speaks of things she doesn't understand." He lowered his chin to his chest and stared at his boot tops. His voice lowered as well. "Whispers fill the air. They say we'll all die someday, that our mum will die like my dad, and when she does, we'll be alone. She told us no, she'd always be with us, but I think she lies to make us feel better." He gazed back up at me with pleading eyes. "Wizards are supposed to be wise. Can *you* tell us the truth?"

I settled down on the flat rock and urged the children to sit beside me, Matthias on my left and Hannah on my right, as I used to do with Mark and Helen in a time so long ago.

I wrapped an arm around each. "Life is complicated as well, and no one—not even a wizard—knows the truth. But wizards have ways to dispel the gloom, if you're open to listen and learn."

Hannah nestled into the crook of my arm and gazed up at me with dark eyes. "Will you teach us?"

What could I say? I'd dug myself a hole, so I stood and loomed over the two, trying to appear wizard-like. "Go home to your mother. I'll consult with my fellow wizards, and if they deem the task worthwhile, I'll join you later."

My words seemed to lighten their load even more than dumping their burdens of gloom had. Both popped up and, after a hurried bow, raced off with a spring to their step.

Once they'd moved out of earshot, I confronted my guide. "Is this how you give me answers?"

"Would you prefer I return you to the small room in your home? I can bring you back with a wave of my hand. I can leave you with the candle lit, and you can watch it burn down."

My eyes narrowed as the children settled to specks in the distance, so easy to abandon and forget. I shook my head. I'd abandoned enough in my life.

"You thought such a quest would be simple?" my guide said.

I sighed. "What will I learn in the village? Will I find answers to my questions?"

He raised and released his slim shoulders in what passed as a shrug. "I can't say for sure."

Far downhill, Matthias and his sister Hannah disappeared into a cluster of cottages. I pursed my lips and blew out a stream of air. "Then I'm bound to follow them to find the source of their gloom."

For more on this book, please visit our website at:
www.EvolvedPub.com/TTTG

ABOUT THE AUTHOR

The urge to write first struck David at age sixteen when working on a newsletter at a youth encampment in the woods of northern Maine. It may have been the wild night when lightning flashed at sunset, followed by the northern lights rippling after dark, or maybe it was the newsletter's editor, a girl with eyes the color of the ocean, but he was inspired to write about the blurry line between reality and the fantastic.

Using two fingers and lots of white-out, he religiously typed five pages a day throughout college and well into his twenties. Then life intervened. When he found time again to daydream, the urge to write returned.

David now lives in the Great Northwest and anywhere else that catches his fancy. He no longer limits himself to five pages a day, and is thankful every keystroke for the invention of the word processor.

For more, please follow David Litwack online at:
Author Website: www.DavidLitwack.com
Publisher Website: www.EvolvedPub.com/david-litwacks-books/
Goodreads: www.goodreads.com/author/show/6439448.David_Litwack
Amazon: www.amazon.com/David-Litwack/e/B008JG79A6/
BookBub: www.bookbub.com/authors/david-litwack
Facebook: www.facebook.com/david.litwack.author
Instagram: www.instagram.com/davidlitwack/
Twitter: @DavidLitwack
LinkedIn: www.linkedin.com/in/davidlitwack/

MORE FROM DAVID LITWACK

David Litwack has produced multiple award-winning books and series across multiple genres, though all of his books carry elements of fantasy and speculative fiction, written in a literary style. Whatever your reading preference, you can always count on David Litwack for entertaining stories loaded with great characters. They might even stretch you a bit and make you think about life, love, loss, purpose....

Be sure to check out each of David's 6 other books to date:
1) Along the Watchtower
2) The Daughter of the Sea and the Sky
3) The Seekers #1: The Children of Darkness
4) The Seekers #2: The Stuff of Stars
5) The Seekers #3: The Light of Reason
6) The Time That's Given

We know you're going to love them.

Since we already gave you a 3-chapter preview of The Time That's Given, on the following pages we'll tell you just a little about the other 5 books.

ALONG THE WATCHTOWER

A tragic warrior lost in two worlds.... Which one will he choose?

WINNER: Readers' Favorite Book Award – Bronze Medal – Fiction Drama
WINNER: Pinnacle Book Achievement Award – Best Literary Fiction
FINALIST: Beverly Hills Book Awards – Military Fiction
FINALIST: Massachusetts Book Awards – Fiction

The war in Iraq ended for Freddie when an IED explosion left his mind and body shattered. Once a skilled gamer as well as a capable soldier, he's now a broken warrior, emerging from a medically induced coma to discover he's inhabiting two separate realities.

The first is his waking world of pain, family trials, and remorse—and slow rehabilitation through the tender care of Becky, his physical therapist. The second is a dark fantasy realm of quests, demons, and magic, which Freddie enters when he sleeps. The lines soon blur for Freddie, not just caught between two worlds, but lost within himself.

Is he Lieutenant Freddie Williams, a leader of men, a proud officer in the US Army who has suffered such egregious injury and loss? Or is he Frederick, Prince of Stormwind, who must make sense of his horrific visions in order to save his embattled kingdom from the monstrous Horde, his only solace the beautiful gardener, Rebecca, whose gentle words calm the storms in his soul.

In the conscious world, the severely wounded vet faces a strangely similar and equally perilous mission to that of the prince—a journey along a dark road, haunted by demons of guilt and memory. Can he let patient, loving Becky into his damaged and shuttered heart? It may be his only way back from Hell.

"This is a book that deserves to be read." ~ *Awesome Indies Reviews*

THE DAUGHTER OF THE SEA AND THE SKY

A thought-provoking look at the line between faith and fantasy, fanatics and followers, and religion and reason.

WINNER: Pinnacle Book Achievement Award – Best Fantasy
WINNER: Awesome Indies Seal of Excellence
WINNER: FAPA Gold Medal – Adult Fiction: General

Children of the Republic, Helena and Jason were inseparable in their youth, until fate sent them down different paths. Grief and duty sidetracked Helena's plans, and Jason came to detest the hollowness of his ambitions.

These two damaged souls are reunited when a tiny boat from the Blessed Lands crashes onto the rocks near Helena's home after an impossible journey across the forbidden ocean. On board is a single passenger, a nine-year-old girl named Kailani, who calls herself The Daughter of the Sea and the Sky. A new and perilous purpose binds Jason and Helena together again, as they vow to protect the lost innocent from the wrath of the authorities, no matter the risk to their future and freedom.

But is the mysterious child simply a troubled little girl longing to return home? Or is she a powerful prophet sent to unravel the fabric of a godless Republic, as the outlaw leader of an illegal religious sect would have them believe? Whatever the answer, it will change them all forever... and perhaps their world as well.

"Author David Litwack gracefully weaves together his message with alternating threads of the fantastic and the realistic.... The reader will find wisdom and grace in this beautifully written story." ~ *San Francisco Book Review*

THE CHILDREN OF DARKNESS
(The Seekers – Book 1)

*A thousand years ago the Darkness came — a terrible time of violence, fear, and
social collapse when technology ran rampant.*

WINNER: Pinnacle Book Achievement Award - Best Sci-Fi
WINNER: Feathered Quill – Gold Medal – Sci-Fi/Fantasy

"But what are we without dreams?"
The vicars of the Temple of Light brought peace, ushering in an era
of blessed simplicity. For ten centuries they have kept the madness at bay
with "temple magic," and by eliminating forever the rush of progress that
nearly caused the destruction of everything.

Childhood friends, Orah, Nathaniel, and Thomas have always lived
in the tiny village of Little Pond, longing for more from life but unwilling
to challenge the rigid status quo. When they're cast into the prisons of
Temple City, they discover a terrible secret that launches the three on a
journey to find the forbidden keep, placing their lives in jeopardy, for a
truth from the past awaits that threatens the foundation of the Temple. If
they reveal that truth, they might once again release the potential of their
people.

Yet they would also incur the Temple's wrath, as it is written: "If
there comes among you a prophet saying, 'Let us return to the darkness,'
you shall stone him, because he has sought to thrust you away from the
Light."

"The plot unfolds easily, swiftly, and never lets the readers' attention
wane... After reading this one, it will be a real hardship to have to wait to
see what happens next." ~ *Feathered Quill Book Awards (Gold Medal in
Science Fiction & Fantasy)*

THE STUFF OF STARS
(The Seekers – Book 2)

If the Seekers fail this time, they risk not a stoning, but losing themselves in the twilight of a never-ending dream.

WINNER: Pinnacle Book Achievement Award - Best Sci-Fi
WINNER: Feathered Quill – Gold Medal – Sci-Fi/Fantasy
WINNER: Readers' Favorite Book Awards – Siver Medal – YA Sci-Fi

Against all odds, Orah and Nathaniel have found the keep and revealed the truth about the darkness, initiating what they hoped would be a new age of enlightenment. But the people were more set in their ways than anticipated, and a faction of vicars whispered in their ears, urging a return to traditional ways.

Desperate to keep their movement alive, Orah and Nathaniel cross the ocean to seek the living descendants of the keepmasters' kin. Those they find on the distant shore are both more and less advanced than expected.

The seekers become caught between the two sides, and face the challenge of bringing them together to make a better world. The prize: a chance to bring home miracles and a more promising future for their people. The cost of failure: unimaginable.

"In this YA sci-fi sequel, Litwack pushes his characters into new physical, mental, and emotional realms as they encounter an unusual, tech-based society. A grand, revelatory saga that continues to unfold."
~ Kirkus Reviews

THE LIGHT OF REASON
(The Seekers – Book 3)

Orah and Nathaniel return home with miracles from across the sea, hoping to bring a better life for their people. Instead, they find the world they left in chaos.

WINNER: Pinnacle Book Achievement Award - Best Sci-Fi
WINNER: Feathered Quill – Gold Medal – Sci-Fi/Fantasy
WINNER: Readers' Favorite Book Awards – Bronze Medal – Dystopian

A new grand vicar, known as the usurper, has taken over the keep and is using its knowledge to reinforce his hold on power.

Despite their good intentions, the seekers find themselves leading an army, and for the first time in a millennium, their world experiences the horror of war.

But the keepmasters' science is no match for the dreamers, leaving Orah and Nathaniel their cruelest choice—face bloody defeat and the death of their enlightenment, or use the genius of the dreamers to tread the slippery slope back to the darkness.

"In this third installment, Litwack gives fans a plot both action-driven and cerebral. All around, a superbly crafted adventure. An enthralling finish to a thoughtful, uplifting sci-fi series." ~ *Kirkus Reviews*

MORE FROM EVOLVED PUBLISHING

We offer great books across multiple genres, featuring high-quality editing (which we believe is second-to-none) and fantastic covers.

As a hybrid small press, your support as loyal readers is so important to us, and we have strived, with tireless dedication and sheer determination, to deliver on the promise of our motto:
QUALITY IS PRIORITY #1!

Please check out all of our great books,
which you can find at this link:
www.EvolvedPub.com/Catalog/

Thank you!